THR~~E~~

DISAPPEAR

JAMES PATTERSON is one of the best-known and biggest-selling writers of all time. His books have sold in excess of 400 million copies worldwide. He is the author of some of the most popular series of the past two decades – the Alex Cross, Women's Murder Club, Detective Michael Bennett and Private novels – and he has written many other number one bestsellers including non-fiction and stand-alone thrillers.

James is passionate about encouraging children to read. Inspired by his own son who was a reluctant reader, he also writes a range of books for young readers including the Middle School, Dog Diaries, Treasure Hunters and Max Einstein series. James has donated millions in grants to independent bookshops and has been the most borrowed author in UK libraries for the past thirteen years in a row. He lives in Florida with his family.

SHAN SERAFIN is a novelist and film director whose works include *Seventeen, The Forest,* and *The Believer.* Among his recent collaborations with James Patterson are *Come and Get Us* and *The 13-Minute Murder.*

A list of titles by James Patterson appears at
the back of this book

THREE
WOMEN
DISAPPEAR

JAMES
PATTERSON
AND SHAN SERAFIN

arrow books

1 3 5 7 9 10 8 6 4 2

Arrow Books
20 Vauxhall Bridge Road
London SW1V 2SA

Arrow Books is part of the Penguin Random House group of companies
whose addresses can be found at global.penguinrandomhouse.com

Penguin
Random House
UK

Three Women Disappear first published in Great Britain by Century in 2020
Paperback edition first published in Great Britain by Arrow Books in 2021
Come and Get Us first published in Great Britain by BookShots in 2016

www.penguin.co.uk

A CIP catalogue record for this book is available from the British Library

ISBN 9781787461918

Printed and bound in Great Britain by Clays Ltd, Elcograf S.p.A.

The authorised representative in the EEA is Penguin Random House Ireland,
Morrison Chambers, 32 Nassau Street, Dublin D02 YH68.

MIX
Paper from
responsible sources
FSC
www.fsc.org
FSC® C018179

Penguin Random House is committed to a sustainable
future for our business, our readers and our planet.
This book is made from Forest Stewardship Council®
paper.

CONTENTS

THREE WOMEN DISAPPEAR

PROLOGUE

ONE
DETECTIVE SEAN WALSH

"LET'S KILL him again in slow motion," I said.

I took a coffee cup from the sink, started the faucet running.

"Assume for a second that it *was* a female killer," I began. "I'm Anthony Costello, accountant to the mob, nephew of top dog Vincent Costello. It's early in the morning, and either the help's asleep or they haven't arrived yet. I'm probably ticked off at having to do my own dishes."

"As ticked off as I am right now?" Detective Heidi Haagen asked.

I ignored her. This was my wife we were talking about. I wasn't going to let the department pin a murder on her—especially not when it was me who sent her to work for Costello in the first place.

"The lady assassin approaches me from behind," I continued, "as I'm rinsing my mug. I've got the water running full throttle because I'm Anthony Costello and I never do anything halfway. The sound makes for nice cover. Lady Assassin tiptoes up behind me and plunges a big old kitchen knife deep into my left shoulder. Probably she's aiming for my neck or spine, but she's no pro—that's obvious from the mess she left behind. Her hands are sweating, and she closes her eyes at the last second."

"We've been over this," Heidi said.

Heidi, my onetime partner, now boss. She was the one who shut me out of this case. Now I was trying to claw my way back in.

"I know," I said. "I know we have, but bear with me. Costello's a big guy. About my height, but a hundred pounds heavier. That first blow brought him down, but it didn't kill him."

I spun away from the sink, dropped to my hands and knees. Heidi rolled her eyes.

"Lady Assassin sidesteps, gets me in the center of my back, but not as deep this time. I drop to my belly and start crawling, trying to get away, maybe headed for the living room, where I keep that Glock stashed in the coffee table drawer."

I pulled myself forward on the tile mosaic floor, grunting and grimacing, playing the part.

"This isn't necessary," Heidi said.

But it was. I had to make her understand—Sarah wasn't capable of killing Anthony Costello.

"She keeps coming at me, again and again, but she's out of breath, losing force. These are just puncture wounds she's inflicting now. I'm Anthony Costello. I'm not going to be done in by my own chef in my own kitchen. So I reach for a chair and pull myself up. Maybe I manage a threat: 'It's my turn now' or 'You're a dead woman'—some stock phrase to make her tremble. I start toward her, then stumble, brace myself against the sink. And now it's me who's scared, because I'm looking at her eyes, and it's clear a switch has flipped. She charges, stabbing wildly. I shield my face with my forearms. The blade finds my gut, my ribs, my thighs. And then she lines up for the kill shot, the tip of the knife pointed at my sternum. In a final burst of energy, I hurl myself out of the way, then stagger and drop. Her final thrust hits the countertop. Here."

I pointed dramatically to a deep gouge in the polished oak. Heidi yawned.

"Sean," she said, "Sunday mornings are sacred. I told you when you called that you'd better have something—"

"Solid and irrefutable, I know."

I went over to the knife block and found one with the same make and model as the murder weapon. Heidi took a step back, which almost made me smile. I held the knife out to her, handle first.

"Sean, I—"

"Just take it."

She did.

"I know you've seen the photos," I said. "I know there were measurements taken, and I know those measurements suggest that the killer was 'above average in strength.' Here's the thing: I asked you to meet me at the scene today because I want you to try it."

"Try what?"

I gestured to the stray hole in the counter.

"You're about five foot ten, right? You hit the gym daily. Bench your own weight. Hell, you could probably bench *my* weight. I challenge you to take the same knife and, with just one thrust, make a hole that deep."

She was less than enthusiastic.

"Even if the department would allow a—"

"Half as deep," I said. "The same gouge, half as deep. Forget what's allowed: I'm fighting for my wife's freedom here."

She glared at me.

"This isn't going to prove anything," she said.

"Just make sure you grip the handle tight. I don't want the blade sliding up your palm."

She gave in. She repositioned the handle in her fist, switched her weight to her back foot, and lunged with everything she had.

TWO

THE RESULT?

Not even one-quarter the depth of the original. The hole was barely noticeable when she pulled the knife back out. We stood staring at the counter. No words were exchanged, no meaningful glances. Then she dropped the knife in the sink and started for the door.

"We're leaving," she said.

"That's it?"

"I told you: it doesn't prove anything."

I followed her outside, onto the wraparound porch of what had begun as a plantation house, rebuilt and renovated over time into a multimillion-dollar mansion. Drive time to either Tampa or Orlando was roughly an hour, but the immediate area looked like the land that civilization forgot. Nothing but kudzu, palm trees, and now police tape in every direction. Heidi lit a cigarette, probably just so she could blow smoke in my face.

"Sarah Roberts-Walsh is a small-boned diabetic who couldn't lift a twenty-pound barbell off the floor," I said. "She *couldn't* have made that gouge in the counter."

Heidi turned to face me.

"Open your eyes, Sean. Stop ignoring the obvious."

"Nothing's obvious."

"Your wife disappeared the same day Anthony Costello was murdered. Maybe the same hour."

"She isn't the only one who went missing that day."

"Yeah, and maybe when we find her she'll have a real good story."

She walked down the porch steps and started toward her car, then turned and came striding back.

"Just what exactly was the wife of a homicide detective doing working for a mob accountant?"

"She was his chef."

"I'm not talking about her job title. How did she meet him in the first place?"

I didn't say anything. I was surprised it had taken Heidi this long to ask the question. I'd had run-ins with the Costello family before. A little over a year ago, I'd arrested Nicholas Costello, Anthony's nephew, for holding up a liquor store on the outskirts of Tampa. After the arrest, evidence went missing, witnesses recanted. It looked bad. It made me look bad. And then Sarah started working for Anthony. Rumors were flying around the squad room: Detective Sean Walsh on the Costellos' payroll. Me, who'd given fifteen years to this job.

"That's your story?" Heidi asked. "Silence?"

"She isn't involved," I said.

"Maybe. Either way, I don't want you anywhere near this."

I watched her drive off, then took out my cell phone and speed-dialed Sarah.

"Hey, it's me again," I told her voice mail. "I'm praying you can hear this. It's been two weeks now. I miss you. I need to know you're okay. I need you to come home. Whatever happened, you need to come home."

I hung up, headed for my car. My phone rang just as I stuck

the key in the ignition. I grabbed it off the dashboard without checking the caller ID.

"Sarah?" I said.

"Next best thing. You got something to write with? 'Cause I got an address."

It was Lenny Stone, ex-cop turned PI. I'd hired him to track down Sarah.

"Where?" I said. "Where is she?"

"About a hundred miles south of the middle of nowhere. Nearest town is Kerens, Texas. Time to dust off that Stetson, partner."

PART I

CHAPTER 1
SARAH ROBERTS-WALSH

October 12
9:30 a.m.
Interview Room C

"FORENSICS FOUND traces of Costello's blood on your clothes, so why don't you tell us what happened?"

We were sitting in a plain white room with a drop ceiling and a mirror I assumed was two-way. Me and Detective Heidi Haagen. She leaned across the metal table.

"This is serious, Sarah," she said. "Your own husband brought you in."

"Where is Sean?"

They were the first words I'd spoken since we sat down. My voice cracked like a teenage boy's.

"Doesn't matter," Haagen said. "He can't help you."

"But I didn't do anything."

"Then just tell the truth."

"Where do you want me to start?" I asked.

"That day. Everything you remember. Begin at the beginning and don't hold back. No detail is too small."

All right, I told myself. *You can do this.*

I gripped the sides of my chair, took a breath, started talking. I kept my eyes pointed straight ahead, away from the mirror. I knew damn well who was standing on the other side.

*   *   *

The morning of Anthony Costello's murder, I woke up to find myself lying on a moss-covered boulder, surrounded by kudzu. I had no idea where I was or how I'd gotten there. I made to stand but my legs were wobbly and my feet kept slipping on the moss. I felt my pockets: no phone, no wallet. For a long while I just sat there, trying to think things through. Maybe I'd gone camping with friends, wandered off by myself, and gotten lost. Maybe I'd forgotten to bring my insulin with me, which would explain why I'd blacked out.

"You're diabetic?" Haagen interrupted.

"That's right," I said. "If I miss an injection, life can get real fuzzy."

She jotted something in her notebook.

"Go on," she said. "What did you do next?"

I yelled for help. I figured if I'd come here with friends, they couldn't be too far away. I shouted and kept shouting, but no one shouted back. I took a deep breath, ordered myself not to panic.

"Anybody hear me?" I tried again. "Please, I need help."

Silence. Nothing but birds fighting off in the woods.

All right, Sarah, I told myself. *It's up to you.*

I lay on my belly, slid down the boulder, and landed ankle-deep in a thick patch of marsh grass. The front of my blouse was stained green. I started to brush myself off, looked down, noticed for the first time that there was blood on my sleeves, blood on my jeans, blood all over my white sneakers. Not wet, but not dry, either. Had I fallen? Been attacked? I scanned my body for any hint of a wound, felt the back of my head for lumps or abrasions. Nothing. The blood wasn't mine.

So whose was it? I struggled to push my mind back but came up empty.

I wasn't wearing a watch, had no idea how long I'd been

unconscious. I looked up at the sky. The light seemed to be growing stronger. I figured it was somewhere between 8:00 and 9:00 a.m. Where would I normally be between 8:00 and 9:00 a.m.? I couldn't remember. I could remember my name, my age, my weight, the fact that I was a diabetic—but where I lived and what I did all day were gone.

I felt dizzy and a little nauseous. Assuming I was right about the time, my last insulin injection would have been late last night, maybe eight hours ago. Eight hours wasn't the end of the world. If I'd passed out atop that boulder all on my own, it might have had more to do with dehydration than blood sugar.

I needed water. I needed insulin. I looked around for a path or a landmark. Nothing. The boulder was lodged at the summit of a small incline. If I was looking for civilization, then downhill seemed like the best bet. I started to walk, then run. The running set off a sharp pain in my right calf. I stopped, knelt down in the grass, and rolled up my pant leg. There was a gash, maybe an inch wide. Something had pierced the thick denim of my jeans. I was wounded after all, though this cut didn't begin to explain all the blood.

"Keep moving," I told myself.

The morning was cool by Florida standards, but my forehead and the small of my back were soaked. I'd been walking for what felt like hours when I passed through a wooded area and emerged in a wholly different world: a painstakingly landscaped and manicured world. Palm trees instead of kudzu, a freshly mowed lawn instead of swamp grass and weeds. And at the other end of that lawn, a house. More than a house: a mansion. An old-fashioned plantation manor refurbished to look as though it were built yesterday.

I'm on someone's estate, I thought. *I have been all along.*

"Hello?" I yelled.

Once again, no answer.

There was a fence along the back of the house separating the lawn from a colorful maze of perennials and fruit trees. I hurried over to the back gate, feeling I'd made it to safety, only to find something that brought me up short and made me wonder if I'd ever be safe again: there was blood on the handle, blood spotting the gate's white wooden planks.

Little by little, then all at once, my memory came alive. I'd been to this house before. I'd been here every day for the last year. I was personal chef to a man named Anthony Costello and his wife, Anna. This was their house. This was where I made three meals a day for them, where I'd made breakfast for Anthony as recently as this morning.

My legs wanted to buckle, but I kept moving forward, through the gate and up the steps to the wraparound porch. The sliding back door was open. I stepped inside.

"Anna?" I called out. "Anthony?"

Nothing. The silence scared me more than waking up on that rock. This time of day, the place was normally bustling. Serena, the maid, would be singing to herself as she polished the dining room table; Anna would be watching *Good Morning Florida* with the volume turned full blast; Anthony would be pacing the marble hallway, cursing into his phone.

"Serena?" I tried.

Still no answer. Something was seismically wrong. I crept like a cat burglar through the dining room, the laundry room, the family room, the living room, the parlor, Anthony's office. Ten thousand square feet of real estate and not a whiff of life.

"It's Sarah," I called upstairs. "Anyone home?"

I'd climbed a handful of steps when the dizziness hit me hard.

Water, I reminded myself. *You need water.*

I made my way to the kitchen. And that was where I found him. Anthony, facedown on the floor, outlined by a pool of his own blood, a kitchen knife lying not three feet away.

CHAPTER 2

"DEAD?" HAAGEN asked.

I shook my head.

"No," I said. "Not yet."

"And still you didn't call 911?"

"I did," I said. "At least I tried. I was in shock."

"I don't believe in shock."

"Denial, then."

"Why don't you skip what you were feeling and tell me what you did?"

I nodded, thinking to myself, *You'll get through this, Sarah.*

At first it didn't occur to me that he might be alive. There was so much blood. So many holes. Gashes up and down his legs, his back. His clothes nearly shredded. I just stood there staring at him. I couldn't look away. I couldn't make myself move.

And then he coughed.

"Anthony!" I yelled. "Oh, my God, Anthony."

I ran across the kitchen, slipped on his blood, nearly toppled, then righted myself and knelt beside him.

"Can you hear me, Anthony?" I said. "I'm calling 911. You're going to be all right."

He made a raspy, muffled sound. I couldn't tell if he was trying to speak. I couldn't tell if he knew I was there.

"Just hold on," I said.

I stood up, spotted my purse lying on the far counter. I riffled through it, turned it upside down, and shook out the contents. No phone. Maybe I'd left it at home. Maybe I'd dropped it in the woods.

I returned to his side, leaned in close, touched his hand.

"You'll be okay, Anthony. I'm not leaving you. I'm just going to find the house phone, all right?"

His eyelids were fluttering, but they wouldn't open. I jumped up, ran to the console in the foyer, but the phone wasn't in its cradle. I sprinted back through the house, thinking, *Blood loss, coma, organ failure.* Thinking every second mattered. No phone in the guest room, the game room, the sun room. I finally found it in the most obvious place: under a couch cushion. I picked it up, dialed. Nothing. The line was dead.

I held the phone away from my ear and looked at it. The buttons were dark. I scanned the room. Everything was dark: the television, the DVR, the hi-fi. I went over to the light switch, flicked it up and down. Someone had cut the power.

There was one hope left. I ran back into the kitchen, took a knee beside Anthony. His eyelids were still fluttering, and his right hand had started to twitch.

"That's right," I said. "Just keep breathing."

I knew better than to move a person in his condition, hovering between shock and death, but I had to access his front pockets. I raised up into a crouch, placed my hands on his side, and pushed. My legs shot out from under me; I landed belly down in his blood. I tried slipping my hand under his waist but didn't get very far. The man weighed three hundred pounds—even before I started cooking for him.

I was at my wits' end, biting back tears, fighting the urge to crumble completely. I wandered over to the kitchen window, stood staring out at the far-reaching wilds of Anthony Costello's estate. And then it hit me: the reason I'd been out there in the first place.

I'd been chasing him.

Or her—I didn't get a very good look. It was dawn. I'd just started the coffee brewing when I heard a door slam. I looked out, saw a figure I didn't recognize struggling with the gate's latch, then saw that same figure tear off across the lawn, headed for the woods.

"And you ran after this phantom figure?" Haagen cut me off. "Like you were one of Charlie's angels? Sorry, but I find that a little hard to believe."

"I must have," I said. "I must have climbed up on that boulder to see if I could spot him."

"And then conveniently passed out?"

"It didn't seem convenient to me."

"Let's get back to the part where you're staring out the window while your employer lies dying at your feet."

"I was collecting myself," I said. "Piecing things together. Coming up with a plan."

"And that plan was?"

"To drive for help."

I'd decided to break my promise, leave Anthony behind while I sped to the nearest gas station and called 911. But when I turned around, he was moving, trying to drag himself forward across the floor. He crawled a few inches, collapsed, then lifted his head and pointed. I walked over to him, crouched down.

"Easy now, Anthony," I said. "Just relax."

He made no effort to speak—just kept pointing. I lowered

myself onto the floor, searched for whatever it was he wanted me to see.

"Oh, thank God," I said.

His phone, lying far back under the industrial-size refrigerator. I ran to the hall closet, fetched a broom, used the handle to bat the phone out. Not a speck of dust came with it: Serena's a maniac for detail.

Cavalry had arrived in the form of a cellular device. My heart was beating hard, my hands shaking. I lit up Anthony's home screen, found a string of missed-call alerts: five in a span of ten minutes, all from "UV," the most recent stamped forty-five minutes ago. "UV" stood for Uncle Vincent, head of the Costello family. Vincent Costello only used the phone for holiday greetings and dire emergencies.

"Oh, no," I said out loud. "Oh, my God, no."

A quick scan of outgoing calls confirmed my suspicion: Anthony had reached out to Vincent just minutes before the missed calls started. His attacker had left him for dead, and instead of dialing 911, Anthony had gone straight to the person who'd always made things right: his uncle, don of Central Florida, the Mafia boss who'd lived to a ripe old age without spending so much as an hour behind bars. Anthony, stuck and bleeding, must have managed a few words, then dropped the phone. A frantic Vincent had tried desperately to get his nephew back on the line.

"All right," I told myself. "Don't panic. Just go ahead and call the paramedics."

I had my thumb on the 9 key when I looked over at Anthony and saw it was too late. His eyes were open and still, and his back had quit rising and falling with every labored breath. I went over and checked his pulse just to be sure. Then I stood and dropped the phone. I may have screamed—I can't remember. Vincent lived in a gated mansion on the outskirts of Tampa, maybe an hour away. He would have sent help of his own. Mobsters who'd be pulling up the drive any minute. And they'd find me, the wife of a cop, alone in the house, dripping with Anthony's blood. Anthony, who'd been killed with a kitchen knife. Me, his personal chef.

CHAPTER 3

"SO YOU ran?" Haagen said. "All the way to Texas?"

I nodded.

"Texas is just where I wound up," I said. "The running was the important part."

Haagen sat back in her chair.

"Let me ask you something," she said. "Just how much of this do you expect me to believe?"

"All of it."

"Every word?" she asked.

Breathing the air in that room was like chewing on thirty-year-old cigarette smoke. I felt tired, cold, anxious, sweaty, frightened, lonely, and above all eager to win Haagen over.

"Every word," I told her.

She folded her hands behind her head and grinned, as if she knew something I didn't.

"Why do you hyphenate your last name?" she asked.

"What?"

"Roberts-Walsh. You hyphenate your last name. Why?"

Changing topic midstream was Heidi's way of keeping a suspect off-balance. It worked. You could never tell what was coming next.

"Sorry," I said, "but how is that relevant?"

"Would you say that you have marital issues, Ms. Roberts-Walsh?"

"*Issues* is a bit vague."

"Problems, then."

"No more so than any other couple."

"So everything's fine at home?"

"Have you ever been married, Detective Haagen?"

She let the question pass.

"What's interesting is that you're very similar to your husband."

"How's that?"

"You're both guarded. You both give the impression that you're holding back. You both pretend to be cooperating when really you're running your own game."

"Maybe you're projecting because you know my husband. I've told you everything I can remember."

She shrugged, seemed almost amused. I took a long look at the mirror I'd been avoiding.

"Maybe," she said. "It's true I know him very well. We were partners for a decade. You know what they say about partners? They're closer than man and wife."

A new way to rattle me: jealousy. I wasn't going to bite.

"Is he on the other side?" I asked. "Is he watching us?"

"Your husband, you mean?" She shifted forward in her seat. "Let me ask you something, Ms. Roberts-hyphen-Walsh. Suppose he *is* there, monitoring, listening, standing idle as you dig yourself deeper and deeper. Why wouldn't he intervene? Barge in here, slam his fist on the table, and order me to stop tormenting his beloved wife? Wouldn't he at least bang on the glass? This isn't going very well for you, you know."

She'd confirmed it: my husband was there, watching. She was talking to him now, not me.

"Could it be because he knows you're guilty?" she asked. "Did the two of you have a heart-to-heart on the drive back from Texas?"

She tapped the manila folder on the table in front of her.

"Or maybe it's the other way around," she said. "Maybe you're protecting him. I mean, however you look at it, it was Sean who set this whole thing in motion."

"You've lost it," I said. "You're off your rocker."

I didn't care anymore about winning her over. If I'd been someone else—someone like Anna, or even Serena—I would have lunged.

"Am I?" she asked. "Tell me, how does a cop's wife end up working for Florida's top crime family? Are you really going to tell me that Sean didn't get you the job? Maybe he wanted you in Costello's house for a reason. Maybe that reason expired. Or maybe you just couldn't take it anymore."

I cocked my head and furrowed my brow like a puppy confused by her master's command.

"Don't you know?" I asked.

"Know what?"

"I was working for you."

"For me?"

"For Tampa PD. I filled out the informant paperwork and everything. I gave weekly reports."

"And you were paid for this?"

"Once a month like clockwork."

"How were you paid?"

"In cash. Sean said that was standard procedure. He said banks left a paper trail that someone like Anthony could easily check on."

"And Sean made these payments himself?"

I nodded.

"And you reported directly to him?"

I nodded again.

She didn't say anything. She didn't have to—her smirk said it all.

Haagen came back after a long coffee break during which I'd been left alone to stew.

"Time to switch gears," she said.

She opened the folder, flipped through the top pages.

"Your medical records," she said. "Type 2 diabetes is no joke. That's what bothers me most about your story."

"I don't follow."

"You say you woke up thinking you'd passed out due to either a missed dose of insulin or dehydration, but we both know you weren't dehydrated: the morning wasn't particularly hot, and you'd only wandered off for a few hours. If you blacked out, it had to be something like insulin shock. Yet you slid down off that rock and were suddenly fine. Nowhere in your testimony do you mention searching for your insulin bag once you got back to the house. Shouldn't that have been your first priority? You know, the way you're supposed to secure your own oxygen mask before you start helping your kids?"

"I was disoriented. And then there was the shock of seeing Anthony like that. I couldn't think straight."

"*Shock*—there's that word again. You know, I did some research."

She held up a sheet of paper and waved it around.

"Diabetics don't usually black out because they missed a dose. In fact, blackouts are very, very rare. No, I think you *invented* your little bout of amnesia because the one detail you can't explain to us is the knife wound in your calf."

"It wasn't a knife wound," I said. "It must have been a rock. Maybe a beer bottle. Anthony liked to host cookouts."

"I asked CSI to look into that. They had an entire class of

cadets from the academy search the area. No rocks sharp or jagged enough to have made such a clean incision. No discarded bottles. Not even a pointy stick."

"I told you: I don't remember how it happened."

"That's okay," Haagen said. "I have a pretty good idea."

She let me chew that over for a long, hostile beat.

"One more thing," she said. "You were alone when you left the house?"

"Yes."

"Which means you were alone when you got into your car?"

"Yes."

"And you didn't take anything with you? Anything that didn't belong to you?"

I hung my head.

"You know what I took," I said.

CHAPTER 4

DETECTIVE SEAN WALSH

WHILE HEIDI was busy grilling my wife, I decided to conduct a little business of my own.

Destroying police evidence is never easy, especially when you're dealing with computer files. Evidence logged through our municipal network is cloned onto two servers downtown. The trick isn't to remove it. The trick is to drown it.

I sat at my desk, picked up the phone, dialed, and waited.

"Hi, this is Detective Sean Walsh with Homicide," I said. "I'm calling to see if you've processed the files for the Danza case, reference number 00527 dash 57. I was looking for them this morning, but couldn't find them in the system."

I told the clerk I'd be happy to hold. I was nothing if not polite. I even hummed along to the tinny Muzak while I sifted through the drawers of my desk, sliding papers I didn't want discovered into an old issue of *Men's Health* magazine. Later that night I'd burn the magazine on a barbecue grill.

"Can I get the last three digits again?" the clerk asked.

Once an admin logged on through his own computer, he'd be the only registered user until he logged off again. It didn't matter if every detective in Florida was searching the database: the network would only recognize the admin. It was a handy flaw in our archaic, underfunded municipal system—one that would allow me to revise the files on Sarah without leaving any record of having done so. Of course, if I somehow got caught...

"Last three digits are 7 dash 57," I said.

Heidi had enlisted a rookie from Vice to gather a phone book's worth of background info on my wife: Wikipedia-style bios of everyone she'd ever dated, her parents' criminal histories (a half dozen parking tickets between them), her transcripts from grade school through culinary school, a facsimile of her medical ID bracelet, copies of her emails, records of every call she placed or received reaching back five years. You name it, it was there.

Before Sarah resurfaced, I'd begun collating data of my own. It was meant to protect her, to bolster the notion that sweet little diabetic Sarah would never hurt a fly. But I saw pretty early on that the puzzle pieces were forming the wrong picture. Not only did Sarah have a motive to kill Anthony but she had twenty-four-hour access to his home.

But then so did Anthony's wife, Anna.

And so did Anthony's maid, Serena.

I looked over my shoulder, pretending to scratch my elbow. My coworkers showed no interest in my computer screen.

"Okay, Detective Walsh," the clerk said. "I'm in the system now, and I see that your request is being processed as we speak. Should be there by the end of the day."

I logged on, found Sarah's case file, saw that I was too late: the content had already been reviewed by the new investigation team. By Heidi. This morning. Just out of curiosity, I clicked on the icon beside Sarah's name. Nothing happened. I clicked on it again. And again. And again. And again.

I'd been blocked.

"Christ," I whispered.

There's nothing I enjoy less than feeling sidelined. I opened a game of solitaire to calm myself down, made it halfway through the deck before my phone started vibrating. I pulled it out of my pocket, checked the caller ID: OLD SCHOOL. My nickname for Vincent Costello.

Great, I thought. *Exactly what I need.*

I didn't answer, and he didn't leave a message. Or rather the call itself was his message: I had five minutes to find a secure line and a private place to talk. I stood, headed for the elevator, did my best to look casual. When the doors opened, my legs nearly buckled: Heidi was standing there, scowling as though I was blocking her way on purpose. Or at least the woman standing there looked like Heidi. Same height, same physique, and a pantsuit right out of Heidi's wardrobe. But this woman was older by a decade, and she was wearing tennis shoes instead of pumps. And Heidi was still in the interrogation room, trying to break my wife.

I smiled to myself as the doors closed. *Jumpy much?* I thought. I was doing exactly what our marriage counselor had accused me of during our one and only session: looking for danger where there was none.

I speed-walked across the parking lot, got behind the wheel of my Jeep, and pulled a burner phone from the glove compartment. Costello picked up on the second ring.

"I shouldn't have to chase you down like this," he said.

He had a painfully deliberate way of speaking—like Jimmy Stewart at half speed.

"I told you I'd call when I had an update," I said. "So far there's nothing."

"Your wife hasn't confessed?"

"My wife didn't kill Anthony."

"For your sake, I hope you're right. Still, you don't seem to be bending over backward to prove her innocence."

"I'm doing what I can," I told him. "Have you found Anna?"

"My men are on the scent. She knows damn well how I feel about her, so I imagine she's being extra cautious. What about the maid?"

"Serena?"

"Is there another?"

"She's in the wind," I said. "But she couldn't afford a bus ticket on what Anthony paid her. I'll find her. Soon."

"Make sure that you do, Detective. I'm running out of reasons to keep you around."

CHAPTER 5

ANNA COSTELLO

October 14
Noon
Interview Room A

"GAWK AT me all you want," I told her, "but I'm not spinning some story just to make your life easier. And if you keep lying to me, telling me there's proof when there is none, then I promise this'll end very badly."

Haagen flashed another blank stare. That seemed to be her specialty.

"Are you threatening me, Mrs. Costello?" she said.

"Oh, Detective, if I was threatening you," I told her, leaning forward so she could see my baby browns, "you wouldn't have to ask."

I leaned back. She sat up straighter. The upright citizen, glaring down her nose. Detective Heidi Haagen, the kind of married-to-her-work sad sack who could suck the fun out of a children's birthday party. I almost felt sorry for her: two days in the box with me and not a thing to show for it. The higher-ups must've been giving her hell.

"Mrs. Costello," she said, "the minimum penalty for threatening an officer is 365 days in jail."

"Yeah, but you won't press charges."

"Why's that?"

"I'm guessing you're already a source of laughs around the watercooler. You really want to arrest a grieving widow because she hurt your feelings?"

"No," she said. "I want to arrest you because you murdered your husband."

I laughed in her face.

"Dirty Harriet," I said. "God, I could use a cigarette."

Haagen looked away as if she was afraid that too much eye contact with me might turn her to stone. She was itching to clock me, but there was a two-way mirror and cameras in every corner. I grinned. With biceps like that, it was a good bet she hit harder than Anthony.

She made a show of sifting through my folder, then started rehashing bits of yesterday's session.

"I asked you about your husband's business affairs," she said. "You refused to answer. That alone is obstruction."

"You asked what part I played in his business. I didn't play any part."

She looked suddenly very glum. I decided to throw her a bone.

"But I never said I wouldn't talk about Tony's affairs."

I waited for the nod.

"Anthony was creative with numbers," I said. "He round-tripped for window dressing while diverting phantom tax obligations offshore."

"English."

"He was an accountant for the mob. He moved money around. More money than his employers knew about."

She wiped a trickle of sweat from her forehead. They must have kept the heat in that room at triple digits.

"If that's true, it would have made him some powerful enemies," she said.

I shrugged.

"My husband thought he was invincible."

"Just to be clear: you're saying he stole from Vincent Costello?"

"I'm saying he got clever in ways the family might not have liked. I never said anything about Vince. Vince isn't someone we talk about."

"I'm sure you'll make an exception," Haagen said. "Let me remind you that you're facing a murder charge."

I hit the table so hard her papers jumped.

"Good," I said. "Go ahead and put me in jail. I'd be safer there. And so would you, if you're hunting Vincent Costello. You think he'd care about your shield? His motto is Buy Them or Bury Them."

"*Them* being cops?"

I didn't say anything.

"Which cops?" she asked. "Who's he bought?"

"Are you Internal Affairs or Homicide?"

She saw I had a point.

"Okay," she said. "We'll come back to that. Who do you think killed Anthony?"

"I don't know. I really don't. But if I were you, I'd be looking really hard at his little black book."

"Little black book?"

The question wasn't rhetorical—I could tell she'd never heard the expression.

"You've gotta get out more," I said. "The women he was screwing behind my back. Except it wasn't really behind my back. If anything, he flaunted it. And he wasn't a stickler about age or marital status or even consent."

"I see," she said, seeming full-on flustered for the first time since we'd started talking. "Do you have any particular women in mind?"

I looked at her as if I didn't know people could be so dumb and still dress themselves.

"Are you interrogating me, or getting me to do your job for you? Think about it. The place wasn't broken into, right? So whoever killed him had access to the house. I'm telling you it wasn't me. Who does that leave?"

A lightbulb switched on.

"Sarah," she said. "He was sleeping with Sarah."

"And?" I asked. "Who else had a key and the alarm code?"

"Serena. The maid."

I gave her a quiet round of applause.

"Then that's where I'd start," I said.

CHAPTER 6

"LET'S GET back to you for a moment," Haagen said. "Tell me again where you were that morning."

I rolled my eyes.

"Asleep," I said. "Medicated. Drugged. I take a nice little cocktail every night. You would, too, if you lived with a monster."

"The screaming didn't wake you?"

"Nothing wakes me. That's the point of the drugs. I tumble out of bed when I'm good and ready."

"Like a rock star," she said, drumming her fingers on the table. "Walk me through it again. From the time you woke up to the time you fled."

I looked around as though I was searching for someone to rescue me.

"Are you serious? We've been over this and over this and over this." I pointed to one of the cameras. "Why not just watch the footage?"

"Humor me," she said. "A little cooperation goes a long way."

So I humored her.

*   *   *

I got up at around ten that morning, and then only because I had to pee. I did my business, thought about hopping back in bed, but my stomach was growling. As soon as I stepped into the hall, I sensed something was off. The house wasn't just quiet, it was empty. Our house was never empty. Especially not in the morning.

I went to the top of the stairs and called Anthony's name. Then Sarah's. Then Serena's. Crickets. I started down the steps.

"Is this a goddamn surprise party?" I yelled. "The surprise better be a vat of coffee."

I crossed through the dining room, noticed the sliding glass door was open, went back to close it. Anthony was always lecturing us about reptiles getting in the house—cottonmouths and gators. He had a real paranoid streak, but maybe this time he had something to be paranoid about, because there was blood all over the door handle, bloody footprints running the length of the deck outside.

I'd have been screaming my head off if it weren't for the benzo haze. Instead, I turned around very slowly and whispered, *"Tony?"* I started searching for him as if we were kids playing hide-and-seek, calling his name softly and looking in places he couldn't possibly be: the hall closet, under the stairs, behind the piano. When I think about it now, it's almost comical: me tiptoeing around and whispering while he lay dead in the kitchen, maybe thirty feet away.

Which is where I found him. This time I did scream. I ran over to him and nearly threw myself on his body. I'm not going to lie: I'd dreamed of doing something like this to Tony more times than I can count, but to actually see it? To see the person you've lived with for fifteen years lying facedown in his own blood, his back and legs oozing from more wounds than you can count? That sobered me up in a heartbeat. I sat there with him for a long while, stroking his hair, replaying our last argument, our first argument, regretting every unkind word in between.

And then the phone rang.

His phone, lying just beyond the reach of his outstretched hand. I didn't think. I picked it up, started to answer, then stopped myself when I saw the caller ID: UV. Uncle Vincent. He knew. Uncle Vincent knew. Tony must have made one last call before he toppled. I waited for the final ring, then tossed the phone back where I'd found it.

Uncle Vincent knew, and he'd blame me. I had no doubt. He never liked me, never made any bones about it. And there'd been an incident, maybe a month earlier. A family gathering. Family in both senses of the word. Tony got drunk. I got drunk. We did what we always did when we were drunk, only this time there was a full banquet hall to watch us go at it, with Uncle Vincent at the helm. Everyone there heard me tell Tony I'd cut his throat the next time he fell asleep. And now Uncle Vincent would be coming for me. Chances were he was already on his way.

"Jesus Christ, Tony," I said. "What am I going to do?"

I was hyperventilating. I actually smacked myself. I wasn't thinking about my dead husband anymore—I was calculating how long it would take Uncle Vincent's men to get here.

I ran upstairs. I knew what came next, what I had to do to protect myself. Every Mafia wife prepares for flight. We come up with a plan and rehearse it as we lie awake in bed. We compare notes. In hushed voices. In back rooms. At birthday parties, bridal showers, barbecues. What would you do if it all fell apart? If the FBI came knocking? If war broke out between the families? If your husband was locked up? Murdered?

Bribes, I reminded myself as I threw together a travel bag. Bribes are key if you want to stay hidden from a man like Vincent.

You don't go on the run so much as you buy your escape. You need capital, but it can't be cash—the courts will strip you of cash. But they can't take your property. Not unless they can prove it was stolen. And I happened to have a fat collection of very expensive, legally obtained jewelry.

CHAPTER 7

EXCEPT THAT my collection had vanished.

I kept the most valuable pieces—a Tiffany tiara, a double-row gem-encrusted bracelet, three pearl necklaces, a blue sapphire Heart of the Ocean replica, an 18-karat-gold locket, five sets of diamond earrings—inside a large cardboard box marked FEMININE PRODUCTS. I kept the box wedged between the piping and the wall of the bathroom sink, hidden behind columns of spare toilet paper. Burglars will riffle through your drawers. They'll tear art from the walls looking for a safe. But they generally steer clear of toiletries. I'd thought I was being clever.

My heart started beating so hard I could feel it in my toes. Maybe, I thought, Anthony had moved my jewels. He always believed his custom-made safe was impregnable, had told me more than once that I was being ridiculous. I ran back through the bedroom and into the hallway, pulled up a corner of the carpeting, and spun the dial on Anthony's sunken vault. Nothing inside but a ledger and some pictures of his late mother.

Maybe Anthony had moved my stash to a more conventional locale. I checked all the places jewelry might normally be kept:

the engraved mahogany case on my vanity table, my dresser drawers, my desk drawers. All empty. Every last piece gone.

Who else would have known to look in that box under the sink?

I thought, *Sarah.*

I thought, *Serena.*

I thought, *Sarah and Serena.*

Had they teamed up to kill Anthony and rob me? The idea didn't sit right. We'd always gotten along, even gone on day trips together when Anthony was away. But then I couldn't remember the last time they'd both been absent on the same morning. At first I felt betrayed. Then I realized it went beyond simple betrayal. They knew my history with Vincent, knew Florida's top crime boss would be only too happy to kill me limb by limb. They'd set me up. It was probably one of them who called Vincent from Anthony's phone.

No more time for thinking. I heard a car pulling up the gravel driveway, moving at top speed, then hitting the brakes hard. I went to the window, peered through the blinds. Vincent had sent his top dogs: Mr. Defoe, a consigliere of long standing, and Johnny Broch, Vincent's go-to muscle. I watched them jump out of their sedan and take the porch steps two at a time. At least they had the courtesy to ring the bell.

Anthony's paranoia was about to pay off for a change. In addition to the obligatory panic room, he'd had hidden passageways built all over the house. The panic room wouldn't do any good. Either they'd wait me out or find their way in: Anthony and Vincent shared the same architect. But the paneling behind the armoire in the front bedroom swung open if you touched it in just the right spot, and behind that paneling was a ladder leading straight to the garage. I hooked my travel bag over my shoulder, heaved the armoire out of the way, and started down.

We had twin cars, his and hers Bentleys—his a four door,

mine a coupe. If Anthony had been really smart, he'd have kept some kind of low-profile getaway vehicle: a Ford Focus or a Hyundai Elantra—something that would blend in once you'd made it past the driveway. It's hard to go unnoticed in a Bentley, but then I guess that's the point.

I got behind the wheel of the coupe, tossed the travel bag on the passenger seat. Anthony must have searched far and wide to find the slowest-moving automatic garage door in Florida. I watched it inch its way off the floor, counted to fifty before it even cleared the front bumper. "Come on, come on, come on," I begged. My nerves got the better of me. I hit the gas too soon, clipped the bottom of the door, heard an unholy scraping as it ripped the paint from the Bentley's hood. Outside, I floored it, saw Vincent's men sprinting for their sedan in my rearview mirror.

I took our winding, gravel access road at eighty miles per hour, kept expecting more of Vincent's goons to pop out from behind the bushes. If they had, I swear I'd have run them over. But the only button men I had to worry about were in the sedan on my tail, Defoe behind the wheel. And they were gaining steadily, as if the Bentley was a Model T and they were driving a tricked-out Aston Martin.

My best hope was to make the highway, then let the Bentley's engine put some distance between us. I ran every red light in the local town, passed a truck around a blind turn, took the on-ramp doing a hundred. They were right there with me. I darted between lanes, looked up to see Defoe grinning, our cars not five feet apart. I got onto the shoulder and floored it. I figured this would end one of two ways: with a caravan of state troopers in my rearview or with a clean getaway. I couldn't allow any third option.

They kept pace for a long stretch, then started to fade. Maybe the Bentley wasn't such a bad choice after all. When there was enough distance between us, I slipped into traffic, got off at the next exit, zigzagged down suburban streets until I was sure I'd lost them.

I pulled into a strip mall and practiced my deep breathing, willing my pulse to slow. Then I started for Tampa, taking back roads all the way.

CHAPTER 8
DETECTIVE SEAN WALSH

ANTHONY COSTELLO was an old-fashioned accountant: he hoarded paper. If he bought a stick of gum back in 1990, he still had the receipt, and he demanded the same from his clients. Lucky for me, he was also cautious, bordering on paranoid. Anthony hung on to every scrap, but he didn't keep any of it—incriminating or otherwise—in the house. He rented adjoining storage units at Pete Owens's Stow-and-Go on the outskirts of Tampa. I know because I helped him find the place.

I first met Pete Owens back when I was working Robbery and he refused to testify against one of his cat burglar tenants. A weekend in jail did nothing to change his mind. That's the kind of guy you want watching your stuff. Pete didn't so much as bat an eye when Anthony signed the lease "Jonathan Dough"—maybe because Anthony agreed to pay triple the rent, plus ten grand for permission to knock down the cement wall between the units.

Of course, I hadn't told Heidi about the Stow-and-Go. Or anyone else, for that matter. Call it pleading the Fifth in advance. Why implicate myself over five hundred square feet that no one knew existed? Not to mention that having Anthony's business files in my back pocket gave me a leg up on my former partner.

I waited for the lunch hour to pass, then drove to the facility, punched in the access code, and watched the steel gates slide open. Anthony's units were at the back, in an alcove beyond the sight lines of his fellow tenants. Picking the industrial lock— Anthony, like his uncle, trusted me only so far—took longer than I care to admit. I stepped inside, flicked on the overhead, pulled the door shut behind me.

If I'd been the one writing Anthony's eulogy, I'd have led with this: *He was the most compulsively organized human being I've ever met.* The walls of the double unit were lined with identical floor-to-ceiling filing cabinets, each cabinet representing a calendar year. Turn to the left once you walked through the door and you could go from 1995 all the way to 2017 without finding a single sheet of paper out of place. I turned to the right. The year I wanted was 2015.

My knees knocked a little as I stood there flipping through manila folders. Something about being in a dead man's storage unit spooked me, as if maybe his ghost was camped out here, contemplating its next move. Lucky for me the living Anthony had made things so easy: Serena Flores's personnel file was right where I'd expected it to be, halfway into a row marked DOMESTIC HIRES.

According to the paperwork, Serena was in her late twenties, just five feet tall, single, or had been when Anthony hired her. Previous address: a town in Mexico called Tecomán. A note penciled in the margins said Tecomán was a drug-smuggling hotbed midway down the West Coast. Maybe Anthony thought Serena would be amenable to more than housework. Maybe he'd offered her a lucrative little sideline, then pressed too hard when she said no. I wondered if that was a motive I could sell to Vincent. Something to get him off Sarah's tail. And mine.

Serena's next of kin—Símon Flores, older brother—lived in the Bowman Heights section of West Tampa. He was a vet tech. The file gave no info beyond his occupation, address, and work number. With any luck, at least one of the three would still be valid. I jogged back to my car, took out the burner phone, and started dialing. A woman answered. I heard barking in the background.

"I was hoping I could talk to Símon Flores," I said, cranking up my slight southern accent. A little charm never hurts.

"Sorry," the woman said, "he's in with a patient. Can I take a message?"

"No, thank you. I'll catch him later."

She'd already told me what I wanted to know: a) Símon still worked there, and b) he was on duty right now.

Fifteen highway miles and a stretch of side streets later, I arrived at Ybor City Animal Hospital. The receptionist was busy handling a small backup of incoming and outgoing customers, some straddling carrying cases, one with a cockatoo perched on his shoulder. I slipped into the waiting room, picked up a magazine, kept my eyes open for a Mexican male in scrubs. An elderly woman sat down opposite me and started weeping at full volume into a floral handkerchief. I figured things weren't looking good for Fido.

I'd called in a background check during the drive over. Símon had come to the US in 2005, applied for and received citizenship in 2014. Nothing on his record said he was anything other than hardworking and upstanding. The kind of guy a sister with a conditional visa might lean on when her employer turned up DOA. Especially if she was the one who'd killed him.

I didn't have long to wait before a Latino in blue scrubs pushed his way through a set of double doors and sat down next to the old woman. The name tag above his breast pocket confirmed he was Símon Flores. I looked him over. North of thirty,

tall, hefty. Not hefty like Anthony, but large enough to get noticed on the street. The way he carried himself—shoulders back,
chest out, eyes full of compassion—you'd have thought he was
the vet instead of the tech. Maybe he'd been promoted. Maybe
he'd put himself through canine med school and was now Dr.
Símon Flores. I hoped it was true. The more he had to lose, the
easier my job became.

He set a hand on the weeping woman's back, called her Carol,
spoke to her in hushed tones. His best guess was that her cat had
eaten a poisoned mouse. The news was more than Carol could
bear. Her weeping turned convulsive. She seemed to want to say
something but couldn't find the breath. I understood what she
was going through. I'd seen the look on her face—equal parts
remorse and sorrow—countless times before. Símon, without
meaning to, had just accused her of killing her cat. He leaned in
and draped an arm around her shoulders. For a second I thought
he was going to kiss her forehead.

"I'm sorry," he said. "I'm so, so sorry."

I could tell he meant it, and that made me glad. Símon had
the kind of bleeding heart that would never turn away—or turn
in—a sister. It was clear now what course I had to take. Con-
fronting him would be the same as warning Serena off, but tail
him and chances were I'd be talking to her before sundown.

"Can I get you anything?" he asked Carol. "Anything at
all?"

I thought, *Yeah, a new cat.*

He gave her a card, told her to call day or night. If you took
away the accent, his English was better than mine.

"Thank you," Carol sobbed. There was a tear in Símon's eye,
too.

I thought, *Better your sister than my wife.*

CHAPTER 9

SARAH ROBERTS-WALSH

October 12
11:30 a.m.
Interview Room C

"THE JEWELS," Haagen said. "You stole Anna Costello's jewels."

"I didn't steal them," I said. "I mean, I did, but I didn't mean to. I didn't even know I had them until it was too late."

"Really?" she said. "You accidentally walked off with six figures' worth of your employer's jewelry?"

Her grin was pure gloating, as if now she'd pinned down my motive, as if she was looking forward to watching me squirm out of this one. I just stared at my fingernails, refusing to take the bait.

"All right," she said, "let's back up. I don't want to miss any of this. You're in the kitchen. You know Anthony reached out to Vincent before he expired. So what next?"

I shrugged.

"For a while," I told her, "I just froze."

I stood beside Anthony's body and couldn't muster a single thought. I couldn't make my feet move. Then the spell broke, and I grabbed my purse and ran for my car. I floored it down that mile-long driveway, desperate to get off the property before Vincent's men could stop me.

"No time to call 911?" Haagen asked.

I thought about it—I did—but Anthony was dead, and if Vincent heard that I'd called the cops, then he'd know it was me who'd found his nephew's body. At the very least he'd want to talk to me. The kind of talk where I was tied to a chair. And if he didn't like what I had to say, there'd be a well-fed alligator somewhere in the Everglades. If Anthony had been wounded, if there'd been any chance of saving him, then I'd have made the call. But he was gone, and there was no point in risking my own life.

"Heroic," Haagen said.

"I'm not claiming to be a hero."

"No, but what you are claiming doesn't make any sense. How did you come by those jewels if you ran right out of the house?"

"I'm getting to that," I told her.

I needed to pull over, collect my thoughts. I was shaking uncontrollably. And bleeding. There was blood leaking from the gash in my pants. I could feel it spilling down my calf. But the only place to pull over was a narrow shoulder, and that would have left me sitting out in the open.

I rounded a bend, saw a cop car idling in a small clearing. My blood really started pumping then. I thought for sure he was waiting for me. I couldn't say if I was speeding or not, but I yanked my foot off the accelerator. Sean taught me never to hit the brake: *It only makes you look guilty,* he said. My eyes shot to the rearview mirror, but the cop didn't budge. At first I felt relieved. Then I figured he was radioing ahead, setting a trap. I braced for a fleet of squad cars, but they never came.

I made it to the nearest gas station, parked in front of the convenience store, and sat gripping the steering wheel.

"Get ahold of yourself, Sarah," I said out loud. "Think."

First things first: I needed to stop the bleeding. I pulled a handkerchief from my purse, took off my belt, leaned forward, and fashioned a makeshift tourniquet. As I was straightening back up, I saw it: a PBS tote bag resting on the seat beside me.

All I knew was that it couldn't be mine. I'm not the tote bag type, and I've never given a dime to public television. Slowly, as if something might jump out and bite me, I reached across and pulled the straps open.

Instead of a rat, I found pearl necklaces, a tiara, a gem-encrusted bracelet. Anna's collection. She'd shown it to me more than once. I'd even say she rubbed my nose in it. Any one of those pieces cost more than I make in a year. Maybe a decade.

"And still you didn't call the police?"

"Are you kidding? That bag was one more reason not to call the police. Someone had put it there. Someone was trying to frame me."

And what could I do but run? From Vincent and the police.

"Any idea who that someone might be?"

"There are only two possibilities," I said.

"Let me guess: the missus and the maid?"

I nodded. It had to be one of them.

"Serena, maybe," Haagen said. "But you think Anna Costello would part with her personal fortune? On purpose?"

I shrugged.

"She'd get it back, wouldn't she? Once I was caught. Meanwhile, she'd count on you asking that very question. What better way to throw you off the scent? And Vincent, too, for that matter. She'd been robbed. She was a victim, like her husband."

Haagen took a sip of water while she mulled things over.

"Not bad," she said. "But I have an alternative theory."

I waited, knowing full well she'd share it with me whether or not I asked.

"Maybe you really did black out," she said. "But it had nothing to do with diabetes. Maybe Anthony caught you robbing his wife. Maybe you only saw one way forward. You hadn't planned on killing him. You figured they'd blame the theft on the maid. Everyone blames the maid. But stabbing a man to death—that's more than a fluctuation in blood sugar. That's a real shock to the system, the kind of thing a mind might try to erase. Don't you think?"

Of course that made sense, but it wasn't what happened. The question was how to convince Haagen, who seemed bound and determined to throw away the key.

"There's just one problem," I said. "If I was planning to blame Serena, then why did I run?"

It was her turn to shrug.

"Maybe you're not that bright," she said. "Or maybe you're the type who's always dreamed of running away, starting over."

CHAPTER 10

I TOLD her I wasn't that type at all. Not consciously, anyway.

As usual, Haagen wasn't buying it.

"Let's focus on the timeline," she said. "I'm guessing you didn't gun it straight for Texas?"

"No," I said, "I didn't."

"So where'd you go next?"

With the tourniquet in place, I pulled out of the gas station, thinking, *Sarah, you need to be anywhere but here.* I needed a safe haven. Someplace where I could patch up my leg, find some insulin, and above all else devise a plan.

Only one destination came to mind.

No way, Sarah, I told myself. *No way do you bring this to her doorstep.*

Aunt Lindsey: my mother's sister, and my only surviving relative. The woman who raised me. An ER nurse who spent her weekdays coaxing strangers away from death's door and her weekends managing a community garden. Aunt Lindsey, the purest heart I knew. She'd give her last possession to anyone who asked.

Which is exactly why you can't ask, I thought.

But there wasn't anyone else. Least of all Sean. If Vincent was looking for me, if the police were looking for me, then Sean would be their first stop. And if he needed to serve me up to save his skin, I had no doubt he'd do it.

An hour later I came skidding to a halt in Aunt Lindsey's gravel driveway. I grabbed my glasses from the glove box, hesitated before reaching for the tote bag. I couldn't leave it in the car, but how would I explain the contents to my aunt? Not that she was likely to demand an explanation.

I dragged my injured leg up the splintering steps and burst through the door. No point in knocking: she never wore her hearing aid at home, and she didn't believe in locks.

"Aunt Linds!" I called out, standing between the twin rubber plants in her narrow, gleaming foyer.

I waited, heard nothing besides the ticking of an antique clock. I set the tote bag beside an umbrella holder and started down the hallway, checking the living room, the dining room, the den. In the kitchen, I stared out the back window, scanning the foliage she let run wild because, as she put it, repairing the ozone was more important than having a neatly trimmed lawn. Never mind the periodic infestations of mice and spiders: every creature had a right to live.

"Aunt Linds? Are you upstairs?"

"I'll be right with you," came a voice from the greenhouse off the kitchen. "I'm just trying to resurrect this basil plant."

A few beats later, she rounded the corner in her rubber clogs, her apron wet and streaked with soil.

"Hey, sweetie," she said. "It's so nice to—"

She stopped short once she got a close look at me.

"What on earth . . . ?"

We stood at arm's length while she studied my wounded leg, my torn clothes, my panicked expression. I could see her counting to five in her head as she took a breath, a technique she'd picked up at the ER.

"You sit down now," she said, pulling a chair away from the table. "Tell me all about it. I'll get you a glass of water."

The promise of a brief rest made me realize just how long I'd been teetering on collapse.

"I will," I promised. "I'll tell you everything. But I have to make a call first."

No need to say it was an emergency. She pulled a cordless phone from the wall, handed it to me, and turned to leave the room.

"I'll just be in the greenhouse," she said.

I called Anna. Twice. The second time, I gathered myself and left a message.

"Anna, this is Sarah. I'm assuming you know by now . . . Listen, I have your jewelry. I have no idea how your collection wound up in my car, but I don't want any part of . . ."

I stopped. I didn't hang up. Instead, I pressed the number 3: message deleted. No good would come from a voice mail. Anything on tape could be manipulated, entered into evidence. I took a breath, then called Anna's pastor, the person most likely to know where she was. Anna's not religious by nature, but sitting on the church's board of directors made her feel a little better about being a mob wife, and she and Father Priatto had grown close. Maybe too close. Sometimes I wondered . . .

The good father picked up on the first ring.

"Hello," I said, my voice already breaking. "This is Sarah Roberts-Walsh, Anna Costello's personal chef. I don't know if you remember me, but we —"

"Of course I remember you, Sarah. How are you?"

"Good. I'm good. I was just . . . I'm trying to get ahold of Anna, and I was wondering if you might happen to know where she is?"

The line went silent. I could hear my own breathing, cycled through the electronic circuits, amplified back to me in the receiver. The call was still active. The father just wasn't talking.

"Father?" I said. "Are we still—?"

"Where are you right now, Sarah?"

"I'm with my...I'm sorry, but why would you ask that?"

"Where are you?" he repeated, his tone cold, clinical.

"Why would you want to know where I am?"

"I think you know why."

I felt suddenly bloodless. The Costellos had judges and commissioners on their payroll. Why not a priest as well? What better informant than the man who hears confession for all the neighborhood cops and thugs?

"I don't," I lied. "It isn't obvious at all."

Aunt Lindsey was standing in the doorway now, looking me up and down, trying to figure out what had gone wrong and how she could set it right.

"Let me give you a piece of very generous advice," Father Priatto said. "You don't know who you're up against. Jail might be the best of your options at this point. I suggest you tell me where you are. I can create a degree of amnesty for you."

"It wasn't me who—"

"Stop right there," he said. "You know what you did. They will come for you. I guarantee it. And when they find you—"

I left him talking to a dial tone.

CHAPTER 11

AUNT LINDSEY bit back her concern long enough to lighten the mood.

"Anna Costello goes to church?" she said. "Now that's a hoot."

I almost laughed.

"I think Anthony uses the diocese to launder money," I said. "Nonprofit status makes for good cover."

"And your detective husband sent you to work for that man?"

My complexion must have darkened a little. Telling her *why* he'd sent me to work for Tony wouldn't have given her any comfort.

"Sorry," she said. "Last thing I want to do is shame you."

"Anyway, I don't work for him anymore."

"I have a feeling that's bad news. What happened?"

I wasn't ready to talk. I needed a prop, something to ease me into the conversation. I looked around for the tote bag, then remembered I'd left it in the foyer.

"There's something I want to show you," I said.

I pushed myself up from the table, took a step, felt my knees buckle. Aunt Lindsey had her arms around me before I could hit the floor.

"Goodness," she said. "Sit back down and let's get you fed."

"It isn't food I need," I told her. "I mean it is, but—"

"Insulin," she guessed. "Why on earth didn't you say something? How long's it been?"

She bolted out of the kitchen before I could answer, returned seconds later with the emergency kit she kept on hand for my visits.

"This'll fix you up," she said.

And then she was on her knees, administering a fifteen-unit shot. The relief came instantly—a fleeting high that could trick you into believing the disease was worth the reward.

When I opened my eyes again, I found Aunt Lindsey in full nurse mode, cutting my jeans open with a pair of scissors, tossing away the makeshift tourniquet, dousing the wound with rubbing alcohol and covering it with gauze. I did my best not to grimace.

"That should hold off any infection," she said.

I watched her pack away her gear, then flit around the kitchen, brewing tea and arranging an assortment of biscuits on a badly tarnished tray.

"That's just to tide you over," she said, setting the tray in front of me and taking a seat. "Now talk."

I started and stopped a half dozen times before I made it to the end. There was so much I couldn't say, so many questions I couldn't answer. I still couldn't remember any of what happened before I woke up on that rock. I didn't know who killed Anthony, didn't know if I'd been there when it happened or if I'd run off beforehand. I couldn't say for sure that it hadn't been me wielding the knife.

"That's an easy one," Aunt Lindsey told me. "You didn't stab that man."

"Because I don't have it in me?"

She nodded.

"When you were ten or eleven, I took you out on a fishing boat. I'm not much of a fisherwoman myself, but it's a useful skill in this part of the world, and I thought I should let you try. You know what you did? You went around setting everyone's bait free."

I shook my head.

"You didn't know Anthony," I said. "He was maddening. He could drive people to—"

"That doesn't matter," she interrupted. "The evidence points to someone else."

I looked at her as if she'd just posed me a riddle.

"What evidence?"

"You said the power was cut, right?"

I nodded.

"And then someone put a bag loaded with jewelry in your car? Hundreds of thousands of dollars' worth of jewels?"

"Yes," I said, starting to wonder if she believed me, if my story was too much for even Aunt Lindsey to swallow.

"Sounds like a multi-person operation to me," she said. "Too many things happening at once. Somebody put in a lot of thought, not only into how to kill him but also how to get away with it. You might not remember the event itself, but you'd damn well remember planning it. You'd remember conspiring to commit murder. You'd remember what was said and where it was said and most importantly who said it. So put the idea that you killed Anthony Costello out of your mind. The only question that matters now is, how do we keep you safe?"

Whether I was a six-year-old who'd just scraped her knee or an adult whose life was hurtling off the rails, Aunt Lindsey always knew how to talk me down. She'd cut through what didn't matter and find the nugget that put everything in perspective. I'd made some wrong turns. My marriage, my job— a woman with her head screwed on right would have said no to both. But I wasn't a killer. I hadn't done the one thing that couldn't be undone.

"Thanks, Aunt Linds," I said.

She sat back in her chair, folded her arms across her chest.

"The jewels are key," she said. "Mind if I have a look?"

"They're in the foyer," I told her. "I'd get them myself, but my leg—"

She jumped up, fetched the tote bag, came back and tossed it on the table.

"Now show me," she said.

I pulled the straps apart, rolled the canvas down until the trove was laid bare. Aunt Lindsey just shook her head.

"The things we choose to care about," she said. "The things we call valuable. In the end, we murder each other over random nonsense."

She went quiet. I waited, knowing there was more to come.

"Sean and Anna did this together," she said.

I stared at her.

"Sean and Anna?"

"Hear me out."

On the surface, Anthony's murder looked like a crime of passion—"clearly" Anna did the stabbing—but there was something larger at play, something to do with money and matrimony.

"Look at the evidence. Look at who benefits. Two bad marriages snuffed out in one go. Anna doesn't have to look over her shoulder. Sean doesn't have to pay alimony. All that's left is for Sean to arrest you so they can get the loot back."

My chin fell to my chest. I didn't know if I was going to cry or fall asleep.

"Even if that's true," I said, "what do I do now?"

"Now," Aunt Lindsey said, "I feed the cook. You need some nourishment. Something that'll stick to your ribs. Then we'll talk about the future."

She went to the refrigerator and pulled out a large Tupperware filled with an old-fashioned, tomato-based stew. She called it her triple threat: three kinds of meat, three kinds of beans, three kinds of vegetables. Ten seconds in the microwave and the room started to smell like an herb garden.

"That's the stuff that made me a chef," I said.

I remember the taste of okra and lima beans, pork and cauliflower. I remember letting out a little moan. And then I remember darkness. I'd fallen asleep with my fork in my hand, my plate still heaping.

CHAPTER 12

"THIS IS all very touching," Haagen said. "Your aunt sounds like a gem. Really, she does. It was good of her to solve the case for you, and it was good of you to pass her insights on to me. Still, if you don't mind, let's stick with the facts. Save the alternative theories for court."

In other words, any attempt to win her over would have the opposite effect.

"You want me to keep going?" I asked.

She nodded.

"Just skip over the parts where your loved ones declare your innocence."

I woke up in the spare room thinking an hour had passed, but really it had been a whole day. My heart began racing before my brain understood why. There were voices coming from downstairs. At first I thought it was Aunt Lindsey's TV, blaring as usual. But it wasn't the TV. A live and heated conversation was unfolding somewhere below me, the deep pitch of a man's voice overwhelming my aunt's soprano.

"Regardless," the man said.

His voice sounded calm and violent at once, a combination I'd recognize anywhere: my husband, Detective Sean Walsh.

"Regardless nothing," Aunt Lindsey said. "You need to leave now."

I slid on my glasses, crossed the hallway to the top of the stairs, and crouched down, listening. I put a hand over my mouth to quiet my breathing.

Sean didn't know I was up there. Not yet. If he had, Aunt Lindsey wouldn't have been able to hold him back.

"I'll leave when I'm satisfied," Sean said.

I could see down into the living room through a narrow gap between the banister's posts. I saw the back of the top of his head. I saw Aunt Lindsey's feet. The two of them were standing inches apart. I told myself that if Sean stepped any closer, I'd come charging down those stairs.

"Why *wouldn't* Sarah run to you?" he asked, pressing.

"I have no idea. But like I said, she's not here. Maybe she realized she should go to the police."

"She didn't go to the police."

"How do you know? Maybe she called another precinct. Maybe they kept it from you for a reason."

Aunt Linds, I thought, *be careful now.*

"You're sure she didn't reach out to you?" Sean asked. "Even by phone?"

"No," she told him. "I mean yes, as in, yes, I'm sure that no, I haven't heard from her."

"Lindsey, let me spell this out for you. Your niece is in trouble. She's in trouble from every possible angle. I know you don't trust me, don't believe my intentions are good. I know you know—or you *think* you know—that she and I have had our difficulties. But I'm the only one who can help her now."

"You're right: I don't believe in your good intentions. But that doesn't change the truth: I haven't seen Sarah or heard from her."

"Really? Then why is *that* here?"

He was pointing.

"What?" she asked.

"That."

I craned my neck. His finger was aimed at the insulin kit. Aunt Lindsey could explain why she kept one in the house easily enough, but could she explain what it was doing in plain view?

"That's just . . ." she began. I heard her brain working to invent a story. I knew Sean heard it, too. "That's just a travel kit. I always keep one for her. You know that. And every few months I re-stock it. As any good nurse would do."

"You're a generous soul," Sean said.

Translation: He didn't buy a word she was selling.

"Listen," he said, "I need your help. I'm launching a statewide search, just in case Sarah's been abducted. I need photos. Lots of photos. Long hair, short hair. Summer clothes, winter clothes. No one has more pictures of Sarah than you."

He turned toward the staircase. Toward me. I yanked my head back. Sean wasn't asking; he was declaring. He knew she kept her family albums in the upstairs study.

"Wait," Aunt Lindsey said.

He was mounting the steps now, his badge flashing on his hip, his gun glistening in its holster. I scrambled away.

"I don't have any photos of her up there," she said.

Sean sniggered, as if she'd just confirmed something for him. He kept climbing.

"You don't, huh? I saw a gallery's worth in your study last time I was here. I'm sure any of them would—"

"No," she said.

I was crouched down at the far end of the hallway, too scared to stand and run.

"Sarah," Sean called, "I love you. You know that. I want to help you. Please don't shut me out. Not now."

I crawled on hands and knees into Aunt Lindsey's bedroom and then into her walk-in closet, hoping the general clutter might give me a place to hide. I heard Sean moving through the upstairs, opening and closing drawers, knocking on doors. Toying with me, like the stalker in a slasher flick.

"You know who I work with," he told Aunt Lindsey. "You know who *she* works for. At a crossroads like this, up against an organization like this? She needs me. Question my integrity all you like, but she needs me."

He opened the bathroom door.

"I could have sworn you had a framed picture of her in here."

"Look, Sean, the scrapbooks—"

"Are in the guest bedroom? Maybe?"

She lost her patience, decided to make a stand.

"You need a warrant, Sean. You can't go through a house without a warrant."

I caught a slight tremble in her voice. She thought I was still lying asleep in the spare room—the room Sean was about to search.

"My little Sarah is nobody's enemy," she added.

"I'm so glad to hear you say that, Lindsey. For once we're in agreement. Unfortunately, it doesn't matter if Sarah is or isn't their enemy: it only matters that they *think* she is."

Step by methodical step, he made his way to the master bedroom. I'd pulled the closet door shut, crept behind Aunt Lindsey's luggage collection, and covered myself with an armful of winter coats.

"Here's one," Sean said.

He was talking about my high school graduation photo. Aunt Lindsey kept it in a silver frame on top of her dresser.

"That picture's twenty years old," Aunt Lindsey said.

"True, but like I told you, I need a wide range. People have to know what she used to look like, what she looks like now, and what she might look like tomorrow."

A quick tour of her dresser drawers, maybe a glance under the bed, and then he was making his way toward the closet.

"Last chance," he said. "If she's in there, why not just tell me? We're all a little old to be playing hide-and-seek."

"How could she be in there when she hasn't even been by the house?"

Her tone—exasperated, fed up with being called a liar—was damn convincing. I hoped Sean thought so, too.

"All the same, I'll just take a peek."

The door opened. I felt every muscle in my body contract. I expected the coats to go flying, expected to see Sean's smug face staring down at me. Instead, I heard him curse, heard his fist slam against the wall. Aunt Lindsey let out a little gasp. Then they went quiet while Sean regained his composure.

"You're a bit of a hoarder, Linds," he said. "I shudder to think what we'll find in the basement."

CHAPTER 13

WHEN I knew for sure he was gone, I pushed my way out of the closet and peered into the hall. Aunt Lindsey was sitting on the floor, knees to her chest, head resting on her forearms. She'd heard me coming but didn't look up.

"God bless you, Sarah," she said. "I don't know how you do it. You're the bravest person I know."

I looked around as if maybe she was talking to someone else.

"Brave?" I said. "I cowered in a closet while you fought my battle for me. I'm so sorry, Aunt Linds. If he'd done anything, if he'd so much as…"

She stared out at nothing. There was sweat trickling down her forehead.

"I failed you," she said.

"What are you talking about? Never—not even once. You've been my champion every step of the way. My hero. It's me who failed you."

I sat next to her, took her hand.

"A child can't fail a parent," she said. "That's what I was, really: a parent. I wanted to do right by you. By your mother. I should have been paying closer attention. I should have been more forceful. Now it's too late. You come to me for protection and there's not a damn thing I can do."

I squeezed her hand a little tighter.

"My marriage isn't your fault, Aunt Linds. And you did do something."

"What's that? Chase him around my home while he hunted you down? Fat lot of good I'd have done if he found you."

"I don't mean that," I said. "You moved my car, didn't you? While I was asleep."

She smiled in spite of herself.

"It's in the church lot down the street," she said.

"And Anna's jewelry?"

"In the attic, wrapped up in your old sleeping bag."

"You know if Sean had seen my car parked out front, I'd be in jail now. Or worse."

Her smile faded.

"And if I'd put my foot down when it mattered, you wouldn't be mixed up in—"

"Shush now," I told her. "I love you. That's all that matters."

Downstairs, she sat me on the couch and brought out her nursing bag. The gash in my leg looked swollen and pink. She was busy tending to it when something—or the absence of something—caught my attention.

"Aunt Linds?"

"Am I being too rough?"

"No, it's not that."

I pointed to the coffee table.

"Did you move my insulin kit?"

She looked over, saw a stack of magazines and an empty space where the kit had been. She stood up. I stood with her. We searched the living room, the kitchen, the upstairs and downstairs bathrooms. The kit was gone. We both knew: Sean had taken it.

He must have figured it would work to his advantage once he found me. How could I run from him when he was holding the thing that kept me alive? Or maybe this was his way of flushing me out. There were only so many places I could go looking for insulin. He was probably camped outside my doctor's office right now.

"I'm so sorry," Aunt Lindsey said. "It's gone."

Then she walked over to me and took my face in her hands.

"Don't worry, child, we'll get through this. Together. You hear me? We're in this together."

I nodded, knowing full well this was my fight, and mine alone.

Next morning, Aunt Lindsey woke up to find the following note on her kitchen table:

Dear Aunt Lindsey,

I know if I delivered this message in person you'd try to talk me out of it, and I know you'd probably succeed, so I'm writing a note because I can't afford to be weak. Not now. I love you. There's no one I'd rather have in my corner, but this is our reality: in order for me to survive, and for you to be happy, I need to disappear. Alone. No forwarding address means no need for you to lie — to the police, or whoever comes calling. I don't want you on the hook for my mistakes. I couldn't bear it if anything happened to you.

There's something else. Something far more urgent. I cooked up a batch of buttered grits for you. They're in the Tupperware on top of the stove. Six stars.

All my heart,
Sarah

PS: As you can see, I've left you both my credit cards. Wait a few days and use them to buy anything you need/want. Use them for my sake, to throw the dogs off the scent. Then destroy them, along with this note.

It took me three drafts to get the wording right, then a fourth to make my penmanship legible. The note felt to me like a good-bye. A permanent good-bye. Because somehow I was sure I'd never see Aunt Lindsey again.

CHAPTER 14
DETECTIVE SEAN WALSH

SÍMON QUIT work at five o'clock sharp, spent an hour pushing weights around a boutique gym, then hit a local fast-food chain, where he sat by the window scarfing a three-tier cheeseburger and curly fries. No doubt about it: the man had assimilated.

From the restaurant I followed him to a ritzy wine bar in Sunset Park. Lucky for me, the place had a glass storefront. I parked across the street, watched through binoculars from behind my Jeep's tinted windows. Símon was halfway through a demicarafe of red when a woman in a sequin dress tapped his shoulder. He hopped up, smiled, gave her a very polite peck on the cheek. For a second I thought it was Serena. Right height and shape, wrong age: Símon's date was robbing the cradle.

They carried on what looked like a lively conversation for the better part of an hour, then made their way to the movie theater around the corner, an indie house showing two titles, one French and one German. Símon was eager to impress.

I looked at my watch, figured I had a couple of hours to kill before they came back out. I hadn't eaten since breakfast. I grabbed three slices at the pizza parlor across from the theater, then strolled over to Símon's Honda Civic and opened the driver's-side door with a slim jim.

I was looking for any sign of Serena: a receipt from a store in Anthony Costello's zip code, one of the ESL workbooks my wife was always giving her, a piece of Anna's jewelry. But the interior was spotless. Of course it was: if Símon played his cards right, he'd have company on the ride home.

I checked the glove compartment. Nothing but the vehicle's registration and an illustrated primer on the flora and fauna of the Everglades. Nothing much in the trunk, either. Just a spare tire, a jack, and a stash of environmentally friendly grocery bags.

Símon was starting to annoy me.

I glanced at my watch. The movie was only a half hour in. Chances were they'd stop for another drink after, maybe even a late meal. Unless Símon's sister planned on crashing date night, there was no point in my continuing to tag along. It occurred to me that I could break into his apartment just as easily as his car. If Serena was there, camped out on his couch, so much the better. If not, there might be something to indicate where she'd gone. I copied Símon's current address off the registration, then locked up and walked back to my car.

Símon lived in Ybor City in a funky but upscale building, a nineteenth-century boarding school that had been converted into condominiums in the nineties. I got past the lobby door with a bump key and some elbow grease, took the stairs two at a time up to his third-floor apartment. For a while, I just stood there listening, hoping to hear a television or radio, something to tell me Serena was home. But the only noise came from children fighting in a corner unit.

I rang the bell just to be sure, then slipped on a pair of latex gloves and let myself in. The lights were off, the windows open. I heard sporadic traffic coming from the street below, but otherwise the place was silent. I switched my phone to Flashlight, passed its beam over the living room, then kept going through the rest of the apartment. No doubt about it: Símon had done well for himself. French doors led to a balcony with a wrought iron railing. The raised kitchen was loaded with stainless steel appliances. Art from multiple continents hung on the walls. The hardwood floors were gleaming. Not a speck of dust anywhere. Not in the bedroom, the bathroom, the study. Almost as if he had a full-time maid.

Well, this was a bust, I thought.

When Vincent called tomorrow for his daily update, I'd have nothing to give him. Unless…

I was on my way out the door when it hit me: what if Símon killed Anthony? It was a theory with no supporting evidence, but still it felt plausible. When it came to women, Anthony was pure predator. His type always is. And Símon, from what I could gather, was pure gentleman. On a day picked at random, I'd seen him cry with an old woman over her dead cat, then greet his date with an innocent peck on the cheek. Símon, champion of the fair sex. He wouldn't take kindly to someone pawing his kid sister.

Maybe I'd laid it on a little thick with Heidi, but I'd meant what I said: it was borderline impossible to believe that a 120-pound woman could bring down a mammoth like Anthony. Símon, on the other hand, acting as Serena's white knight—that was easy enough to picture. Maybe he'd gone there to beat some manners into Anthony. Maybe his rage had gotten the better of him.

The idea struck me so hard that, without realizing it, I backed up and dropped onto the couch. But before I could think things through, I heard keys jangling outside, and then Símon's front door swung open.

CHAPTER 15

ANNA COSTELLO

October 14
2:00 p.m.
Interview Room A

I NEEDED a place to hole up, gather myself. My first instinct was to book a room at the Four Seasons. Anthony and I spent our last anniversary there. We got into a blistering poolside fight, and then I didn't see him again until two in the morning, when he stumbled in and passed out facedown on his side of the bed. Believe me, if I was going to kill him, I'd have done it then.

The problem with the Four Seasons—and the Peninsula, the Ritz-Carlton, the Regency—was that I'd need a credit card, and even if I weaseled my way in without one, I'd run the risk of being flagged by the staff. The Costello payroll reached far and wide, and then there were the wannabe thugs looking to ingratiate themselves with Vincent. I wasn't above slumming it at a Super 8, but even that would be risky: a Bentley, even a scratched one, wouldn't exactly blend in with the Hyundais and tractor trailers.

Meanwhile, I had to get off the street, at least for the six remaining hours of daylight. I pulled into a parking garage, drove up to the third level, and took a space between a minivan and a Ford F-150. No way to spot me unless you happened to turn your head as you were driving past. I figured I'd shut my eyes until dark, then drive straight out of Florida, put as many miles as I could manage between me and my dead husband's family, then pawn the Bentley for a fraction of its worth and buy a one-way ticket to Buenos Aires. I've always wanted to learn the tango.

I didn't sleep. If I can't fall asleep in my own bed without swallowing a bucket of pills every night, then how was I going to drift off in a parking garage in the middle of the day? Especially knowing I was Uncle Vincent's new most wanted? Still, I tried. I draped a scarf over my eyes and angled my seat back as far as it would go.

Which is why I didn't notice Defoe walking up behind the Bentley with a crowbar. He'd smashed in my rear passenger's side window and was fiddling with the lock by the time I had the key in the ignition.

"Don't you dare!" he shouted. "Get out of the car. Now."

I cranked the engine, shifted into reverse, stomped on the gas. Defoe leapt out of the way, but not before I clipped his leg. Johnny Broch materialized from between two SUVs, ran at the Bentley as if he might tackle it, then hurled himself onto the hood of a Fiat when I switched to Drive and laid on the gas again.

"Stop!" Defoe yelled. "We just want to talk."

He was upright, hobbling at full speed toward his sedan. I might have asked him why he had his pistol out if he was only looking to chat. Broch, who was an easy six feet six inches and must have weighed three hundred pounds, half slid, half fell off the Fiat. He and Defoe made an unlikely pair: two thugs fat and fit, tall and short, young and old. I was running from Laurel and Hardy.

It's hard to burn rubber in a parking garage. I lost my side mirror turning onto level two, nearly massacred an octogenarian and his shopping cart as I blurred down level one. Then I did something I've only seen in movies: I took out the boom barrier at the attendant's station. Plowed right through it and dragged the remains skidding and sparking into the street. Pedestrians screamed, scattered, then screamed again when Defoe's sedan came barreling after me.

The only direction I had in mind was away. I spun right at the first corner, then turned hard into an alley after I saw traffic backed up at the next light. I had the Bentley pushing seventy when a small slab of cement by the back door of a restaurant sent the car careening into a dumpster. The airbag nearly knocked me unconscious. By the time I'd scrambled out from under it, Defoe was limping toward me, his minion at his heels.

"Enough, Anna," he said. "It's time to come with us."

I'd forgotten just how heinous his skin was close up—taut and glistening, as if someone had taken a cockroach shell and spread it over a human face.

"Can't do it," I said, leaning with one hand against the Bentley, waiting for my breath to come bounding back.

"Come on now, Anna," he said, patting his leg as if he was summoning a dog.

Here's a free survival tip: always do the opposite of whatever your would-be assassin commands.

Which is to say I ran like hell. I was guessing they couldn't kill me until Vincent got his alone time. More importantly, I was guessing I could outrun a fat man and a gimp. One perk to being the wife of mob royalty: you spend a lot of time at the gym. With the crumpled Bentley blocking the alley, the only way they could follow was on foot. I figured as long as I didn't trip and face-plant, I'd live to see another day.

"Go on, go on!" Defoe shouted. "Stop her before she makes the street."

Then I heard tires screeching, and I knew Defoe was planning to hightail it around the block and cut me off on the other side.

Unfortunately for me, this alley was the length of an airport run-way, and I hadn't cleared a third of it before I crashed.

A quick glance over my shoulder told me I had nothing to fear from Broch, who was too top-heavy to keep pace. Now all I needed was for downtown traffic to keep Defoe at a crawl. I dug deep for an extra gear, gasped my way through the homestretch.

And then I saw my escape route: a city bus. It was pulling past the alley and up to the curb as I hit the street. I ran after it, leapt aboard just before the driver shut the doors, then started for the back.

"Hey, miss," the driver called after me. "Forget something?"

I hadn't taken a city bus since college. I searched my pockets, threw change down the chute until the light turned green.

The smart play would have been to duck out of sight, but I had to know. I walked past rows of empty seats, crouched down, peered out the back window.

Defoe and the man-child were standing beside their double-parked sedan, craning their necks in every direction but mine.

I was safe. For now.

CHAPTER 16

BUT PROBABLY not for much longer. Not unless I found a way to get Vincent Costello off my back.

I exited three stops later, in front of a strip mall lined with the kind of stores my brain is programmed to ignore: a comic book shop I'd bet my life sold weed out of the back, one of those cook-your-own-food Mongolian barbecues (Anthony always thought they looked like fun; my argument was, what's the point if you have to do all the work?), an antiques store with busted GI Joes and ancient lunch boxes in the window. Crap, crap, and more crap. And crappiest of all: a women's discount apparel store with half a roll of duct tape holding the front window in place.

Like it or not, this was a new day for me, and new days require new outfits. I held my breath, stepped inside. It was suddenly clear to me what people meant by *off-the-rack:* half the merchandise was lying trampled on the floor. The place itself looked trampled. The drop ceiling was buckled from water damage, the blue synthetic carpet was worn through to the concrete foundation, and the long, dark cracks in the drywall reminded me of my grandmother's spider veins. Even the security cameras hadn't been updated since the seventies.

In other words, the place was perfect. I didn't have to search hard to find the kind of outfit Anna Costello would never be caught dead in: acid jeans, a pink sweatshirt with GLAMOUR GIRL scrawled across the chest in purple glitter, a pair of those rubber clogs patterned with geometric cutouts, plastic sunglasses sporting neon-green frames, and a handful of sparkly rainbow hair clips that I planned to stick at random intervals all around my head. I could sit on Vincent Costello's lap and he still wouldn't recognize me.

I took my haul up to the counter and paid—this was one place I could use my credit cards without fear of a Costello hearing about it seconds later—then carried the drawstring plastic bag back to the only dressing room and swapped my new clothes for the old ones. I looked like a cross between a high school cheerleader and the last woman standing at the local casino's boilermaker Thursdays. It would work just fine. Where I was going, I'd fit right in.

La Torre Bar (formerly La Torre Bar and Grille, but the latter part of the name was dropped when not even the most hardened wino would eat there) was five miles to the north, in a neighborhood I'd heard about but never visited. I decided to hoof it in my new clogs. I had time to kill: Victoria wouldn't be there before happy hour, anyway.

Victoria Maria Elena Costello. Anthony's first wife. In his more affectionate moments, Anthony called me "the upgrade." Victoria kept the Costello name in part to piss off Anthony and in part because it came with major benefits. No one fires a Costello. No one assaults or insults a Costello. And men don't hit on a Costello uninvited. Not even drunk men.

All that came in handy for Vicki given that she poured the drinks at La Torre. By the time I arrived, my new sweatshirt was a darker shade of pink, and my feet felt as though they'd been rubbed raw. The bar sat between a bodega and an abandoned storefront. A gaggle of aging men hung outside the bodega playing cards and smoking cigars. I cocked my head and winked at them: a new personality to go with my new wardrobe. Then I gave myself a silent pep talk and pushed through the bar's saloon-style doors.

The interior was all felt pennants slung crooked against wood paneling. The sawdust on the floor was probably the same sawdust they'd laid out when the place opened three decades ago. At a little after five, only the hard-core regulars were in attendance—drunks of both genders with sunken mouths, busted capillaries, clothes that would fall apart if they were ever washed. Of course, the population would look much the same at 8:00 p.m., 10:00 p.m., midnight.

She was standing behind the bar, chopping up lemons, with a black rag slung over one shoulder. She hadn't changed much since the last time I saw her. Fake hair, fake eyelashes, fake nails, fake tits, and none of it particularly well maintained.

"Hiya, Vicki," I said.

She hated it when anyone shortened her name. Victoria sounded to her like royalty, and falling from Anthony's castle to this hole-in-the-wall had done nothing to slow her ego.

"I know you?" she asked.

I took off the Cracker Jack–prize sunglasses.

"Know me?" I said. "You hate my guts."

She glared across the bar, her jaw working double time. Vicki's one of those people who can make the act of chewing gum look and sound like a war crime.

"Oh, yeah," she said. "You're the lying, thieving, flat-chested whore. Anthony find a newer model yet?"

I grinned. I felt oddly pleased with myself. Her insults held no sway anymore. Nothing she said could faze me. I needed information from her, and that was it.

Namely, I needed to know who might want Anthony dead.

Because while I believed either Sarah or Serena was involved, or maybe both of them, I didn't believe they'd acted alone. I didn't believe they'd done the stabbing. Combined they added up to about half Anthony's weight. Maybe Serena turned off the alarm, let the killer in. Maybe Sarah sprinkled my husband's eggs with powdered Valium. But the move against him had been sanctioned by a higher power. Maybe Vincent's men weren't coming after me to avenge Anthony. Maybe they were just finishing the job.

If anyone could cut through the maybes, it was Victoria. She'd been hands-on with his business interests—especially his extracurricular interests, the side deals he didn't want Vincent to know about. She was the one who convinced him he wasn't getting his due. It took a while, but her relationship with Anthony went south because she pushed too hard, wanted his fingers in more and more pies. That's part of why I played deaf and dumb in my marriage. The other part was that I really didn't want to know.

"I'm trying to imagine what brings an Italian American princess like you to this shithole on a weekday afternoon," she said. "I'm not coming up with anything that makes my life better."

"I've got questions," I said. "Questions I'm pretty sure only you can answer."

"Anthony did something to you, didn't he?"

She was gloating. The poor thing really had no clue, and I wasn't about to break the news until she told me what I wanted to know.

"In a way," I said. "I'm not involved in his business dealings like you were. I was wondering who . . ."

"He's in bed with?"

I nodded.

"You looking to hurt him? 'Cause if that could be done, believe me I'd have done it. Anthony's protected from every angle.

As bad as I wanted to see his little empire collapse—an empire I more or less built for him—I wasn't going to get myself killed trying."

"It isn't that," I said. "I just want to be prepared."

An elderly patron at the end of the bar called out for a fresh pint. Vicki told him to keep his pants on.

"I don't believe you," she said. "But if you want to make a play against Tony, it won't be me who stops you. Nothing would make me happier than to see you both go down in flames."

"That's sweet, Vic," I said. "So tell me: where is he vulnerable? Most likely to get in trouble?"

"You asking who would come after him?"

I gave another nod, felt the hair clips knocking against my skull.

"Granted, my information's dated, but I'd look to the boys in blue."

"The cops?"

"That's right, hon: the cops. Tony blackmails them. Gets them to do his bidding. *His,* not Vincent's. You starting to see the picture?"

It was a much bigger and uglier picture than I'd imagined. I leaned hard against a stool. Vicki smiled, enjoying herself.

"Could be one of the cops is after him. Could be Vincent himself. But the question you need to ask yourself is, how does Tony know which cops are dirty? Who's feeding him the intel? 'Cause that person has a hell of a lot to lose. Could be he wants out."

"You know who it is, don't you?" I said. "Give me a name."

She laughed. Her laugh was as fake as the rest of her.

"I'm not a rat, hon. But then I'm guessing you don't really need me to tell you."

It was a good guess.

"So what is it?" she asked. "Death threats? A pipe bomb through the bay window?"

"No," I said. "Anthony's already dead."

I'd like to say I told her the truth because I thought she should know, but the even bigger truth is I got a kick out of watching her face turn colors beneath all that rouge.

"What are you talking about?"

"He was stabbed to death. I found him this morning in our kitchen. I'm no expert, but it looked like a crime of passion. I'm sure those dirty cops will come knocking at your door any minute."

She picked up the knife she'd been using to cut lemons and pointed it at the door.

"You bring this shit to me?" she said. "Get the hell out or I swear to God I'll do you the way they did Anthony."

"Vicki, I—"

"You think I'm stupid? You're here asking questions because you know it's *you* they're coming for next. You've got 'Loose End' tattooed across your forehead. And now I've got to worry about your deathbed confession: 'I didn't know anything about anything until Victoria spilled her guts.' You're lucky we're standing in a room full of witnesses."

On cue, the drunks stumbled off their stools and gathered around. The poor dears thought they were really quite threatening; I could have knocked any one of them over with my little finger. I took a last look at Vicki and told myself it was better to be the widow than the ex.

CHAPTER 17

I DAMN near wore out those rubber clogs walking the seedier streets of East Tampa, looking for some hole to crawl into. I had a hundred dollars cash in my wallet, enough to rent a motel room for a night—maybe two if the room came with a mirror on the ceiling and an hourly rate. There was a surprising shortage of choices, and I wasn't about to stop one of the locals and ask for a rec. Not without backup.

And that was the thing: I had no more backup. Anthony and I had more than our share of problems, but I always knew that if any man so much as laid a finger on me he'd end up trampled by an army of Costellos. At least that was true yesterday. Now that same army was hunting me. For the first time in a long while, I understood what it meant to be alone.

My Fitbit logged twenty thousand steps before I came across the Jackalope Inn, a circa-1970 structure with teetering breezeways and rusted-out railings—the kind of establishment that feels incomplete without a SWAT team huddled in the parking lot. *Perfect,* I thought. *Even I wouldn't think to look for me here.*

Inside, the man behind the bulletproof glass told me it would be forty bucks for the night. I spent another five bucks at the vending machines, coming away with a Diet Coke and a bag of almond Mars bars—my first meal of the day. The room was more or less what I'd expected: a sagging twin bed, flea market paintings, peeling wallpaper, a carpet I'd make sure never to touch with my bare feet. What I hadn't anticipated was the odor. It was as if somebody had sprayed every inch of the place with synthetic fruit punch. Whatever stench they were covering up didn't stand a chance.

I switched on the TV in hopes that the voices might calm me. Big mistake. The Jackalope Inn only offered local channels, and at the ten o'clock hour they were all showing the nightly news. Anywhere I flipped, there he was: a full-screen headshot of my recently deceased husband. I didn't want to watch, but I couldn't look away. So I sat there chomping on Mars bars (almond my ass—not one lousy nut in the whole bag) and listening to the pundits make uninformed guesses about who whacked Vincent Costello's portly nephew. Surprise, surprise: my name came up. Some ace reporter had already managed to obtain from an anonymous source a "firsthand account" of the knock-down-drag-out Anthony and I had at his uncle's party—the one where I threatened to kill Anthony in his sleep.

Of course, there were other suspects. Anthony did work for the mob, after all. It was perfectly plausible that I'd been framed, in which case I was either lying at the bottom of a swamp or locked in a closet somewhere with duct tape over my mouth.

Listening to that crap was giving me a full-blown panic attack. I pictured Vincent sitting on the edge of his overstuffed recliner, watching the same program, growing more and more convinced that it was my turn to die. I switched off the TV, but the sounds of bellowing drunks and blaring sirens didn't do much to calm me down. Someone was walking back and forth along the breezeway outside. *Defoe,* I told myself. It had to be.

The more I thought about it, the more convinced I became that I wouldn't survive the night.

Which is why I picked up the motel phone and made the call. The only call I could think to make.

"Nine one one, what's your emergency?" the operator asked.

I hemmed and hawed, gave her something less than the full story.

"You stay put now," she said in the kind of soothing voice that truly anxious people find maddening. "Help is on the way."

She didn't say what kind of help. I went to the window, pulled back the heavy curtain just far enough to peer outside. The Jackalope faced the kind of cityscape that sends urban dwellers running for the country. Busted streetlamps, heavily graffitied storefronts, potholes you could climb down into, delinquents gathered on every corner. But no Defoe. No Broch. Still, my legs were trembling, and I had to fight to keep down all that chocolate and syrup.

I was expecting either a squad car or a sedan, so at first a Jeep pulling into the lot below didn't register. Then I saw who stepped out of it: Detective Sean Walsh, Anthony's friend on the force. The man Anthony had tried to convince me was nothing more than a golf buddy who owed him a few favors. The man Vicki wouldn't name. Was he here on behalf of the Tampa PD or the Costello family? Or had he come, as Vicki had suggested, to tie up one last loose end?

I didn't stick around to find out. Just like in the movies, I shimmied out of the narrow bathroom window, grabbed on to a tree branch, and lowered myself down. The back of the motel faced an abandoned lot. I started across at a full gallop, tripping over rubble, scraping my palms as I pushed myself back up. I didn't know where I was headed or what I'd find on the other side, and I didn't care. All I wanted was to put distance between me and Sean.

Which is exactly what I failed to do. Sean wasn't gimpy like Defoe or bulky like Broch. He was the type to count calories and measure his body fat after his morning run. He came up on me out of nowhere, had me pinned to the ground before I knew I was in a fight.

"Hi there, Anna." He grinned.

I didn't hesitate to scream my head off. Sean let go of one of my wrists, clamped a hand over my mouth. I clawed for his eyes but couldn't find them.

"Easy now," he said. "You called us, remember?"

Us. Was it possible that even the 911 operator moonlighted for the Costellos? Or had she unwittingly forwarded the call to one of Anthony's blackmail victims? Or to Sean himself?

"Yeah," I said, once he took his hand from my mouth. "It was a false alarm. So sorry to waste your time."

He lifted me to my feet but didn't cuff me. He didn't Mirandize me, either. There was nothing at all coplike about his behavior, which made me halfway certain I was headed for a pair of concrete boots.

I tried sweet-talking him as he led me back to the Jeep.

"Listen," I said, "I don't snitch. I won't tell anyone anything about anything. I don't know anything. Anthony kept me in the dark. Whatever secrets the two of you had died with him. I promise you, Sean. All I want now is to get as far from this tropical shithole as possible. There's money in it if you help me. You don't have to do this."

"Do what?" he asked.

I didn't say anything. He waited a beat, then burst out laughing.

"You think I'm here to . . . what? Whack you? You've got it all wrong, Anna. I'm here to help. Like you said, Anthony kept you in the dark. You're new to this kind of thing. I figure you might need a little coaching."

I leaned across the table until Detective Haagen and I were sitting eyeball to eyeball.

"And that's what he did," I told her. "He coached me. All the way to the station. He told me all about you. Sorry, but he isn't a fan. He said if I wanted to stay out of prison I should dodge your questions, claim I found the body and panicked. Nothing more to it. Meanwhile, he'd get Vincent off my back, hand him the real killer."

"Detective Sean Walsh said all of that?"

"Yes. But then if I believed him, I wouldn't be sharing it with you right now, would I?"

I watched her think it over. For a cop, her poker face was downright lousy. I could see she wanted to believe me. She wanted to believe I was giving her testimony that would end her ex-partner's career. At the same time, she was afraid of being duped by a mob widow who might very well be lying through her teeth to save her own hide. In the end, she stalled.

"I'll have to talk to the DA," she said.

"Fine," I told her. "Meanwhile, can I go? I've told you everything I know. Everything from the moment I found Anthony to right now. I'm tired as hell, and I need about three showers."

She looked confused.

"But where would you go?" she asked. "Back to the Jackalope? Wouldn't a cell be the safest place for you? If what you say about Sean is true, we might be able to work something out."

I gave her a trademark Costello sneer.

"You mean witness protection?" I said. "Detective, you've been inside my home. Hell, at this point you probably know it better than I do. You really think a bungalow in Tempe is gonna cut it?"

Now she looked worried, and I knew damn well what she was worried about: dead women tell no tales, and they sure as hell don't show up to testify in court.

"Don't sweat it," I told her. "I'm the three Rs: resourceful, resilient, and rich. I won't make any more mistakes."

She shrugged.

"I can't hold you. But I do need you to keep close."

"Fine by me," I said, standing.

Of course, legally speaking, I could have shut down that interview any time the mood struck me. Haagen was right to be cautious. I hadn't lied to her, but the truth I'd shared was purely by design.

CHAPTER 18

DETECTIVE SEAN WALSH

LUCKY FOR me, the lovebirds paused in Símon's doorway for a long, loud kiss. It gave me just enough time to duck out onto the balcony.

If Símon had lived on the second floor, I might have jumped. At most I'd have sprained an ankle or tweaked a knee. Nothing a frozen steak couldn't fix. But that third flight would land me in the hospital. There'd be a report. Heidi would hear about it. She'd figure out soon enough that Símon and Serena were siblings, and then she'd come hard after my badge. I couldn't risk that. My only option was to hunker down and wait it out.

I watched Símon and his date through a small gap in the curtains covering the French doors. They'd decided to take their nightcap at home. Símon, it seemed, wanted to showcase his stainless steel martini mixer. Either he was a little drunk already or he didn't spend much time in his kitchen. It took a lot of opening and closing of cabinets before he had the gin and the vermouth and the olives lined up on the counter.

Meanwhile, my mind was running scenarios, none of them very pleasant.

My biggest fear was that Símon and his lady friend would

choose to sip their cocktails under the stars. In that case, the best I could do would be to hide my face and shoulder my way past them. Símon had pounds on me, but I had sobriety and surprise on my side. I slipped out of my blazer, prepared to hold it like a cape in front of my head.

But the evening didn't take that particular turn. These were working people with early start times. They could only fit so much into an evening. Once Símon found a pair of tiny plastic swords for the olives, they carried their martinis straight to the bedroom. I quit holding my breath, let out what felt like enough air for four people. Then I waited some more just in case Símon came back in search of snacks.

That was when I saw it, lying there on the small wrought iron table. A bright blue workbook called *English on Your Lunch Break*. I remembered when Sarah bought it. She took the title literally, had visions of tutoring Serena over grilled-tomato sandwiches and sun-brewed iced tea. The two of them were close—almost like sisters. Together, they made life under Anthony's thumb bearable.

Seeing the book here now, my pulse turned electric. I scanned the rest of the balcony, spotted a small, tan duffel bag hidden behind a potted ficus tree. I walked over, opened it, found a stash of women's clothes and toiletries. Things were looking up. So much so that I almost forgot I was on the verge of getting busted for B and E.

Priorities, I told myself. *Time to get the hell out of here.*

I opened the French doors just wide enough to slip through, then walked heel to toe across the living room. There was a jazz record playing somewhere in the recesses of the apartment. Símon was pulling out all the stops. Part of me felt jealous: Sarah and I hadn't been on anything like a date in as long as I could remember, and lately our bedroom was strictly for sleep.

Back at the Jeep, I pulled out a flask from under the spare tire and did some drinking of my own. Then I spent an hour circling the block until a spot opened up directly across from Símon's building. Serena had been there. She'd been staying there. Date night or not, there was a chance she might come back. The fact that she'd hidden her belongings behind a tree on the balcony only confirmed she was on the run. Whether she'd done something or was afraid of being blamed for something remained to be seen.

Unlike most cops, I love a good stakeout. There's an adrenaline rush that comes with putting yourself in a position to see what nobody wants you to see. The adrenaline helps me think. And I had a hell of a lot to think about, starting with how I'd play it when Serena made her appearance. I couldn't, despite direct orders, turn her over to Vincent. I'd be disposing of the person most likely to swear up and down that Sarah was no killer.

The more I thought about it, the more I became convinced I could pin it on the brother—whether he'd done it or not. All I needed was a little time to build the case. Meanwhile, I had to get word to Heidi's three main suspects. Apart from the fact that they ran, Heidi had nothing on them. Nothing concrete. All they had to do was point the finger at each other, keep my ex-partner turning in circles. I'd tell them exactly what to say. Have Sarah implicate Serena, Anna implicate Sarah, Serena implicate Anna. Or maybe have each of them implicate the other two. Heidi would be blinded with reasonable doubt. Sarah would remain free.

A plan was starting to take shape. I worked it out one piece at a time. The siblings were my ticket back to a humdrum life. First, find Serena and put in a call to the tip line; second, hand Símon over to Vincent with a note that read "He killed your nephew." It would be awfully damn convenient to have Símon disappear while Serena was in the box with Heidi. He'd look like a man who knew his sister was about to flip. And when

Heidi's team searched Símon's condo, they'd find a few of Anthony's prized possessions sitting on the top shelf of his bedroom closet.

Little by little, the lights went out in the buildings around me. I found myself kicking around the same question into the wee hours: did the fact that Serena was staying with Símon make it more or less likely that he killed Anthony? I mean *actually* killed Anthony. And if not him, then who? It wasn't one of Vincent's men. The killing was too personal, too sloppy. A pro wouldn't stab him twenty-seven times, then leave the body behind. Who else had the motive *and* strength? Maybe Serena found herself a boyfriend. Maybe Anna had taken a lover. Maybe Sarah had, for that matter: I'd have been too checked out to notice.

But why dwell on maybes when there was a flesh-and-blood brother tailor-made for the part? The truth didn't matter at all next to what I could prove. And if I could just find Serena, I was pretty sure I could prove that my wife hadn't killed Anthony Costello.

CHAPTER 19

SARAH ROBERTS-WALSH

October 15
8:30 a.m.
Interview Room C

I DROVE out of Aunt Lindsey's little township before sunup, bleary from lack of sleep and feeling as though my calf might combust at any moment. I had nothing with me but Anna's collection. Not even a change of clothes. I'd thought about leaving Aunt Linds a diamond or a sapphire, but if Sean or his cronies came back with a warrant, they'd lock her up for receiving stolen property. They'd do it just to draw me out. And it would work. I'm not brave or strong or fierce or healthy, but no way could I let my aunt spend even one night in jail.

First things first: I needed to convert those jewels into cash. A week ago that would have been easy. Anthony knew people. Sean knew people. A half million dollars' worth of jewels would have fetched a half million dollars in bills.

But now everything had changed. I'd have to take whatever a pawnshop was willing to give me.

There's a long string of cash-for-goods joints on Hillsborough Avenue, mixed in with the liquor stores and tattoo parlors, but unfortunately pawnbrokers don't tend to be early risers. Not as early as Aunt Lindsey, anyway. The best I could find was an 8:00

a.m. open. That left me with two hours to kill. Two hours is a long time when you can't be seen in public.

I bought a latte and two slices of lemon pound cake at the drive-in window of a Starbucks, then sat in the parking lot sipping and nibbling. The sugar and caffeine made me queasy, but at least there'd be no chance of my drifting off. I wouldn't let myself sleep again until I found a bed in a town or city where I knew nobody, and where nobody who knew me would think to look.

At 8:00 a.m. sharp, a skeletal man with a slick comb-over and a bad case of scoliosis opened the door to Quick Money Pawn & Gun. I gave him ten minutes to get settled, then followed him inside, tote bag hanging from my right shoulder. The place was a junkyard with a roof over its head. You couldn't take a step without tripping over an appliance or a box of comic books. Rifles and guitars hung side by side on every wall. Bicycles dangled from the ceiling. Power tools filled a metal shelving unit stuck precariously in the center of the store. Boxes of cheap cigars stood ten deep at the far end of the counter.

The owner was smoking one now, eyeing me from behind a glass display case cluttered with knives and watches and the kind of costume jewelry Anna Costello wouldn't be caught dead wearing. I walked over to him, set the bag on the counter, kept the straps drawn tight.

"My first of the day," he said, turning his head to blow out a ring of very rank-smelling smoke. "What can I do you for?"

I had to wonder how many sad and desperate women had been here before, standing where I now stood, hoping this greasy stick figure of a man would pay enough for their baubles to get them out of town.

"I've got something—some things—I'd like to sell," I said.

I stopped there. I had a whole sales pitch planned, but my

voice was quaking, and I knew the more I talked the more I'd give myself away. Instead, I just opened the bag.

He took a long look inside, and while he looked it dawned on me that he might very well have ties to the Costello family. Pawnshops need protection. More protection than most businesses. On top of which they're an invaluable source of intel. A handgun just came in? Who sold it, and who got clipped the night before? Someone pawned a sixty-four-inch TV and a set of silver steak knives? Who got robbed, and how much would they pay to get their stuff back? I cursed myself for the risk I was taking, but it was too late now. Besides, I didn't exactly have an abundance of options.

"Interesting," the man said. "Very interesting."

Interesting? It had to be the biggest haul his little shop had ever seen.

"You are looking to sell all of this?" he asked.

I nodded.

He started sifting through the bag, cautiously at first, but then two pieces in particular caught his attention: Anna's antique silver locket, and a high-clarity blue sapphire pendant that Anthony had given her quite publicly at a banquet celebrating their tenth anniversary. The broker set them on his palm, held them up to the light.

"I need to look at these under the glass," he said. "Please wait here—I'll just be a moment."

I started to protest, but before I could get out a word he'd turned his back to me and slipped into a side room. I thought about sacrificing those two pieces and running off with the rest. What if he was on the phone to the police? To Vincent? Maybe he'd recognized the sapphire. Maybe he'd been at that banquet.

Not yet, Sarah, I told myself. *Hold your ground.*

After what felt like a dozen lifetimes, he came back, grinning from ear to ear. I guessed this was his salesman persona.

"Sixty thousand," he said. Just like that.

"For the two pieces?"

"For all of it."

I studied his expression. He wasn't joking. It was enough to snap me out of flight mode.

"Sixty thousand?" I said. "They're worth ten times that."

"Yes," he said, "but how much is discretion worth?"

I took a step back, stumbled over a crate of naked Barbie dolls.

"Discretion?" I said.

"I've been at this a long while," he said. "You and I both know those jewels don't belong to you. We both know how you came by them, and we both know that whoever you took them from has far more resources than you do."

I reached for the bag, grabbed the closest strap. He grabbed the other.

"How do you know this isn't a sting?" I bluffed.

He sniggered.

"Like I said, I've been at this awhile. I can tell the difference between a setup and a getaway. There's a window in my office. I took down your license plate. I'll know who you are five minutes after you walk out that door. Is sixty thousand starting to sound fair?"

I nodded, felt my face turning colors.

"I should think so"—he smiled—"given what you paid for them."

The stacks of bills fit neatly inside Anna's tote bag.

CHAPTER 20

"YOU PAWNED Anna Costello's half-million-dollar collection for sixty K?" Haagen said. "Now that's priceless. I can't wait to see the look on her face."

She laughed herself silly, then put on the brakes and fixed me with her most damning stare.

"You realize you just copped to a felony?" she said, glancing up at the camera.

"But I didn't take the jewels—I just found them."

"That's what every burglar says."

"I didn't know what else to do. I was just trying to survive."

"Yeah, they say that, too."

I started biting my nails. She reached across the table, pulled my hand away.

"We'll get to that charge later," she said. "Let's keep our focus on the timeline. I'm guessing you're on your way to Texas?"

"Sort of," I said.

I hadn't planned on holing up in Texas. I didn't have any plan at all except to get as far from Tampa as possible—far from Vincent and Sean and anyone who would care that Anthony was dead.

I got on the interstate headed west and told myself I wouldn't slow down until the sun had set and risen again. I drove out of Florida, through Alabama, and into Mississippi. I drove through Mississippi and into Louisiana. I didn't see the time or the states go by. I don't remember pulling over for gas or to clean out my wound, though I know I must have. I was in the zone. On autopilot. All of me save what I needed to keep the car moving forward had shut down.

I finally stopped eighteen hours and thirteen hundred miles later, at a diner in a flat and dried-out wasteland where nothing seemed to grow—not trees or shrubs or even grass. Nothing but a sprawling vista of dirt in every direction. And two buildings: a restaurant with a hand-painted sign out front that read THE DINER THINGS IN LIFE and a large and only slightly dilapidated farmhouse maybe fifty yards past the diner.

I couldn't say for sure what state I was in. I'd stopped keeping track. I only knew that my gut was churning from lack of food and my head was buzzing from lack of sleep. Coffee and flapjacks would give me the strength I needed to get back on the road. I'd worry about getting some rest later.

I heard country music playing inside. I figured it would be one of those backwater eateries where everyone turns and stares as you enter, then whispers about the outsider who's eating alone. Carrying a PBS tote bag wouldn't help matters, but I wasn't about to leave sixty thousand dollars sitting in my car.

A tiny Liberty Bell hanging above the entrance rang when I entered. A minute later, a waitress came charging through the kitchen's double doors, carrying a pot of coffee in one hand and a pitcher of water in the other.

"Anywhere ya'd like, hon," she said.

The place was nearly empty, the only customers a sun-beaten family of four in a booth by the window. I took a stool at the counter, set the tote bag at my feet, and hooked the foot of my uninjured leg through the straps. At first I was alone, but then an elderly man in a John Deere baseball cap came back from the gents, sat two stools over, and buried his head in a newspaper.

Be friendly, I told myself. *But not memorable.*

"Peaceful in here," I said to the man, then smiled. "Like we might see a tumbleweed roll by."

He didn't so much as glance in my direction, but the waitress, who was fiddling with the cash register at the opposite side of the counter, gave a little snort.

"As long as it's a *payin'* tumbleweed," she said.

She walked over to me with a menu.

"I'm Doris," she said. "I own the place. Special today is split pea."

"I'm Michelle," I told her. "This might sound dumb, but I just pulled off the highway, and I'm a little disoriented. Can I ask what town we're near?"

"You headed west?"

"East," I said.

"Oh, you from Phoenix? I got cousins in Prescott. Next town east from here is Kerens. Sixty-one miles. Not much of a town compared to Phoenix. Doubt it has a hundred people in it. Love your hair, by the way."

She had the Texas accent, but you couldn't call it a drawl. She talked faster than any New Yorker, almost as if she was trying to clear room for the next thought. She was younger than Aunt Lindsey, but not by much, and she had a similar air about her— as though she'd treat you with kindness but wouldn't be taken for a fool.

"Sixty-one miles," I repeated.

To a town with no population to speak of. What were the chances anyone would think to look for me there?

I glanced around at the decor before opening my menu. There were truck parts hanging wherever you'd expect a poster or a sign. An air horn painted in polka dots dangled from a hook above the fountain soda machine. A mud flap decorated with stick figures and an arrow pointed to the restrooms in the back. A radiator grille separated patrons from the area behind the counter. A side mirror jutted out from a support beam like a fancy light fixture, in contrast to the chandelier made out of a semi-size tire. The wall behind the counter was plastered with license plates. All in all it was an homage to the interstate, without which this place couldn't exist.

"I see you're noticing my Great Wall," Doris said, nodding toward the license plates.

"I like it," I said. "A travel theme."

"More like a departure theme: every state worth leavin'. Which is to say, every state but Texas."

So I *was* in Texas, somewhere between the interstate and a town called Kerens.

"Coffee's free with waffles," she said. "Just so you know."

"I'll take waffles, then."

"Good choice. They ain't killed no one yet."

I smiled, handed her the menu, went back to perusing the Great Wall. Mixed in with the license plates was a sign that read HELP WANTED.

"Any chance you're hiring a cook?" I asked.

"Waitress. I've got bunions on my bunions. Why, you lookin'?"

"Maybe," I said. "But I'm a chef."

"Don't need a chef. Need a waitress, though."

She gave me a wink I couldn't quite interpret, then headed into the kitchen.

My mind started racing. I'd been thinking I'd push on for Mexico just like every fugitive in every movie, but as plans went, that one had its flaws. First and foremost, I'd have to cross the border with a sack full of sixty thousand dollars. Second, if I made it across the border, I'd be driving blindly into a country I knew nothing about, and I'd have to learn the ropes in a language I barely spoke. Then there was the question of how long sixty grand would last given that I was unlikely to score a work visa.

But Texas was a different story. I spoke the language. I was employable. No one would look at me twice. And if they did, they wouldn't know what they were looking at: the Costellos' network petered out around Pensacola, and my disappearance wasn't exactly national news.

I'd have to ditch the car, buy a used one someplace that accepted cash and wasn't fussy about paperwork. Maybe I'd get a Ford F-150, circa 1980. Something old and cheap, but functional. Something that would blend in. I'd waited tables before, during and just after college. I could make this work. Maybe not forever, but for as long as it took Vincent and the cops to give up on me.

By the time Doris returned with the waffles and coffee, my mind was made up.

"I want to apply," I said, standing and extending my hand as though the job interview had already begun. And as I stood, the straps hooked around my ankle sent me lurching out over the counter while the bag itself flew backward. Bundles of the pawn-broker's bills spilled out across the linoleum floor. The old man spun his head in my direction as if he was seeing me for the first time. I dropped to my knees, started shoving thousand-dollar stacks of cash back into Anna's tote bag. I figured when I was done I'd bounce up and run for the door.

Doris stepped out from behind the counter and stood there watching me with her arms folded across her chest.

"And you want to waitress for me?" she said. "Whatever trouble you're running from, it must be bad."

Something in her voice told me I had nothing to fear. Not from her, anyway. I looked up, flashed a timid smile.

"You own that big yellow farmhouse?" I asked.

"Maybe."

"I'll give you a hundred dollars if you let me use the shower."

She studied me hard.

"I'm guessing there's a reason you can't go to a motel?" she said.

"More than one."

She dug her fingers through her thick gray curls while she thought it over.

"All right," she said. "Eat your waffles and meet me out back."

CHAPTER 21

I FOUND Doris standing by an industrial-size dumpster, a shotgun dangling from one hand. I cursed myself for being so goddamn dumb, for tagging along after a woman I'd met five minutes ago as if she was some kind of savior, as if she didn't have her own set of problems that sixty grand might fix. Whether she was planning to kill me or just rob me, I had it coming.

"Perfect day for target practice," she said, glancing up at a cloudless sky. "Can see a hundred miles in any direction."

I took a slow look around. She was right: no point in running.

"Guess I won't be taking that shower," I said.

There's a calm that comes with having lost all control. I set the bag full of money that wasn't really mine on the ground at my feet, raised my hands, and backed away. It became suddenly clear to me how far I was from anyone and anything I knew.

Doris looked at me and lost it. She laughed until her gut couldn't take any more.

"You're no career criminal, that's for sure," she said. "Hell, I'm not even pointing this thing at you. What is it? Abusive husband? Handsy boss? You can tell me—I'm familiar with both."

I lowered my arms—slowly, in case the situation might still go sideways.

"So am I," I said.

She sauntered over to me, held out the gun.

"Take it," she said.

For a long beat I just stared.

"Are you serious?"

"Is the trouble you're in serious?"

I nodded.

"Yeah, I thought so," she said. "Look at you, meetin' a stranger in a Texas back alley here where no one can see, all 'cause you got some seat-of-the-pants notion that you might hide out and play waitress. You see what I'm sayin'?"

"I think so," I lied.

"I'm saying we need to get you ready."

She thrust the gun at me so hard I had no choice but to accept it. I thought I understood then: she was looking to make a sale.

"How much?" I asked.

She ignored me, pointed across the yard to a wooden trellis with old coffee cans hanging from its frame. A makeshift shooting range.

"Think you can bull's-eye one at this range?"

I pushed the gun back toward her. She refused it.

"I wouldn't know how," I said.

"Well, that's what we're doin' here, ain't it? I once taught a twelve-year-old girl to fire that thing, and she wasn't exactly what I'd call precocious. I figure I can teach you, too."

The question was, did I want to learn? Sean was always after me to take up shooting. He booked sessions at a firing range, gave me a Glock for my thirtieth birthday. I made him cancel the sessions, return the gun, and buy me a new set of stainless ware instead. I'm not the killing type. That isn't me pleading my innocence—it's just the truth.

But things had changed since I turned thirty. There were people who wanted to hurt me. Professionals who inflicted pain for a living. Even sixty-one miles outside of Kerens, Texas, there was a chance I'd end up serving one of Vincent's men. Maybe Vincent himself, if his stomach started growling at exactly the wrong spot on the interstate.

"Okay," I said. "Maybe you've got a point."

"You ever fire a gun before?"

"No. But I've been around guns."

"What's that mean?"

"It means I know how. I've just never had a reason to."

She pointed to the trellis, which was maybe twenty feet away.

"Knowing and doing are two different things," she said. "Let's start with a coffee can. They're small, but at least they don't fire back."

I pressed the butt plate against my shoulder, shut one eye, and stared down the front sight with the other.

And then I froze.

"If you believe Sun Tzu, the battle's won before it's fought," Doris said. "Visualize the Maxwell House guy's face exploding and then go on and pull that trigger."

I took a deep breath, aimed, and froze some more. I've never performed well in front of an audience. As a kid, I wanted more than anything to be a singer. Aunt Lindsey bought me some lessons, and by the time I finished with them I could carry a tune better than most sixth graders. What I couldn't do was make myself walk out onstage come talent night. The vice principal tried to shove me out of the wings, but I grabbed on to her leg and wouldn't let go. Sometimes I think that's what drew me to the kitchen: the chance to work quietly behind the scenes.

"I'll make you a deal," Doris said. "Hit the target and you win a free shower."

I adjusted my grip.

"And if I miss?"

"Then I get to laugh at you guilt-free. That's a twelve-gauge—it'll be like hitting the side of a barn with another barn."

"That's it? You get to laugh at me?"

She thought it over.

"And I get a night's free labor. You cover the dinner shift for nothin'. Sound fair?"

"Plenty fair."

Come on now, Sarah, I told myself. *You can do this.*

And I did. I held myself steady and squeezed that trigger. And Lord knows if I hit the target, because the recoil landed me flat on my ass. I looked up to see Doris holding her sides.

"Hot damn," she said. "I didn't know it was possible to miss from this close. I mean, you must've hit something somewhere, but I've never seen those cans so still."

She reached out to take the gun back.

"I was gonna let you have it for two hundred, but—"

I held on to the barrel.

"Let's up the stakes," I said. "One more shot. If I make it, you put me on as *chef* for a day. If I miss again, you get a free waitress for a full week."

She backed up a step.

"Go for it," she said. "But I can't say I like your odds."

I took careful aim, concentrated with everything I had, promised myself the battle was already won...and then fell on my ass a second time. When I got back up, I saw the coffee cans hanging undisturbed.

"Well," Doris said, "you better nap some after your shower, 'cause Thursday's a busy night at the Diner Things in Life."

CHAPTER 22

DETECTIVE SEAN WALSH

I SAT parked outside Símon's place until sunup. Serena didn't show. She must have packed an overnight bag and headed to a local motel in case Símon got lucky. Chances were she'd be back by breakfast, but I couldn't risk hanging around any longer—I had a 7:00 a.m. shift to make.

I thought about calling in sick, but knowing Heidi, she'd have sent someone to check on me. Though she had yet to say it out loud, I was a top suspect in her high-profile case, and I couldn't afford to draw attention to myself. I stopped home for a shave and a change of clothes, then gunned it for the station house.

I had plenty of practice hiding sleepless nights from my superiors, and this particular sleepless night would be easier to hide than most. Heidi wanted me to chaperone a rookie assigned to his first homicide. Busywork, pure and simple. For once I didn't mind.

The kid's name was Randolph. He was short and lean, almost frail-looking, and tried to hide his bad skin under a layer of cover-up that seemed likely to melt right off in the Florida sun. He'd been some kind of celebrity on the beat, risen through the ranks at lightning speed. At twenty-six years of age, he was biologically young enough to be my son. That wasn't his fault, but there were other reasons not to like him. Randolph was a smug little company man, the type who'd rat you out for parking too far from the curb if he thought it might endear him to the brass. Any detective on the squad who had more than a year or two until retirement was sucking up to him already, thinking one day soon he'd be signing their OT slips.

The case was a stone-cold whodunit: a homeless man found knifed to death under a pedestrian bridge near the Tampa River-walk. We rode over in a department-issue sedan, Randolph behind the wheel. I'd have been fine with quiet, but Randolph wanted to chat. He wanted to know all about the Costello case. Mostly he wanted to know about Sarah. What was it like having my wife in the box with my ex-partner? He didn't know how I could concentrate. I must be worried sick. How was Sarah holding up? Had she ever run off before? Had she been acting differently in the days leading up to the murder?

"You know, they say some women can sense a natural disaster before it happens. Earthquakes, tsunamis, tornadoes. Not that they know exactly what's coming—only that it's big. Maybe it's the same with homicide?"

The little bastard was fishing, looking for a tip he could pass on to Heidi, something to raise his profile and ruin my life.

"Listen, Randy—"

"It's Randolph."

I smiled, knowing that from this moment forward his name would forever be Randy. I was about to tell him where to go with his thinly veiled interrogation when it dawned on me that two can play this game.

"What's the over-under in the office pool?" I asked.

"What office pool?"

"Don't you mean *which* office pool? There has to be more than one. Does homicide detective Sean Walsh's wife go to prison for murder? Does Detective Walsh keep his job? Hell, I bet there's even one on whether or not I set the whole thing up. Everybody knows I had a relationship with Anthony Costello. Maybe I'm framing my own wife?"

I'd raised my voice without meaning to. That's what an absence of sleep will do for you: your ideas might be good, but the execution falls apart.

"Nobody's saying you framed Mrs. Walsh."

Mrs. Walsh? That small sign of respect told me I had him running scared. His biggest fear, I knew, was that I'd ask for names—a tally of who was for me and who was against me.

"What *are* they saying?" I asked.

"Not much," he lied. "I mean—"

"Nobody's saying I was on the Costello payroll? Nobody's saying I got in so deep there was only one way out?"

He started hemming and hawing. I cut him short.

"Because if they are, you can tell them this: I was working Anthony. That's what the golf games were about. That's why I put Sarah in his house. I wanted to be the one to read Vincent Costello his rights. Anthony always seemed weak to me. I figured sooner or later he'd let something slip. Something I could use. It was stupid—I see that now—but ambition got the better of me. That promotion should have been mine, not Heidi's."

A motive I figured Randy of all people would understand. I just hoped he'd pass his new intel along.

By the time we got to the crime scene, the unis had it roped off and locked down. There were enough squad cars along the perimeter to patrol a small town, all with their lights flashing and sirens muted. Lookie-loos were gathered on the bridge above, faces pressed against the chain-link fencing. I hoped a good Florida rain would come along and soak them to the bone.

"You nervous?" I asked Randy.

"Me? Why would I be?"

"Let's go find out."

We got out of the car and walked over to the police tape. The boy in blue who greeted us was almost literally a boy: wiry from the neck down but with the last of his baby fat clinging stubbornly to his cheeks. When he spoke, his voice wobbled like a kazoo. I looked from him to Randy and had a sad thought for the future of Tampa law enforcement.

"What do we know?" I asked.

Randy shot me an I'll-ask-the-questions look.

"Not much," the infant cop said, pointing over his shoulder to a cadaver slumped against the underside of the bridge. "No ID, no witnesses that we can find. He must have been here all night. A jogger called it in."

"Cause of death?" Randy asked.

"Well, it looks like someone—or someones—beat him real bad. Then, when he was down, they dropped a cinder block on his head."

Randy looked past the tape while he slipped on his latex gloves and scrub booties. I looked with him. It wasn't a pretty sight. Not for Randy, anyway. Not if he was hoping to clear his first case. A brigade of Tampa's homeless had decamped in a hurry. There were beer cans and cigarette butts and liquor bottles scattered everywhere. Overturned shopping carts stood among the ruins of a cardboard city. It would take CSI days to sort through it all, and chances were every print they pulled would come back a hit. Young Randy was turning a little green around the gills.

"I've seen worse," I told him.

He looked at me as if this was the world's cruelest practical joke and he knew damn well I was behind it.

CHAPTER 23

"SHOULD WE go take a look at the body?" I asked.

Randy nodded, then shook himself all over like a diver about to plunge into icy water. But just as we started to duck under the tape, my phone rang. Somehow I knew before I checked: it was Vincent "Old School" Costello.

"Sorry," I said. "I have to take this."

If anything, Randy looked relieved: nobody wants a chaperone overseeing his first date. I walked back to the sedan, leaned up against the trunk, shoved my work phone into my front pocket, and pulled the burner from my back pocket.

"I've located her," I said.

"Then why isn't she sitting in front of me now?"

"I know where she is," I said. "I mean, I know where she's staying. I'm just waiting for the right moment to pick her up."

"The right moment has passed, Detective. I understand why you didn't bring Sarah to me. She's your wife. There are demands even I can't make. But the maid is different. I'll give you until sundown, like in a western flick. If the girl isn't in my possession by then, certain disquieting facts—facts that would put your fitness to serve in question—may become public knowledge."

Reminding him that I'd collected certain disquieting facts of my own would have won me a one-way trip to the Everglades.

"I understand," I said, but by then I was already talking to a dial tone.

I kept the phone pressed to my ear, sat on the trunk of the sedan with my feet on the bumper, pretending the conversation was still in full swing. I needed a moment to let the sweat dry. Sunset was a tight deadline, especially with a John Doe threatening forced overtime. And Vincent wasn't the type to make idle promises. Whatever file he had on me would be in the hands of every local newscaster come morning. Vincent wouldn't worry about my stink blowing back on him. He thought he was invincible. Maybe he was right: forty years is a long reign for a mob boss.

What I needed now was a reason to slip away, to leave Randy on his own for however long it took me to find Serena. But bringing Serena to Vincent wasn't an option. As far as I knew, Sarah was Serena's only friend in the US. I needed a Sarah ally in the box with Heidi, someone who'd swear up and down that Sarah and Anthony were on the best of terms. The only way I could square that with Vincent would be to hand him Anthony's killer, or someone who could pass for Anthony's killer—namely, Símon. Then Sarah would be off the hook all the way around, and I could go back to being a cop and nothing but a cop. There were a lot of moving parts, and all of them had to click into place before nightfall.

Impossible, I told myself. Ditch Randy now, and Heidi would sic Internal Affairs on me with an order to kill.

And then I finally caught a break. It came in the unlikely form of Marty the Mute, a vagabond I'd busted for drunken loitering almost weekly when I worked Vice. He was tugging on the hem of my blazer. I looked down at him. His beard had gone gray in the last decade, and his wino nose had turned a deeper shade of red, but the waiflike frame remained the same. Even wearing what must have been all the clothes he owned, he couldn't have weighed more than a buck twenty. I mouthed a fake good-bye into the phone, then hopped down off the sedan.

"Marty," I said. "It's been a minute."

He held out his wrists as if to say "Cuff me." Marty was always the type who preferred prison to the street.

"Wish I could, buddy, but I'm working a murder."

He nodded vigorously, pounded his chest with a tight fist.

"What, you?" I asked.

More nodding. Marty's life hadn't exactly panned out, but he'd always seemed harmless, even gentle. His rap sheet was a laundry list of petty offenses, and no way could I see him hoisting a cinder block high enough to cave in a man's skull. I figured he viewed this as his chance to go inside for good.

"I tell you what," I said. "Flip your hands over. Let me see your palms."

He obliged. Sure enough, the skin was scraped to the bone. I decided to test him.

"We going to find your prints on that two-by-four?" I asked.

He looked confused, started drawing a rectangle in the air with his fingers, then mimed lifting something really heavy. There were tears in his eyes. They seemed legit.

Hot damn, I thought. *You really never know.*

"Do yourself a solid," I told him. "Hold back on the remorse. You'll get a longer sentence."

I cuffed him, read him his rights, put him in the back of the nearest squad car, and signaled for one of the uniforms to go fetch Randy. A few minutes later, my junior colleague came stomping up to me, looking as if his little world was about to implode.

"I thought you were my partner for the day," he said. "So far all you've done is take a phone call and drag me away from the scene."

I got the feeling he was rehearsing his report to Heidi.

"Sorry, but I was busy solving your case for you," I said.

"What?"

I jerked a thumb toward the squad car. Marty looked to be singing silently to himself in the back seat.

"He confessed?"

"Not in so many words."

I laid it out for him, told him about my history with Marty, said he'd find corroborating fingerprints all over the cinder block. Then I asked for my reward.

"The collar's all yours," I said. "But I need a favor."

Randy left me the sedan, drove back in the squad car with Marty and the uni who'd greeted us at the scene. I stuck a siren on the hood, made it crosstown in record time. I was sweating as though it was mid-August, and my head was spinning from the all-nighter, but at least I had the presence of mind to dial the animal hospital and make sure Símon's hangover hadn't turned into a sick day. It hadn't. If Serena was at the apartment, then she didn't have her big brother around to protect her.

An elderly woman pushing a grocery cart let me into the building without asking any questions. I hightailed it up two flights, rang Símon's bell to the tune of "Pop Goes the Weasel," hoping to sound playful and innocent. Serena didn't answer, so for the second time in as many days I broke my way into Símon's condo. The glasses from last night's tryst were sitting in the sink alongside the morning's breakfast dishes. Otherwise, the place looked just as tidy and unlived-in. I started for the back rooms.

"Serena," I called. "Siesta's over. Come out, come out, wher-ever you are."

No response. No stirring that I could hear.

"Policía," I tried. "We need to talk."

I counted to ten, then started opening doors. Spare room

empty, bathroom empty, bedroom half ransacked but also empty. I made a beeline for the balcony. There was a newspaper and a half drunk cup of coffee on the table where I'd found *English on Your Lunch Break* the night before. The small, tan duffel bag brimming with Serena's things was gone, too.

My gut started churning. I dropped onto one of the wrought iron chairs, held my breath until the nausea passed. I'd missed her. She'd been here, and I'd missed her, and the only place I knew she might be headed now was roughly a thousand miles away, a country where even the Costellos had no pull.

CHAPTER 24

SARAH ROBERTS-WALSH

October 15
3:00 p.m.
Interview Room C

THE BEST shower in the world is the one that's long overdue. I watched the blood and dirt, and whatever else had clung to me since I woke up on that boulder, swirl around the drain of Doris's claw-foot tub and vanish. Then I stood under the spray awhile longer because that warm, pounding water felt so damn good.

Afterward, I changed into a DINER THINGS IN LIFE T-shirt and a pair of jeans Doris said she never wore because the fit was too snug. Downstairs, in her sprawling farmhouse living room, my hostess greeted me with a cold beer.

"Let's take a load off," she said, pointing to a pair of over-stuffed recliners. "The dinner rush won't start for an hour or so. I'll go fetch us some snacks."

I sunk deep into my chair, sat looking the room over. It reminded me of an enormous booth at a high-end flea market. Besides an abundance of antique furniture, there was a faded Navajo rug spread across the center of the floor, a wagon wheel chandelier hanging from the ceiling, a bookcase crammed with hardback encyclopedias and well-worn dime novels. Collections of cacti occupied every windowsill; randomly placed figurines and kachina dolls seemed to be crawling all over one another atop the fireplace mantel. Above the mantel was a very formal portrait of a man with a thick red mustache sporting a flannel hunting jacket. I wondered who he was. I wondered how long Doris had lived here.

She came back carrying a bowl of pitted olives and a glass canister filled with pretzel rods, set them on a TV-tray-style table between the recliners, and took her seat.

"Now, I'm not one to pry," she said, "but since you're a guest in my home, I need at least some of your story. Starting with who or what you're running from."

It was a fair request. I started out slow and guarded, but before long I forgot who I was talking to; it was as if I was recapping it all for myself, trying to make sense of how I wound up in a place I'd never heard of, running from a crime I didn't commit. Which isn't to say I laid out every detail, but I did give her more than the broad strokes, more than I should have considering that we'd only just met. Once I caught myself, I changed the subject. I pointed to the almost life-size portrait above the fireplace.

"Your husband?" I asked.

"Was," she said. "I've been widowed five years."

"I'm sorry."

"Why? You didn't kill him. Since we're sharing, I'll tell you who did. Turns out we have a common enemy. It was the cops murdered my Jeffrey."

"The cops?"

"Right on this highway, about three exits east of here. They tried to make it look like he'd done it himself, but I'm no fool."

I didn't know what to say, so I just waited.

"Jeffrey ran a shipping company. Six drivers, six trucks. Cops around here are as crooked as the letter s. They want a piece of everything, and God help you if you won't pay. Well, Jeffrey wouldn't pay. So one morning I got a call. Jeffrey had one belt too many and drove his semi into a gantry pole. Jeffrey was a drunk, so that sounded about right. But then I went down to the scene. In addition to being a drunk—or maybe because he was a drunk—Jeffrey had a gut I wouldn't wish on my worst enemy. Acid reflux, hiatal hernia, something called a Schatzki's ring—there wasn't anything right with that man's stomach. Only liquor he drank was tequila. Agave tequila, 'cause he couldn't tolerate wheat or barley or rye or any of it.

"Well, they let me take a last look at my husband, and what did I find? Bottles of Jim Beam scattered all across the floor of the cab. They got that one detail wrong, and some nights that's what I'm most angry over. 'Cause that one detail is enough for me to know, but not nearly enough for me to prove a thing."

"You think they wanted you to know?"

"Honey, I'm sure of it. There are vindictive people in this world, and mostly they're the ones who crave power. Which is why you're going to need a good cover story. A better story than the one you've got now, *Michelle*."

I said I agreed. I started to tell her my real name, but she held up a hand.

"Let's stick with Michelle. We can build around that. For now, we should get over to the diner. I'll put you on kitchen duty for tonight. Not sure how smart it'd be to have a fugitive circulating among the clientele."

Kitchen duty meant mopping the floor, doing the dishes as they came in, fetching ingredients from the walk-in freezer, making sure Doris's coffee cup was never less than half-full. Peeling carrots and potatoes was as close as I came to actual cooking.

On the one hand, it was busywork, but on the other hand, I couldn't see how she got by without more help. For a cut-rate diner in the middle of nowhere, the place was hopping. Which isn't to say there were people spilling out into the parking lot, but the steady stream never let up. And Doris was pulling double duty, cooking *and* covering the tables her lone waitress couldn't handle.

When the last customer had left and the OPEN sign was turned to CLOSED, Doris came to keep me company while I finished the last of the dishes.

"You've got a work ethic on you," she said. "I'll give you that much. Now let's see what you can do with this."

She handed me a slotted metal spatula. At first I was confused. I thought she wanted me to wash it.

"Looks like it's already clean," I said.

"I'm aware of that. I wanna see what kind of chops you've got behind a skillet."

She pointed to the stove, where she'd already laid out a half dozen eggs.

"You choked down my waffles earlier. We both know I can't cook worth a damn. Truth is, quality or lack thereof doesn't move the needle on your bottom line when 90 percent of your business drifts in off the highway. But since you fell out of the sky, I figure, why not make the place respectable? At least for as long as you stick around. So how about it? Wanna prove to me you're ready for the breakfast stampede?"

"Yes, ma'am."

"Call me that again and the deal's off. Meantime, make me an omelet I can't forget."

An omelet is like the scrapyard of breakfast foods: you can throw in just about anything you want and end up with a meal that's at least edible. I ran around the kitchen searching out the real crowd-pleasers: cheese (at least two kinds—one sharp, one mild), butter, onions (shallots are better, but Doris didn't seem to have any in stock), mushrooms, finely chopped ham, spinach and/or kale.

Doris sat on a stool, watching me dice and mix, watching me angle the skillet as needed to make sure all the egg was getting cooked. When I was done, I slid the finished product onto a plate and handed it over.

"Oh, no," Doris said. "Let's do this proper."

She walked through the kitchen's double doors and took a seat at the counter. I followed on her heels. Half joking, Doris pulled a paper napkin from one of the dispensers and fashioned it into a bib. I set the plate in front of her, gave a little bow, then stared anxiously as she took the first bite.

"Well, well," she said. "These are the tastiest unborn chickens I ever put in my mouth."

I was sweaty and aching and tired, but I couldn't stop myself from grinning ear to ear.

"So I'm hired?" I asked.

"Think you can do what you just did thirty times in an hour? I mean, you can cook—but can you line cook?"

She had a point. I'd never before had to ply my trade in a high-volume environment. But having your back to the wall gives you a new kind of confidence.

"Easy as breathing," I said.

She thought it over.

"I'll give you three hundred a week to start, plus room and board—board being whatever you want to fix for yourself here at the diner. It's not the best deal in the world, but it's what I can afford."

For the second time that day, I thrust my hand across the counter.

"Deal," I said.

CHAPTER 25

"SO GLAD you found your place in the world," Haagen said, looking at her watch, "but can we speed this along?"

"You're the one who asked for every detail."

This was the closest I'd come to talking back.

"Every *relevant* detail," she said.

"I thought the relevance was for you to decide?"

She didn't have anything to say to that. Her interruption only made me want to go slower. Detective Haagen, with her ramrod posture and her smug little frown, was becoming someone I seriously disliked.

"So can I continue?" I asked.

She nodded and snarled at the same time.

It took me a couple of days to get settled, a full week to make every item on the menu my own, but from there it was smooth sailing. I added ginger and lemon to the roast chicken, pepper and a touch of paprika to the cheddar burger. I got rid of the powdered mashed potatoes and started from scratch, adding a healthy dose of onion and garlic. Once we sold out of the frozen pies, I replaced them with my own homemade recipes: almond flour and vanilla extract in the key lime, Granny Smiths and a touch of sour cream in the apple.

The customers weren't increasing in number, but they were eating more, coming back for seconds and sometimes thirds. I even got the line cook lingo down:

"Two Ts on the hoof, sticks in the alley, and my radio's waiting," Doris would yell.

"On it," I'd yell back.

Still, every time the little Liberty Bell above the entrance rang, I'd feel a quick jolt of fear, like maybe it was a state trooper or a fed or a plain old cop come to haul me away. This fear meant that, as much as possible, I kept to the kitchen, out of sight of the customers.

When I did venture through the double doors, I seemed to get noticed. Once, as I was on my way to the restroom, a trucker at the counter stopped me to say how much he'd enjoyed his flapjacks. Then he gave me a long once-over.

"Your name's Michelle, right?" he said.

I nodded.

"You're her, aren't you?"

"*Her?*"

"You were in that movie? What's it called? The one where you drown at the end?"

I'd started to claim mistaken identity when a customer two stools down said, "Michelle! That's Michelle Brown. You researching a role? Gonna be in one of those trucker serial-killer flicks?"

By now, every head at the counter was turned toward me.

"Give us a little Shakespeare," yelled a man in a Texas Rangers cap seated at the far end. It sounded like a catcall.

"I don't act anymore, fellas," I said, and walked away.

The *fellas* was me playing to my audience, trying out a word Sarah Roberts-Walsh would never use. I liked it. It felt like something Marilyn Monroe or Mae West might say. I thought, *Maybe this is my cover story. Michelle Brown, failed actress. Maybe that's who I am now.*

Meanwhile, life as Doris's housemate was going just fine. At first I had trouble sleeping in the palatial but rickety spare bedroom, where I made a nightly roundup of spiders and moths before switching off the light. The ancient windows that looked as though they might disintegrate if you so much as tapped them did nothing to block out the not-so-distant hum of the highway, and the sound of a car driving past Doris's property would have me sitting bolt upright in bed. Little by little, though, I calmed down. The highway became white noise. I stopped noticing local traffic. And fourteen-hour days on my feet had me falling asleep before my head hit the pillow.

Doris and I were so busy at the diner that just about the only socializing we did outside of work was during target practice. Every day, between lunch and dinner, Doris had me out on her meadowlike lawn, shooting at cans.

"Someday you might actually hit one," she joked.

The problem, for me, was the recoil. I couldn't pull that trigger without being knocked backward, without the bruise on my shoulder turning a new and darker shade. Day after day, I looked like a comic practicing her pratfalls. Until the day I didn't. Until the day—which at first didn't feel any different from any other day—I found my balance and cleared the field.

"Well, I'll be," Doris said. "We're going to have to find you smaller cans."

Roughly three weeks into my new life, Doris announced that she had a gift for me. She was waiting at the bottom of the stairs, before sunup, as I came stumbling down in my all-white line cook's outfit. I could smell coffee in the background—about the only thing Doris made at home.

"Here you go," she said, handing over a small box meticulously wrapped in shiny polka-dotted paper, a red bow sitting on top.

My morning fog lifted. I felt half-giddy, half-embarrassed: shouldn't it have been me giving Doris a gift? I hugged her, then took the box and carefully peeled away the wrapping. Inside, beneath a bed of yellow rose petals, I found a forged driver's license featuring my photo and borrowed name: Michelle Brown. Michelle was thirty (a generous guess on Doris's part), weighed 120 (another generous guess), and lived on Serpentine Road in Phoenix, Arizona.

"How did you…"

"I may be a hick," Doris said, "but I'm a hick with resources. Consider it a housewarming. And don't ask any more questions."

I'm not ashamed to say that I got a little teary. Doris put herself at risk. She committed a crime on my behalf. More importantly, she believed me. I hugged her again, held on until she pushed me away.

"Just do me a favor," she said. "Make this an honest-to-God rebirth. Figure out who you want to be, and pour all of it into Michelle. No more letting men set your course for you. Michelle's a shitkicker who takes no guff."

"I promise," I said.

"Good. Now let's go feed some hungry truckers."

Up until then, I'd made no effort to check in on my old life. Not by phone or text or email or postcard. I'd been dying to hop on Doris's laptop and google "Hunt for Sarah Roberts-Walsh," but I didn't dare: even search items can be traced these days. But that afternoon, Michelle decided to skip target practice and head to a nearby laundromat, pockets weighted down with quarters. Doris had a machine of her own, but what I wanted was a good old-fashioned pay phone, and the Happy Laundry Laundromat had one of the few remaining public phones in the state.

I smiled at the attendant, headed straight for the back wall, started feeding coins into the slot.

"Hello?" Aunt Lindsey said.

"Aunt Linds?"

"Sarah?"

"Listen," I said, "I can't talk for long, but I need to know if you're okay."

"Me? What about you? Are you calling from—"

"No, nothing like that."

"Oh, thank God."

Inside, I felt as though I might dissolve just from the sheer comfort of hearing her voice, but I stuck a smile on my face for the sake of the laundromat's patrons, tried to make it look as though I was sharing good news. And in a way I was.

"I'm fine," I said. "Better than fine. I've landed in a good place."

"Of course you have," she said. "That's just your style."

"Anyone been asking for me?"

"Oh, yes, a steady parade. I think there's even a cop parked down the street."

I hoped it was a cop.

"Don't worry," she said. "I didn't tell them anything more than I told Sean: 'Ain't seen her.' And now that's been true for too long. God, I miss you."

"Me, too, Aunt Linds," I said. "I love you."

And then I hung up.

I thought I'd feel homesick to the point of breaking, but driving back to Doris's place I was nearly bouncing in my seat. Hearing Aunt Lindsey's voice reminded me that there were people out there who could be trusted. People worth loving. It made me believe that Doris was real, that she wasn't on the internet right now, checking to see how much she'd get for turning me in.

That night, I fell asleep before my head hit the pillow. I dreamed of lazy beach days with Aunt Lindsey, when I was a child and she was still young. Sloping sandcastles and rainbow ices and the tide carrying us backward. The kind of days that dropped by the wayside once I hit my angry teenage years.

And then I woke up. I couldn't say what it was that woke me. Maybe a truck had backfired? Maybe Doris had taken a midnight bathroom break? The plumbing was about what you'd expect from a hundred-year-old home on the prairie.

I glanced over at the clock, then rolled onto my side. That was when I saw him, standing in the doorway, the right side of his blazer tucked behind his gun. I knew who it was before that tall, lean frame came all the way into focus.

"Hello there, Sarah," Sean said.

CHAPTER 26

I SQUINTED through the darkness. He stood silhouetted against the lamplight like a cartoon villain. It was almost comical.

"Sorry to wake you," he said. "But really I have no choice."

Slowly, I reached toward my nightstand, fumbled for my glasses—glasses I only wore when Sean was around, as if somehow they'd make him think before raising his fist.

"You have a lot of choices," I said.

"Not really. Not since you ran from the scene of a murder. That was your choice, but somehow it seems I'm the one paying for it."

"That's a situation *you* created."

"Did you kill him?"

"No," I said. "Did you?"

If he'd been close enough I would have felt the back of his hand one more time. Instead, he switched on the light, stepped inside, shut the door behind him.

"In case you're thinking of running again, there are two sheriffs parked out front. They did me a favor, let me come in alone."

He started toward me, then stopped and sat on the edge of the bed. He reached over, took my hand.

"I've been worried sick about you, Sarah," he whispered. "I suppose you don't believe me, but it's true."

I couldn't move. I couldn't even flinch. As powerful as Sean was, as quick as he was to dole out a slap or a kick, it was the gentle, reassuring voice that I'd come to fear most. Because the longer the calm, the more violent the storm.

"Please just go," I said.

"You know I can't, baby. The only question is whether you're going to make me break out the cuffs."

For a while we just stared at each other. I could imagine the nostalgia in his eyes, and I have to admit I felt it, too. Not for him, but for the man I'd convinced myself he was, back when he was wooing me and I was letting myself be wooed.

"Okay," he said. "We'll do this the hard way."

He stood, took a step back, pulled out his handcuffs, and twirled them around one finger.

"You want to pretend I'm the bad guy and you're all sweetness and light, but the truth is—"

"Get your ass on the ground!" Doris screamed.

The door flew open so fast I couldn't tell if she'd pushed it or kicked it. And then she was standing there with her twelve-gauge pointed at Sean's jewels. At first Sean didn't react. Then he looked back and forth between me and Doris, his smile growing wider and wider.

"I said on the ground."

She pumped the shotgun for effect. Sean didn't blink.

"Doris," I said, "it's okay."

"Now!" she yelled.

"Lady—"

"Shut your mouth. Before you launch into an avalanche of bullshit, you should know that killing doesn't scare me, and neither does getting killed. Everything I love's been butchered by bastards like you. And so help me you're about to pay for it."

Sean let her anger simmer for a moment, then turned solemn.

"This has nothing to do with you, ma'am. I recommend you back off."

"Kneel," said Doris. "Lock your fingers behind your head."

"I can't do that."

"Sean," I said. "Sean, just please don't—"

"There are armed deputies outside," he told Doris. "That shotgun you're holding will make short work of me, but I hope you were telling the truth when you said you're ready to die."

She stepped closer, then—in a move I wouldn't have thought a woman her age could pull off—kicked his legs out from under him.

"Now you're on your knees," she said.

Sean ignored her. He looked up at me.

"You sure this is what you want?" he said. "I can still help you. I want to help you. I love you, Sarah. Don't tell me it's over between us."

"You know it is, Sean. It was over even before all of this."

"I don't believe that. You don't believe it. I'm the only one who—"

"Shut your goddamn mouth," Doris said, inching forward, pressing the barrel against his ear.

But Sean was losing his patience.

"I'm going to count to five," he said, "and if I don't hear that gun hitting the ground, I'm going to forget you're a lady."

"Just do what he says, Doris."

"Not a chance. I've gone that route with men like him. Even when you give them what they want, they find a way to ruin you."

"One," Sean said.

"Come take his gun," Doris said.

"What about those sheriffs outside?"

"Two," Sean said.

"Let 'em take me away. He's an intruder in my home. I didn't hear him identify himself. All I heard was threats. Your home is your castle in Texas. No way a jury convicts me."

"Three and four," Sean said.

Doris gave the twelve-gauge another pump. Sean smiled. I knew that smile. It meant he was about to have some fun. I couldn't let that happen. Not to Doris. I threw myself at the man who'd come to drag me away, wrapped my arms around him, clung to him like body armor.

"I'll go with you," I said. "Okay, Sean? I'm going back with you."

"You'll regret this," Doris said. "This moment right here. Every hour of every day."

"It's over, Doris," I told her.

She turned and walked out of the room. I loosened my grip on Sean. We stood, brushed ourselves off.

"You have the right to remain silent," he told me.

CHAPTER 27
DETECTIVE SEAN WALSH

IT WAS another shot in the dark, but I jumped in the sedan and floored it to the airport. Traffic was heavy, then light, then heavy again. I parked at the Departures curb, left the siren spinning on the dash, bolted inside, and scanned the boards. Flight 201 for Mexico City, gate 16. Scheduled to take off in just under an hour.

My badge got me through customs without any hassle. I took the escalator two steps at a time, shouldered my way past men and women of all ages. When I got to the gate, the seating area was already packed. I stood back and searched.

Families, businesspeople, what looked to be a high school marching band traveling in uniform. The women were all too old or young, tall or short, thin or fat.

I checked the adjacent gates, the nearby restaurants, bars, shops. No sign of Serena anywhere. I walked back to gate 16, dropped onto a bench with my head in my hands, and wondered if there was any way I might board the flight myself. I felt like a gambler who'd bet his home and lost. Now it was just a question of who'd come to collect the debt: Vincent or Heidi.

And then, when I looked up, there she was—exiting the ladies' room directly across from where I was sitting. She was wearing a straw sun hat with an enormous brim and a plaid scarf that she'd pulled up over her mouth, but it was her. Same slim build, same jet-black hair. And she was carrying a small, tan duffel bag. I hunched forward, dropped my head back into my hands, waited for her to pass.

I counted to ten, then dared a look over my shoulder. She was sitting by the window, gazing out at the runway traffic, looking as though she didn't know what to do with herself, as though she might never know what to do with herself again. I'd have felt sorry for her if it weren't for the fact that I had my own future to protect. Mine, and Sarah's, too.

And then it occurred to me: *Now what?*

Things would go much better for me if I wasn't the one to take her downtown. Vincent wouldn't like that one bit, and neither would Heidi. This wasn't my case. She didn't want me anywhere near it, and the fact that I kept pushing would only ratchet up her suspicions, make her turn over rocks I couldn't have disturbed.

I squinted at the gate's monitor. Forty minutes until boarding. I got up, walked as far away as I could without losing sight of that tentlike hat, and took out both phones: business and burner. Heidi and Vincent. Good and evil, at least in the eyes of the law. I balanced one phone in each palm, thinking maybe I'd just go with the heavier of the two.

The cop phone won out. I called Randy. I figured I'd throw him another career booster. He picked up on the first ring, didn't let me get out more than a hello before he started jabbering.

"Looks like Marty's confession is legit," he said. "Like, 100 percent legit. We're talking slam dunk. I—"

"That's great, Randy—"

"Randolph."

"Sorry. I'm glad you're batting a thousand, but I need you to listen—this is important."

"Okay."

"Tell Heidi that Serena Flores, housemaid to Anthony Costello, is sitting at gate 16 in the Tampa airport, waiting to board a flight to Mexico City."

"Right now?"

"Right now. But listen, this can't come from me."

"So who's it supposed to come from?"

"Tell her you put out feelers. One of your informants got back to you. Trust me, this is bigger than a homeless guy's murder. You'll probably get a commendation."

"And you're just handing it to me?"

I could see his eyes turning into little sergeant's badges.

"I'm the gift that keeps on giving. Now go!"

And it was true: I had more gifts to give him. Or at least one more gift: a very large veterinarian named Símon Flores. I'd keep feeding Randy tips. He'd be my conduit to Heidi. The next tip would have something to do with Anthony Costello's files on Serena and several other choice items turning up in Símon's apartment. Of course, Símon would be gone and buried by then. Vincent would see to that.

I hung up, headed into one of those airport junk stores, and bought the tackiest outfit I could sling together: a Hawaiian sweatshirt, a HAIL TO THE GATORS baseball cap, mirrored sunglasses. Then I went into the bathroom and changed. When I was done, I stood for a beat checking myself out in the mirror. I certainly didn't look like Detective Sean Walsh. Not at first, second, or third glance. I was all set to sit back and watch the show, no matter who came for Serena.

By then, I figured I'd given Heidi a big enough head start. I walked back to gate 16, pulled out the burner phone, and dialed Vincent's number.

"I'm assuming you know better than to call without good news," he said. "So, do you have her?"

"Not exactly. I got a tip."

I told him where she was. I told him how long he had to come get her.

"I thought I was clear: that's your job, Detective."

"But here's the thing: I'm at a murder scene on the ass end of town. I couldn't get there in time if I wanted to."

"How reliable is this tip?"

"One hundred percent."

I hung up. I figured this way I'd at least have an argument to sell. *I told you, Vincent. I went straight to you, as soon as I heard. It's not my fault my boss got the same tip. Besides,* I'd say, *I have something better than Serena: I have Anthony's killer.*

With the hour of departure approaching, flight 201 looked to be packed. Not a spare seat anywhere in the waiting area, and plenty of people siting on the floor. I leaned against a support beam and watched. Serena had pulled her hat over her face as though she was napping. Trumpet-playing members of the marching band decided this would be a good time and place to tune their instruments, at least until their chaperone told them to cut it out. Between the band and a half dozen newborns, it was going to be a very unpleasant flight for a whole lot of passengers.

Countdown to boarding hit the fifteen-minute mark. I couldn't stop myself from casting glances in every direction. If no one showed, I'd have no choice but to bring her in myself. Heidi would come down on me hard, and Vincent would have his boys give me a world-record tune-up before outing me to the press. But once Serena set foot on that plane, there'd be nobody to say Sarah didn't do it.

A flight attendant cleared his throat into the sound system, announced that the plane was ready to begin boarding. I stutter-stepped forward, then pulled up short. Two airport rent-a-cops had entered the seating area. They were walking the rows, comparing each female face to an eight-by-ten photo. Serena spotted them. Even from a dozen yards away I could see the blind fear take hold. She broke into a full-out run, but it didn't do any good: the taller of the two men was on top of her before she cleared the waiting area. I watched them cuff her, lead her away.

At first I figured Heidi had sent them. It wasn't her style, but maybe she got caught in bumper-to-bumper traffic, called ahead. Then I realized: they were Vincent's men. They had to be. Airport cops on the up-and-up wouldn't have left Serena's bag behind.

CHAPTER 28

THEY LED her away in the opposite direction of the main terminal. I followed, trailing a few yards back. The crowd of moving bodies made it easy to blend in. I pulled out my cop phone, got Randy back on the line.

"Pretend you're talking to your snitch," I said. "Is Heidi on her way or not?"

"We're just through customs. We'll be there in—"

"We?"

"Me, Detective Haagen, and a handful of uniforms. It was my tip. She told me to throw Marty in a holding cell and tag along."

"So she didn't call the airport police? Tell them to pick up Serena?"

"Why would she? Like I said, we're here now."

Meanwhile, the airport cops were steering Serena down a side hallway leading to an unmarked metal door. I hung up on Randy.

Think, think...

"Officers," I called, running after them, waving my arms, pretending to be out of breath. "Officers, please wait."

They turned toward me, looked none too pleased. One of them

held up a hand as if to say "That's far enough." Serena turned, too. Her face was streaked with mascara, and she was in bad need of a Kleenex. If she recognized me, she didn't let it show.

"There's an unattended bag at gate 16," I said, which wasn't exactly a lie. "I heard some kind of rattling coming from inside. It sounded like a grandfather clock gone haywire."

"We'll send someone over," the short one said, sounding bored and impatient.

Up close, the duo looked more formidable than I'd imagined. The tall one could have dunked on Jordan any day, and the short one made up for his lack of height with a barrel chest and anvil arms.

"I took a picture of the bag," I said. "So you'd know what to look for."

I held up my phone as if I wanted them to see, then flipped it around and hit Video.

"Smile," I said. "You're going to be on the six o'clock news."

That got their attention.

"Mike, go handle this," the pituitary case said.

"What are you, some kind of nutjob?" Mike asked, stepping toward me.

"Maybe," I said. "Why not ask Vincent?"

He stopped in his tracks. I flashed my badge just long enough for him to glimpse the shield.

"Let's have a private word, Mike," I said. "Tell your partner to stay where he is."

The truth is, they could have jumped me right there. They could have jumped me, and they could have taken me. There wasn't any foot traffic in this corridor, and anyone peering down the hall would have seen two cops making an arrest. Mike seemed to be weighing the options. Luckily, he thought better of it. I pulled him off to the side.

"Listen," I said. "I'm doing you a favor. I've got you on video, walking away with the prime suspect in a murder investigation. I'm telling you, drop it. Tampa PD is descending on gate 16 right now. They'll want to know who paid you. Maybe you'll stand up under a police grilling, but do you think Vincent will take that chance? Let her go, and I'll erase this video. Right here and now, while you're watching. All you have to do is tell Vincent the cops beat you to her."

He was anxious now. There was sweat on his brow and he couldn't make himself stand still. I knew what he was thinking: *Do I back down or go to the mat? Which scores more points with Vincent Costello?* Because say what you will about our local mob boss, but he pays way better than the Tampa International Airport Police Department.

"You'll make it up to him," I said.

His puffed-out chest deflated a full inch.

"Yeah, all right," he said.

Then, to his partner: "Cut her loose."

Serena bolted without a word. I gave each of my colleagues a no-hard-feelings handshake, then turned and followed her. By the time I got to the gate, the spectacle was in full swing, Serena kicking and thrashing like a snared cat while Heidi and Randy held on for dear life. The unis formed a small phalanx on either side, ready to catch her if she broke loose.

"*Ayúdame!*" Serena screamed. "*Por favor…*"

I joined the circle of onlookers, pushed my sunglasses up the bridge of my nose, and bent my knees until I was just able to see over the shoulder in front of me.

"We *are* here to help you," Heidi said. "You understand? We're the good guys."

Serena lashed out with her feet, hooked her ankles around a bolted-down chair, and kept on screaming. My Spanish is less than functional, but I'm pretty sure she said that cops are the real murderers.

To Heidi's credit, they didn't tase her or bend her arm behind her back or even wrestle her to the ground; they just held on until the fight died down, then calmly escorted her out of the terminal.

When they were gone, I sat for a minute and watched the passengers finish boarding. Part of me still wished I could fly standby, especially now that I knew there'd be at least one empty seat.

CHAPTER 29

SERENA FLORES

October 21
4:00 p.m.
Interview Room C

"WHAT DID she say?" Haagen asked.

Detective Nuñes—a first-generation American whose accent told me her family came from the north—gave me a sad look, as if she hated to betray one of her own.

"She said there's something sinister here."

"Sinister? Sinister how?"

I pretended not to understand. Nuñes translated. I sat back, looked over the dreary, windowless room: a scratched-up metal desk, hard-backed plastic chairs, surveillance cameras in every corner, those fluorescent lights that look like ice cube trays. *How in the world did I end up here?* I wondered.

"I'm the victim," I said. "You have no right to keep me."

"Ah, you do speak English." Haagen smiled. "Maybe you should tell us how you're the victim when Anthony Costello's the one in the morgue?"

I thought it over. There was a phrase I copied maybe a hundred times in my high school English class: "The truth will set you free."

"How far back do you want me to go?" I asked.

"However far you need, just so long as you tell us everything you know about Anthony's murder."

*   *   *

I went back a full year.

We were standing outside the upstairs guest bathroom. Me and Tony. Usually he liked the help to call him Mr. Costello, but when I first got here, the double *l*s came out a *y*. He said it made me sound like a cartoon. The *th* in *Anthony* wasn't any easier, so we settled on Tony.

"How many times do I have to tell you?" he asked, holding up a green hand towel with a small soap ring in the middle.

"I'm sorry," I said. "It won't happen again."

"I wish I could believe that. Once more, and I start docking your pay. Now get out of here. Go find something to clean downstairs."

I turned to walk away. Dressing me down was nothing new. I hardly even noticed anymore. But this was the first time he'd threatened me. Soap washes out. That's the point of soap. But when the towels cost six hundred dollars per set, they aren't towels anymore: they're little museum pieces that no one should touch.

"Hold on," he called after me. "We need to talk about that vaccination. Did you make an appointment like I asked?"

I searched for a white lie but came up empty.

"I was going to do that later," I said.

"Later? I asked you weeks ago. I told you it was a priority. For your visa, but also for my health. This is my busy season. I can't afford to be getting sick."

"I understand."

"*You* can't afford for me to be sick. You think Anna will pay your salary?"

I shook my head.

"Wait here a second," he said.

He stepped into the bathroom, came back holding up a pill bottle in one hand and a cup of water in the other.

"Normally I wouldn't share these, but since you work under my roof, giving one to you is the same as giving one to me. An ounce of prevention."

"What are they?"

"The next best thing to vaccination. They prevent colds, the flu, pneumonia—you name it. Now come take one."

The question I was too afraid to ask: *If you're already taking them, then how can I get you sick?*

"I'll go to a clinic tomorrow," I said.

"Sorry," he said. "You had your chance."

That was a lie. He hadn't talked to me about this weeks ago, like he claimed. He'd mentioned it in passing the day before, at breakfast.

He had me follow him into the bathroom, then watch as he took two pills and mashed them down to powder with the end of a toothbrush. Then he brushed the powder into the cup, swished the water around, and handed the cup to me.

"Here," he said. "The medicine makes its way through your system more rapidly once it's dissolved."

What choice did I have? My visa, my livelihood—everything depended on this man. I didn't even have enough money for a flight home. I took the cup, tried to hide the fact that my hand was shaking. He smiled as I drank it down.

"Very good," he said. "Very good."

It wasn't until later that I realized this was a trial run. He wanted to see if the taste of the drink would make me gag or grimace. It didn't. It tasted like nothing. That pleased him.

"Go on, now," he said. "I think there's some broken glass in the game room. Anna was stumbling around drunk last night, as usual."

I didn't feel dizzy right away, or if I did, then I don't remember it. I only remember waking up eight hours later, lying fully clothed on top of the covers in one of the guest bedrooms, with no sense of how I got there. My head was aching. I thought I might vomit. Then I looked over and saw him, standing in the corner and buttoning up his shirt.

It took me two tries to push myself off the bed. The exhaustion felt like a weight pinning me to the mattress. I turned my back to Tony, smoothed out the duvet, then started for the door. He stepped in front of me.

"You're lucky," he said. "You know that, right?"

I nodded, kept my eyes on the floor.

"Tell me why you're lucky."

I shrugged. All I wanted was to get away from him.

"You see, I hate it when you do that. Why do you nod like a sheep when in fact you have no idea what I'm talking about?"

I didn't say anything.

"You're lucky because I didn't write you up. Normally, when you make one of your patented blunders, I write a little note and stick it in your file. That file will follow you wherever you choose to go in this country. That's how it works here. Do you understand?"

I said I did.

"You understand that I've been very nice to you? That I've given you a break?"

I knew what he was really asking. He was asking if I was going to tell anyone about the "vaccination." He was asking if I planned to report him.

"You are very nice to me," I said. "Thank you for being so nice."

He let me pass. I got as far as the front gate before I started retching. When I was finished, I wiped my mouth with my sleeve and kept walking to the highway. On the bus ride home, I made a vow never to return to that place again.

CHAPTER 30

THE NEXT morning, I woke before dawn, packed a small suit-case, and started for the Greyhound bus station. But I didn't make it any farther than my building's front steps. There was a car parked by the fire hydrant across the street. A big, expensive-looking American car. A man got out. I recognized him, but at first I couldn't say from where. Then I remembered. It was Detective Sean Walsh. I'd seen him before, when he visited Anthony or came to pick up Sarah because her much smaller, much less expensive car was in the shop.

He waved me over. I thought about running, but what good would it do?

"Get in," he said.

I walked around, climbed into the passenger seat, held my suitcase on my lap. He started driving. I didn't bother to ask where we were going.

"How are you doing, Serena? Sarah tells me you work your tail off. She's very fond of you, you know."

I nodded. No one in this country had been kinder to me than Sarah. How she wound up married to Detective Walsh and working for Tony was a mystery I couldn't even begin to explain.

Walsh took the entrance ramp onto the highway. For a while neither of us said anything, but I could tell he wanted to talk.

"I need to ask you something," he said. "Are you being treated well? At your job? Are the Costellos good to you?"

"Please, don't take me there. Not today. I feel sick."

He steered onto the shoulder, brought the car to a screeching stop. It felt like something he'd planned ahead of time—as if he was putting on a show.

"If you don't want me to take you there, then I won't," he said. "I can drop you off wherever you want. The suitcase tells me that's either the airport or the bus station. But I need to be very clear about something first."

He turned to face me.

"This isn't the kind of job you just walk away from. There will be consequences. With a man like Anthony, there are always consequences. You understand what I'm saying, don't you?"

I kept staring straight ahead.

"I'm saying you can't leave Anthony Costello to wonder what might happen next, because if he starts to wonder, he's going to assume the worst. He's going to think you're a threat. This isn't a man—or a family, for that matter—you want to threaten."

"I'm no threat to anyone."

He took a deep, dramatic breath, then tugged back his blazer and tapped his badge.

"You're a friend of Sarah's," he said. "That means you're a friend of mine. If something's wrong, I want to help. So I'll ask again: are the Costellos treating you well?"

I'm not stupid. I knew who he worked for. I knew what he was really asking. I knew what would happen if I said no.

"I couldn't be happier there," I lied.

"Good girl."

A half hour later, we were parked in front of Tony's gaudy

modern-day castle, the home I'd only just sworn never to set foot in again.

"Remember," Sean said, "if you have any trouble, you come to me."

I thought he'd drive off, but instead he followed me inside. I headed straight for my maid's quarters: a small room where I was allowed to keep a few belongings and where I sometimes slept when Anna and Tony had one of their all-night dinner parties. I shut the door behind me, sat on the edge of the cot, and took long, deep breaths. I thought about calling Símon, my brother, but what could he do against men like Tony and Sean? How could I tell him what happened to me? Besides, Símon had his life here, a life he'd worked hard to make, without help from anyone—least of all me. The last thing I wanted was to cause trouble for him.

Before long, I heard shouting in the kitchen. Sean and Tony were arguing. At first their voices were just loud enough for me to hear, but little by little the volume swelled. They took their fight out onto the deck and closed the sliding doors, but I could still make out every word.

"I can't keep bailing you out like this," Sean said.

"You can keep doing whatever it is I tell you to do. You're my errand boy, remember?"

"This is getting too ugly."

"Oh, you have no idea how ugly things can get. Keep making yourself useful and maybe you won't find out."

They yelled back and forth some more, and then everything went quiet until I heard Sean's car peeling out of the driveway. I sat as still as I could for as long as I dared, afraid Tony would turn his rage on me.

But he ignored me. Morning, noon, and night, we didn't so much as cross paths.

Back home in my studio apartment, I got on my knees and

prayed for the first time since I'd left Mexico. I prayed for a way out, a way back to the broken-down little coastal city I'd dreamed of leaving my whole life. I prayed until the sun came up and it was time to catch the bus and report to work all over again.

CHAPTER 31

"YOU HAVE beautiful hair," Tony said. "It's a shame to tie it back like that, where no one can see."

Slowly, even gently, he slid the band from my ponytail, then used his fingers like a comb until my hair was hanging loose around my shoulders. We were standing in front of a hallway mirror, Tony looming up behind me.

"See?" he said. "Isn't that better?"

I nodded.

"And those pants don't work at all," he continued. "They look like scrubs. A woman with legs like yours shouldn't hide them. Let's get you a pair of those fitted jeans the girls are all wearing."

I wanted to scream, to run, to turn and gouge his eyes out. But I couldn't let him know what I was thinking. For such a big, important man, Tony was deeply insecure, even paranoid. Once, I saw him pick up a chair and break it over the dining room table just because Anna teased him about eating a third cannoli. If he knew how disgusting I found him, he'd have beaten the life out of me, then called Sean to come clean up the mess.

"Maybe try a little lipstick, too," he said. "Red is your color."

Of course, he only behaved this way when Anna wasn't

around. If she spent the day at home, which was becoming more and more rare, Tony either stuck to his office or went golfing with Vincent or Sean. Anna didn't seem to mind. Neither one of them looked happy when they were together.

He kept after me for months. Then one day I saw him alone in the dining room, grinding up more of those pills. Instead of a toothbrush, he was using a wooden mortar and pestle, and instead of a cup of water there were two wineglasses sitting beside a half-empty bottle. I knew those pills couldn't be for me. Anthony didn't need to wine me or dine me. I was just his little Mexican maid. I slipped away before he caught me watching. Whatever he was planning, whoever he was planning to hurt, I didn't want to know about it.

I went into the laundry room, transferred a load from the washer to the dryer, then emptied a fresh basket into the washer and switched both machines to their loudest settings. I told myself I wouldn't leave that room no matter what, not until Tony had done whatever he was going to do. But ten minutes later I heard his voice calling me from somewhere on the other side of the house.

"Serena! Serena!" Over and over again.

I walked toward the sound of my name as if I was in a trance. I found him in the living room, with Sarah. She was lying unconscious on the floor.

"Help me do this," he said.

He gestured in the direction of the stairs. I didn't say yes. I didn't say no. I just stood there, afraid to so much as blink.

"Now!" he said. "You take her feet."

I obeyed. I'd never felt so much like a coward.

I'd left my country not because I was poor or afraid or even unhappy: I left because I wanted a first-rate education. My plan was to save up, go to a fancy American law school, then return home and fight the cartels. I was going to challenge myself, see what I was capable of. *Well,* I thought as we hauled my only friend up the stairs as if she was just another piece of furniture, *now you have your answer. Now you know who you really are. You work for the criminals, not against them.*

We dropped her on a bed in one of the many guest rooms.

"Shut the door on your way out," Tony said.

As if I needed to be told. Downstairs, I finished up the laundry, mopped the kitchen floor, vacuumed the family room. Anything to keep myself from drifting over to the bottom of the stairs. I prayed Anna would come home and find them. If she told the cops, they'd listen. She might even get Vincent to listen. In the Costello family there are laws you break and laws you don't, and God help you if you get the two confused. But Anna was babysitting her nephew in Orlando. She wouldn't be back until after midnight, if she came back that night at all.

An hour later, I heard Tony calling for me again. He didn't sound agitated or angry or ashamed. He needed me for another chore—that was all. We carried Sarah to the downstairs den, propped her up in an armchair.

"When she comes to," Tony said, "tell her it was an insulin blackout. You understand? An insulin blackout. Let me hear you say it."

I repeated the words back to him.

"She's had them before," Tony said. "She ought to be grateful: another employer might not put up with the lost time."

I stayed with her, made sure she kept breathing. Half the night was gone before her eyes opened. I wondered if I'd been unconscious that long, too.

"Whoa," she said, blinking her eyes as though fighting off a spotlight. "I feel like I've been run over by a semi."

"No," I told her. "You passed out. Tony says you missed your insulin."

I stuck to his lie because the truth would have changed Sarah the way it changed me. I couldn't sleep at night without pushing the dresser in front of my door, without getting up again and again to make sure the windows were locked. I kept a can of pepper spray and an enormous carving knife on the floor beside my bed. I didn't want any of that for Sarah. I hadn't protected her against Tony—the least I could do was spare her the constant, gnawing fear.

"Maybe," she said. "God, what time is it?"

"Late. Just wait here. I'll be two minutes."

I ran to the kitchen, fetched a glass of orange juice and a bottle of aspirin. By the time I got back, Sarah had drifted off again. I set the glass and bottle on the coffee table, then stretched out on the floor at her feet. Without meaning to, I fell asleep. When I woke a few hours later, the sun was just coming up. And Sarah was gone.

I sat down in the armchair where she'd been sleeping and told myself that I had to do something. I had to make sure that what had happened to Sarah would never happen again.

That was when I decided to be brave. That was when I decided to kill Anthony Costello.

CHAPTER 32

"SO YOU'RE confessing?" Haagen said. "You killed Anthony?"

"No, I didn't."

"But you wanted to."

"But I didn't."

She brought an open palm down hard on the table, looked at me as if I was a toddler refusing to eat my peas.

"Can you believe this?" she asked Nuñes.

Nuñes just rolled her eyes. I couldn't tell if the gesture was meant for me or her partner.

"All I'm hearing from you is motive," Haagen said. "A damn good motive, too. Maybe even self-defense. Hell, if you told this story to a jury, you might get off with a slap on the wrist. Maybe the judge would deport you and let that be the end of it. So why not cut to the confession? What happened in that kitchen? Tell me and I'll put in a good word with the DA."

"You aren't listening to me," I said.

I wanted to cry—not out of fear or anger or anything like remorse, but out of pure, deep-in-my-bones frustration. Talking with Haagen could do that to you. She'd bat your words around like cat toys, tune out whatever she didn't want to hear, and keep pushing until you broke. I guess that's her job, but beneath the hard-nosed facade she seemed to be enjoying herself a little too much.

"Oh, I'm listening," she said. "And you know what I think? I think somebody hired you to help them kill Anthony Costello. He deserved it, right? He was a bad guy. He did horrible things. To you. To people you cared about. Anyone in your position would have wanted him dead. So who was it you let in the house? Who did the stabbing?"

I didn't say anything.

"You know, don't you? You could solve this for us right now."

I nodded. We'd been squared off on opposite sides of a cold metal table for hours. It was time to bring the day to an end.

"I know," I said. "But he didn't pay me, and I didn't let him in. He did what he did all by himself."

"Who?"

"You know who."

"Tell me anyway," Haagen said. "Tell me all of it."

I started to look for Sarah, but I knew, I could feel it—something was off in the house. Something very bad was about to happen. Then I heard it: shouting, coming from the kitchen. Tony and another man. They were fighting over what sounded like the end of a business arrangement. It must have been their arguing that woke me.

"Sorry," Tony said, "but things don't work that way. They only work the way I want them to work."

"Oh, that's all changed," the other man said. "You've played your name for all it's worth. It's open season now. Uncle Vincent won't come to your rescue. Not this time. You're an embarrassment. You'll be lucky if you get a shallow grave."

The voice was familiar, but I couldn't place it. Not at first.

"You think he'll believe *you*?" Tony said. "You think you can ruin me without ruining yourself?"

I crept out of the den and tiptoed into the dining room. From there, I could see part of the kitchen through the open doorway—the part Tony was standing in. I watched him raise his fist, watched the veins bulge in his neck. He lunged forward. I heard a body slam into the refrigerator. I heard glass shatter. I heard cursing and stomping. And then I heard a gasp as Tony came staggering back into view, clutching his gut.

"You son of a bitch," he said, his voice strained and wet, as if his mouth was clogged with soup.

I saw the blade before I saw Sean. He held it out in front of him like a bayonet and charged. Tony fell to the floor but Sean kept stabbing him, his arm rising and thrusting, rising and thrusting. I clamped my hands over my mouth, ducked under the dining room table.

When Sean was done, he wiped the blade on Tony's pants, stood for a while with his hands on his knees, then straightened up and walked down the long entrance hallway as if he was in no hurry at all. I didn't dare move until I heard the front door pull shut.

"By *Sean*," Haagen said, "you mean Detective Sean Walsh?"

I nodded.

"The one who works in this building? The one who's married to your friend Sarah?"

I nodded again. Her voice was calm and even. It seemed as if she'd known all along, as if this was the very story she'd been pushing me to tell. She exchanged a look with Nuñes, then turned back to me.

"You can prove it?" she asked. "You have proof that it was him?"

"No," I said. "I don't have—"

"You're saying Detective Sean Walsh committed murder, and you're saying it on the record. You better be damn sure you're right. Sean's cleared a lot of cases in this department. Every one of them will be opened again. We're talking untold man-hours. Criminals will go free. So let me ask you again: do you have proof?"

I leaned forward, looked her dead in the eyes.

"No," I said. "I don't have proof. But I saw where the proof went."

CHAPTER 33

DETECTIVE SEAN WALSH

MY PLAN was to stop at Pete Owens's Stow-and-Go on the way to Símon's apartment. I had Serena's file on the seat beside me, but I needed something more, something that belonged to Anthony and couldn't be copied or reproduced. Something Vincent would recognize.

There was a pistol from the Civil War that Anthony kept locked away in his storage unit because he was afraid the help might steal it. He'd inherited the gun from his father, Vincent's brother. Vincent had hoped to inherit it himself. That was the closest uncle and nephew ever came to a major clash. Once the relic turned up in Símon's apartment, there'd be no doubt: Anthony would have clung to that pistol until the undertaker pried it from his icy hand.

As plans go, this one felt foolproof. I was already rehearsing my exit speech: "I've handed you your nephew's killer," I'd say. "I'm done now. It's time for me to walk away."

I was stopped at a light a block from the Stow-and-Go when they hit me: squad cars, unmarked cars, a goddamn armored SWAT truck. There was even a helicopter circling above. The sirens drowned out every other sound. Shock and awe meant a high-risk, high-profile arrest. The news vans wouldn't be far behind.

At first it didn't compute. I thought they were raiding the Stow-and-Go, swooping in on Pete and his band of thieves. I was thankful I hadn't arrived five minutes earlier. But then I heard Heidi's voice bleating at me through a loudspeaker, and I saw what must have been half the Tampa police force take cover behind their vehicles, Glocks and rifles pointed at me.

"Sean Alexander Walsh," Heidi said, "I need you to step out of the vehicle with your hands on your head. Nice and slow."

I did as I was told. The chopper hovered so low to the ground that the wind off its blades had my blazer flapping and my hair blowing in every direction. I stood at what felt like the junction of a thousand spotlights, my mind spinning through every possible scenario. Only one seemed likely: Vincent had given up on me a day too early, leaked my file straight to the precinct.

Heidi, dressed in Kevlar, crept up on me with her Glock raised. A small fleet of uniforms kept pace behind her.

"Sean Walsh," Heidi said, "you're under arrest for the murder of Anthony Costello."

Murder? It was more than I could process. Without thinking, I took a step forward, dropped my arms to my sides. Heidi and her entourage cocked their guns in unison.

"Hands, hands, hands!" she screamed.

Then: "On your knees. Now."

She let one of the unis pat me down and cuff me. She'd have done it herself if she wasn't getting such a kick out of pointing that gun at my head.

"You have the right to remain silent," she said. "Anything you say—"

"What the hell is this?" I shouted. "Have you lost your goddamn mind?"

"—will be used against you in a court of law . . ."

I wasn't listening.

"You know where I was that day," I said. "I was on shift. I was working a scene on the other end of Tampa. You know that."

She kept on reading me my rights. I looked around at the small army assembled to hunt me down. You'd have thought I was Pablo Escobar.

"Search it," Heidi said.

A crew of gloved detectives descended on the Jeep. I'd worked alongside each and every one of them. They were my colleagues. My friends. I'd been to their weddings, seen their kids baptized. If they had any regrets about what they were doing, it didn't show on their faces.

Heidi signaled for me to get to my feet. Together we watched Jimmy, Beth, Tom, and Samuel strip my car down to the studs. They tore out the carpet, dropped anything that wasn't nailed down into an evidence bag.

"Come on, Heidi," I said. "What is this? What do you think they're going to find?"

Crickets. She wouldn't look at me, wouldn't talk to me. My partner of more than a decade.

"Anything?" she called.

Samuel came trotting over, holding up a clear plastic bag. Inside was a Navy SEALs custom-engraved six-inch commemorative blade.

"No gross residue," he said, "but the size and color match."

"This is insane," I said. "Samuel, do you really think I'd hide a murder weapon in my own damn car? You think I'd drive over to Anthony's and kill him with my own monogrammed knife? Am I really that stupid? Samuel, look at me."

But he'd already turned his back and walked away. Heidi held up the bag, studied the knife.

"All right," she said to no one in particular, "let's wrap this up."

Two uniforms I'd never seen before steered me toward the back of a squad car. The news vultures had arrived in force. There must have been a dozen cameras on me. I figured, why not give them something worth filming?

"I've got shit on every one of you!" I screamed, swinging my head around, eyeballing my former friends and colleagues one by one. "You think I'll forget this? You think I'll go quietly? I'll bring down every one of you. You think *I'm* stupid? You just flushed your careers down the goddamn toilet. I'm taking this prime time. The story of the Tampa PD is about to be writ large. Think about that when you're kissing your kids good night."

I felt a hand on my head, pushing me down into the car. I took a last look around. My eyes settled on Heidi. She gave my stare right back, then broke into a wide and vicious grin.

PART II

CHAPTER 34
SARAH ROBERTS-WALSH

MOST OF what people say about jail is true. The roaches are so big you can hear their footsteps. Showering is a spectator sport. The guards are at least as terrifying as the inmates. And every meal is one part powder, two parts grease.

Luckily, the subhuman chow came in handy for me. Once my fellow inmates found out I could cook they went from wanting to have some fun with the newbie to making sure I didn't break so much as a fingernail. We had access to a microwave and an electric kettle, which was pretty much all the equipment I needed. Twenty-four hours into my stay they were calling me M.S.—short for Martha Stewart, another inmate who famously brightened up her tier.

My shtick was this: I'd take whatever someone bought at the commissary and turn it into something they might actually want to eat. You'd be amazed at what you can do with a packet of ramen noodles. Crush them up, boil them to mush, then tamp the mush down and let it cool and you have the wrap for a burrito. What you fill it with is up to you, but the most popular items were American cheese and fake sausage, two of the pricier commissary foods.

As for dessert, Oreo cookies make a nice base for mini cakes and pie crusts. Break them up, mix the crumbs with Kool-Aid or cola, and you've got a kind of batter that fluffs out like a yeast after just a few minutes in the microwave.

If you're feeling fancy, you can scrape away the creamy center and use it later as icing.

In short, I was accepted—even celebrated. Which isn't to say I'd ever want to go back to jail, but I learned something about myself I never would have guessed: when my back's to the wall, I find a way to survive.

All told, I was incarcerated for three days and three nights. On the morning of what would have been the fourth day, a CO the inmates called Gangrene because of her mossy-colored skin told me to come with her and leave my blanket behind. Once we were off the tiers and out of the cellblock, she handed me off to a young social worker in a turquoise pantsuit. Her name was Karen, and her handshake was limp bordering on submissive— as if it was her way of saying *I'm no threat*.

I was being released—Gangrene had made that much clear— but Karen wondered if she might have a word with me first.

"A kind of exit interview," she said.

I had no objections. The truth is, I didn't know where I'd go once they let me walk back through those gates. I followed her into a small office that was tiled with yellow subway tiles and furnished with a laminate desk and plastic chairs. It reminded me of my high school principal's office, only smaller.

"You know that the police have arrested your husband for the murder of Anthony Costello?" Karen asked once we were seated.

"I heard rumors," I said. "I didn't know for sure if they were true. There are a lot of stories flying around this place."

"You don't seem surprised," Karen said.

I tugged at the collar of my orange jumpsuit—a nervous tic I'd picked up in no time at all.

"I guess I'm not," I said. "Sean is a violent man. Anthony was a violent man. Something was bound to give."

Karen plucked a paper clip from a tray on her desk and started straightening it, then bending it back to its original shape—her own nervous tic.

"I'm just wondering why you didn't come forward with a full report."

"Full report?"

"About the abuse. The physical abuse in your marriage."

She made her voice sound as if she was consoling me when really she was blaming me for something. After all those hours in the box with Heidi, I'd played enough games to last me a lifetime.

"You might as well ask why I didn't report the rape," I said.

"The rape?"

I rolled my eyes.

"Don't you people talk to each other? Anthony Costello raped me. He drugged me, and then he raped me."

A piece of paper clip broke off in her hands. She was blushing. Her cheeks turned phosphorescent under the cheap overhead lights. I was glad I got a young one. Karen couldn't have been more than a year or two out of social work school. Maybe less. Maybe this was her prison internship.

"I didn't know," she said.

"Neither did Sean. Or at least I didn't tell him. You know why?"

She shook her head.

"Because Anthony would have denied it. More than denied it—he would have claimed the sex was all my idea. He'd have said he fought me off for as long as he could stand it, but I just kept coming on to him. And Sean would have believed him. And I think you can guess what would have come next."

Karen hesitated, cleared her throat, reached for a fresh paper clip. I hoped for her sake that she really was an intern.

"But isn't that all the more reason to come forward? Tell the authorities?"

I decided to break out the props. I opened my mouth wide, pointed to two shiny, fake molars on the left side.

"You see that?" I asked. "Last winter, Sean and I were walking downtown, doing our Christmas shopping. We got into a fight over how much to spend on my aunt. My aunt is more like my mother. She raised me. She's all I've got in the way of family. Her eyesight had taken a bad turn, and I wanted to get her a large-screen TV. Sean said she was just an aunt. He said aunts get fancy soaps or gourmet chocolates, not expensive TV sets. It escalated from there. Next thing I knew, he was slapping me around in the parking lot behind Macy's. There were people all around. When I started screaming, he switched from slapping to punching. He hit me so hard, he knocked these teeth out.

"Back then, I was brave. I called the cops. I filed a report. And then I waited. For weeks. For a full month. I didn't hear anything back. Meanwhile, Sean was on his best behavior. We got that television set for Aunt Lindsey. He brought me flowers, took me to fancy restaurants. He swore up and down it would never happen again. He said he loved me. He actually made me believe he'd changed.

"So I decided to let him off the hook. I called the precinct to retract my statement, say I wouldn't press charges. And guess what they told me? There was no report. Either it had vanished or it had never been filed.

"Do you see what I'm saying, Karen? Sean had the power to erase history. I wasn't just up against him. I was up against a brotherhood. A state-sanctioned gang. That was when I knew he'd lied. He hadn't changed at all. He'd do it again. And again, and again, and again. And one day he'd go too far. He'd beat me dead, and no one would do a goddamn thing to stop him. So don't talk to me about reports. Don't talk to me about what I could have or should have done, because you weren't there."

After that, Karen didn't have much to say for herself. She walked me to pick up my belongings and my street clothes. I changed in a handicapped bathroom, signed a piece of paper, and was on my way.

Outside, I waited for the shuttle bus back to the city. It was raining, which seemed about right. I thought of Sean. I felt more like a patient leaving the hospital than an inmate leaving jail. I'd survived the torturous injection, gagged down the vile medicine, and now the disease was cured. I had the rest of my life to look forward to, and the fact that I had no plans didn't bother me one bit.

CHAPTER 35
ANNA COSTELLO

I OPENED my eyes when they absolutely wouldn't stay closed any longer, then rolled onto my side and switched the alarm clock to Radio. This morning—if you can call 12:30 p.m. morning—the local DJ was playing Martha and the Vandellas: "Nowhere to hide / Got nowhere to run to, baby..." I laughed out loud at the irony, then got up and danced a little.

I never would have guessed that New Orleans was my kind of town. Jambalaya gives me the trots. Dixieland makes me twitch. But so far, I couldn't find a single thing wrong with my post-Anthony life. I enjoyed sitting on my wrought iron balcony with a dark roast in the morning and a gin fizz at night. I enjoyed looking down on the cobblestoned street where tourists and locals mingled and sometimes clashed. I even enjoyed the smell of fresh horse manure from the buggy tours that passed under my window every hour like clockwork.

But most of all I enjoyed being alone. It beat the hell out of tiptoeing around that soulless McMansion, doing my best to steer clear of the man who only spoke to me when he wanted someone to scream at, only touched me when he wanted someone to slap around. My marriage had become a nonstop game of hide-and-seek.

Which isn't to say that my old life didn't haunt me. Coffee and gin cured a lot, but they couldn't keep the uglier memories at bay. I'd be sitting on the toilet, swimming in the hotel pool, finishing a crossword puzzle in bed, when out of nowhere I'd flash on an image of Tony, Vincent, Defoe, Broch. They came at me like monsters rearing their heads in a children's pop-up book. Tony spitting in my face because I'd scraped his Bentley when I was backing out of the garage. Defoe grinning at me through a shattered rear window. Vincent whispering in my ear that sooner or later Anthony would snap and kill me—not because Anthony was evil, but because, as wives go, I was "my own special ring of hell."

Of course, there was still plenty to fret over in the here and now. I'd been following the investigation from afar. I knew Sarah was out of jail, and I knew Sean was locked up. I'd even managed to get Serena on the phone. Haagen pushed her to the brink, but she stood tall. Serena, more than anyone, put Sean behind bars. When I talked to her, her voice was half nerves and half exhaustion, but there was some hope, too. She'd moved in with her brother and was starting a new job, working in the cafeteria of a downtown public school. Spooning out mashed potatoes was a far cry from what Serena wanted to be doing, or was capable of doing, but she'd be treated well, and the school system would pay for night courses. She'd be Serena Flores, Esquire, soon enough.

It felt as though the three of us had turned a corner, but that didn't mean we were in the clear. Anthony was dead. Sean was staring down a life sentence. But skeletal old Uncle Vincent still loomed large. Who knew what story Sean was feeding him? Chances were he'd say he'd taken the fall for Sarah, play the devoted husband to keep from getting shanked. And Vincent, who seemed to think that women were made to lay traps for men, wouldn't be hard to convince.

Or maybe Sean would point the finger at me. That would be the smart play. As I said, there was never any love lost between me and Vincent. It wouldn't take much to convince him that I'd killed his beloved nephew. Besides, as he saw it, I was costing him money just by staying alive. A lot of money. Between the house, the yacht, the luxury cars, and the offshore accounts, I stood to inherit a sizable fortune—a fortune Vincent believed was rightfully his.

Anthony wasn't all the way stupid, but the Costello empire-building gene had skipped right over him. If the playing field had been level, if he'd been born into a nice middle-class family in the suburbs, he might have wound up managing a restaurant or owning a car wash. I'd put his absolute ceiling at real estate agent. But with Vincent backing him, he'd gone crashing through that ceiling. In other words, Vincent made Anthony wealthy, and now Vincent felt that wealth should revert back to him.

And with me out of the picture, it would. Anthony had no other next of kin. My guess was that Vincent planned to help me commit suicide. Probably with a noose or pills. Something that would leave a clean corpse for the medical examiner, who was most likely in Vincent's pocket anyway. *Not a bruise on her apart from what she did to herself,* this hypothetical coroner would say. *Suicide, open and shut.* The distraught wife just couldn't go on.

All that to say: I was still jumpy as hell. In the morning, I expected to pull back the curtains and find Defoe standing on my balcony. At night, before I went to bed, I spilled a garbage bag of crumpled newspaper over the floor so no one could sneak up on me. I even cut back on the sleeping pills for fear the noise wouldn't wake me.

Of course, Haagen would come hunting for me, too, once the trial was underway. I'd be witness and widow—the person who humanized Anthony for the jury. Maybe the DA would offer me some kind of temporary protection, put me up in a swank hotel for the duration. But the trial would end, and unless Sean was convicted beyond a shadow of a doubt, my straits would be no less dire. Vincent had to walk out of that courtroom without a doubt in his head. Then, if I had to pay him off, I would. Meanwhile, the staff at this boutique hotel knew me as Jane Pepper, and I wore my curly red wig morning, noon, and night. I even wore it to bed.

And yet, part of me felt so free. All that was missing was a companion. Someone I could talk to without worrying that they'd turn on me—or turn me in. To Vincent. To Haagen. Someone I trusted. Someone who had as much to lose as me.

CHAPTER 36

SHE TURNED up the morning of my fifth day in New Orleans. I might have complained about the hotel's security. There was no call from the concierge, no bellhop announcing her arrival: just three soft knocks at the door. It was a knocking I recognized. It used to mean, *I don't want to bother you, but breakfast / lunch / dinner is ready.* Truth be told, it always bothered the hell out of me. I wanted to scream at her to stand up tall and give that door a good, hard whack. Now, though, there wasn't any sound I'd rather hear.

"Just a minute," I said.

I changed out of my satin robe and into jeans and a T-shirt — my way of saying we were equals now. Then I opened up. She'd lost weight. Sarah never had much of an inch to pinch, but now she was out-and-out skinny. I was half concerned, half jealous.

I didn't say anything. Neither did she. She stood in the hall, looking me over, hands hidden in her coat pockets. I had to wave her in, then step aside so she didn't run over my foot with her gargantuan suitcase.

I went first.

"You crazy, deluded, devious backstabber," I said.

She cocked her head, made her little gourmet chef hands into fists.

"At least I fight my own battles," she said. "I don't hide behind my money."

"Can't hide behind what you don't have."

"Yeah, and I'm no one's trophy bitch."

"And I'm no murderer."

"No, you just hire it done."

That was enough. She broke into a smile. Then we were hugging each other, laughing and crying at the same time. It was our code: if our reunion opened with mutual accusations and confessions, it meant neither of us was wearing a wire. It meant that, as far as we knew, we were in the clear.

After Sarah freshened up, we headed down to the hotel's five-star restaurant, took a seat on the terrace, and ordered giant prawns and even larger hurricanes. Three drinks in, we were trying our best to be quiet and civil.

"To us," Sarah said, raising her glass.

"The three of us."

"Serena really came through."

"We all did," I said. "The trophy wife, the maid, and the cook. Who'd have thought we could pull it off?"

"Not Sean. He thought he was going to swoop in and save us all."

"He should have been saving himself. Did he give you the speech?"

"All the way from Texas. He wanted me to say you'd paid Serena, then Serena hired her brother. Longest car ride of my life."

"He wanted me to say that I'd paid you, then you paid Serena, who in turn paid her brother. Every finger pointing in a different direction. He kept saying, 'That's how we beat this. Confuse them until they throw up their hands.' We have to assume he'll use the same strategy in his defense."

"Too little, too late," Sarah said. "In the end, we had the better plan."

"Underestimate us at your own peril. Mob man and cop boy couldn't fathom being brought down by three little women. Speaking of Sean..."

I dug into my pocketbook. Sarah set her drink down.

"Take a look at this," I said, handing her a newspaper clipping. "It's worth framing."

She read the headline aloud: "Bail Set at $5 Million for Detective Accused of Murder."

"The third paragraph from the bottom says the amount is unprece—"

"Five *million*?" She was shell-shocked. "I don't care how much Sean was reeling in on the side—no way he comes up with that kind of cash."

"That's what the judge had in mind. Apparently he gave a long lecture on the *disease of corruption* in the Tampa police force."

"To our husbands," she said, taking her glass back up. "Two diseases we've finally cured."

We clinked rims. Then Sarah turned serious. Serious is Sarah's default mode. Whether she was baking a soufflé or conspiring to commit murder, she always seemed to be thinking of the worst possible outcome, holding it up in her mind's eye like a threat. That was how she motivated herself. All stick and no carrot.

"It isn't over, you know," she said. "We need to rehearse."

"What *now*?"

Sarah took out her glasses, slid them up the bridge of her nose. Glasses with sheer plastic lenses. Glasses she bought when Sean started hitting her, as if four eyes would somehow make him a gentleman. She was wearing them now in order to appear more lawyerly.

"Until the three of us are all set in our new lives," she said, "we can't afford to waste a second."

"I wish you'd thought of that two hurricanes ago," I said.

"I mean it, Anna. Sean is wily. He has resources. So far we're ahead, but we can't forget we're playing in his world."

"All right, all right," I said. "You go first. I'll take small sips between questions."

She cleared her throat, sat up ramrod straight in her chair.

"How would you describe your marriage to the deceased?" she began. "Was it happy? Were you what people call soul mates?"

"Soul mates? Who's defending Sean, a Hallmark card?"

"Anna, this is important. Get into character."

I shut my eyes, shook myself semisober.

"Yes," I said, "we were happy. There were ups and downs, but on the whole I'd say we did better than most couples."

"Hmm... The ups must have happened in private, because people I've talked to only seem to remember the downs. Is it true that at your own wedding you threatened to castrate him if he so much as glanced at one of your bridesmaids?"

"If I didn't love him, I wouldn't have cared."

"You must have loved him a whole lot, because I have witnesses on record saying that you threatened to slit his throat when he fell asleep, to burn down the mansion with him in it the next time he passed out drunk, to lace his shampoo with sulfuric acid, his iced tea with antifreeze, his underwear with—"

"Yeah, and he threatened to run me through a meat grinder. It was *The War of the Roses* at our house. We fought. We were passionate. But we never would have hurt each other."

"Maybe not, but would you have paid someone to hurt Anthony?"

"What?"

Sarah shot me a look that said, *Nice job. Your surprise seems genuine.* I thought, *Maybe I should bring a hurricane to court with me.*

"It's been widely reported that three women disappeared immediately after Anthony Costello's murder: you, Sarah Roberts-Walsh, and Serena Flores. What hasn't been reported is that something else went missing. Something very valuable. Your jewelry. A half million dollars' worth, maybe more."

"I don't know where my collection went."

This was one bald-faced lie I'd told Haagen. I was confident I could repeat it without tipping my hand.

"Really? Because Sarah Roberts-Walsh told detectives that she sold every one of the pieces."

"That's what I heard."

"No, don't say that," Sarah scolded. "Don't pretend to have heard."

"I have no idea what Sarah did or didn't do. The jewels aren't worth much unless you know how to fence them and I doubt she figured that out."

"You doubt that, huh?"

"She's a cook, not a jewel thief. She wouldn't have the stones to take them, and even if she did, she wouldn't have the slightest idea how to fence them."

"Do you also doubt that Sarah had access to Detective Walsh's collection of knives? Do you doubt she had access to his vehicle? To the Jeep where the murder weapon—a monogrammed knife—was so conveniently discovered?"

"Oh, please," I said. "Sarah Roberts-Walsh is about as dangerous as a retired librarian. If I was going to pay someone to kill my husband, it sure as hell wouldn't be her."

"So who would you hire?"

I pretended to be looking over the courtroom.

"I didn't hire anyone," I said. "But if I had, it would have been someone like him. Someone who traveled in Anthony's circle. Someone who knew how to handle himself. Someone who might stand a chance against a three-hundred-pound man who grew up in a mob family."

Sarah nodded.

"The defense would have objected until he was blue in the face, but you got your point across. Now you grill me."

"Later," I said. "I've got something to show you first. Something I don't like to leave unguarded for too long."

CHAPTER 37

BACK IN my room, I slid a titanium suitcase out from under the bed, knelt down, and undid all three locks.

"What's this?" Sarah asked.

"My collection," I said, popping open the lid, pulling away a layer of neatly folded sweaters to reveal a little over a million dollars in tightly wrapped stacks of bills. "I meant it when I said you wouldn't know what to do with them."

"How did you . . . ?"

"Doesn't matter."

"This looks like a lot more than we told Haagen."

"You think I went around advertising their real value? Remember, that's half for you, half for Serena. I'm not paying you off. This is so the two of you can start over, like we agreed. You're the ones who . . . who did the heavy lifting. I'm so sorry. I just couldn't—"

"He was your husband. Of course you couldn't."

"You were right about Sean. He was so convinced the killer had to be male, he never stopped to think that two women might have done the job. I guess we fooled the forensics team, too."

"The blades were identical. Sean was so in love with that knife, he had to have the black *and* the silver handle."

"Lucky for us."

"Doesn't get any luckier."

I looked over at her. She wasn't convulsing or gnashing her teeth or even blinking. She was standing dead still while tears rolled down her cheeks, one on top of the other.

"Hey," I said. "Hey, what's wrong?"

As if I had to ask, but a stock phrase was the best I could come up with—the crisis equivalent to clearing your throat.

"I loved him once, you know?" she said. "It wasn't supposed to be this way. This wasn't in our vows. Now I'm getting rich off of . . ."

She couldn't bring herself to finish the sentence. I shut the suitcase, stood, and put an arm around her.

"First of all," I said, "half a mil doesn't make you rich these days. And second, what do you think would have happened to you—to me—if we'd just sat back and left our fate to those men? You said it yourself: Sean would have killed you sooner or later. And even if he hadn't, you'd have spent the rest of your life scared out of your mind, never knowing when the next trip to the ER was coming."

She nodded, wiped away tears with the heel of one palm.

"And me?" I went on. "You know firsthand what kind of animal Anthony was. I used to think I loved him. Really, I was seduced by everything that came with him. The house and the cars and the jewels, but also the celebrity. Being able to walk into any restaurant and get a table on the spot. Having people wait on me, even at home. I grew up outside of Jackson. Not poor, but nowhere near rich. Just average. Everything about me was average. I never had any talent, never saw myself as anything more than a secretary or a shop clerk."

Sarah's tear ducts had stalled out. She was listening now—taking a break from her story to hear mine.

"But then I met Anthony. At a minor-league baseball game, if you can believe it. It turned out his uncle owned the team. Anthony saw me sitting up in the bleachers with my girlfriends. I wasn't the prettiest of the group, but it was me he invited to join him in the family suite.

"After the game, he introduced me to the players, then took me for a drive along the coast in his Jaguar. I was hooked. It felt like the big time—as big as it gets in Central Florida. I didn't see what was coming any more than you did. But it came. For both of us. We grew up in our marriages, and then we saw our mistakes. Our husbands were bad men, and they had all the power on their side. We did the only thing we could do. Don't call it murder. Call it survival. Because that's what it was: them or us."

Sarah patted my arm. She looked thoughtful, as if she was about to share some life-altering insight. Instead, she asked for a Kleenex. I laughed out loud.

"A Kleenex and champagne," I said. "Not because we're celebrating, but because it's there and we might as well drink it."

I took two half bottles from the minibar. They cost more than two full bottles, but this wasn't the time to be frugal.

"Plastic cups, or straight from the bottle?" I asked.

"Straight from the bottle."

"That's my girl."

We sat across from each other on the twin beds, drank without toasting, seemed for a long beat to have run out of things to say. Then I had an idea.

"Let me see those sham glasses of yours," I said.

She looked confused but dug them out of her pocketbook without asking any questions.

"And that snapshot in your wallet of you and Sean at Niagara—let me have that, too."

"Why?"

"Because we're going to burn it."

"Burn it?"

"And these awful reading glasses, too."

The frames were bright yellow with patches of brown—the most pitiful pair Sarah could find. I put them on, pushed them up the bridge of my nose.

"Weakest prescription money can buy," I said. "Luckily you don't need them anymore, since Sean won't be coming at you anymore. Time to let go of the past."

I took the metal wastepaper basket from under the desk, filled it with pages from the *Tribune,* then dropped in the glasses and the photo. As a show of solidarity, I pulled out of my pocket a leather key chain with AC & AC branded on one side and tossed it in. A present from Anthony on the occasion of our third anniversary. By then, the romance was already dead.

"Come on, now," I said.

She followed me onto the balcony. Below us, the street was starting to come to life. Fast-talking front men were out fighting for business, luring tourists to their restaurants, bars, clubs. A street musician with an accordion was butchering the theme to *The Godfather.* Everywhere people were singing, holding hands, climbing lampposts. A few flames on a balcony would only add to the festivities.

Sarah sat on a wrought iron chair and watched me strike the match.

"I don't know," she said. "Maybe this isn't such a good idea."

She was turning emotional again. The alcohol brought it out in her.

"Of course it's a good idea," I said. "The best idea I've ever had. We're protecting your future self. Ten years from now, do you really want to stumble on those glasses and lose a night of your life to nostalgia or guilt or whatever you happen to be feeling just then? All triggers have to go. Otherwise, we'll never be free."

She gave me a reluctant nod. I let the match fall. With no accelerant, the burn was slow, but once the flames took hold they shot up a good three feet above the basket. Someone on the street yelled something about a Thelma and Louise weenie roast. I saw myself as the independent and tough-minded Louise, even if it hadn't been me who wielded the knife.

Sarah leaned forward until the fire's glow reflected on her skin. She wasn't crying, but her face was somber as hell. I put a hand on her back.

"Believe me," I said, "I wish it was different."

And I really did. I could have ripped my hair out thinking about all the ways I wished things were different. I could have collapsed on the floor and screeched in tongues. But Sarah had been so strong—it was my turn to be strong for her. Later, I knew, I'd have all the time I needed to be weak. I had my own hard moments ahead.

CHAPTER 38
DETECTIVE SEAN WALSH

AT LEAST they cared enough for my well-being to stick me in solitary, though even then I wound up next door to someone I'd put away: Marty the Mute. At least he made the place a little quieter. Sometimes we'd play hangman by passing a slip of paper back and forth through an air vent. I lost every round. It made me wonder who else Marty might have been if he'd made the effort.

Otherwise, there wasn't much to do in my cell besides sit and steam. Sarah's betrayal was like a gut punch. The best memories were the hardest to cope with. Walks on the beach. Airboat rides through the Everglades. Trips to Niagara Falls, New York City, Yellowstone Park. All tainted now. We'd started in love and wound up strangers. Wasn't it supposed to be the other way around?

I was deep into a set of prison cell push-ups when a flabby corrections officer with bad skin announced I had a visitor. My first thought: Sarah had come around, wanted to talk things through with me before she set the official record straight. I saw in a flash how willing I was to forgive her, even if she never forgave me. And yes, I'd done plenty that needed forgiving.

I worked out a short speech in my head as the CO led me to

the visiting area. I'd let her know that she had my attention now. I understood who I'd been, and I wouldn't be that person anymore. I was done playing fast and loose with our wedding vows, with the policeman's oath of honor, with every promise I'd ever made. Whether we stayed together or split, I'd love and cherish her, for richer or poorer, in sickness or in health, until the end of my days.

But it wasn't Sarah I found waiting for me: it was Defoe, Vincent's right-hand goon. One look at him and I forgot all about my little mea culpa. I was spitting mad again—angrier at Sarah than I'd ever been before. Like we'd set up this rendezvous and she'd sent Defoe in her place. Defoe, the ugliest man on two feet. All pockmarks and scars, oil and dandruff. I've seen bodies in every state of decomp, but I always had a hard time looking Defoe in the face.

He gave me a little nod as I took my seat. I nodded back. The thick prison glass between us seemed to magnify his deformities. We reached for our handsets at the same time. Defoe got right down to business.

"Our mutual friend is very displeased with your current situation," he said.

He had an unnerving way of talking through his thin smile, almost without moving his lips.

"He couldn't come here and tell me himself?" I said.

"I assume you're joking. It's good to see you still have your sense of humor. You'll need it in the days ahead. Of course, how many days you have left depends to a large extent on what you say now."

"How many days I have left?"

"I mean behind bars."

Defoe wasn't the brightest, but he had too many years' experience to threaten me outright in a state-run facility where any and all conversations might be recorded.

"You're a lawyer now?" I asked.

"A liaison."

The way I felt just then, I could have plowed my fist through the glass and squeezed his neck until his nasty head popped.

"What is it you want?" I asked.

"I want to look you in the eyes and know the truth."

"About what?"

"Are you guilty as charged?"

"How do you think I'm going to answer?"

"How you answer doesn't matter: your eyes will tell me what I need to know."

I sucked it up, leaned forward until my nose was touching the glass, and let him have a good long look.

"No," I said.

His smile got a little fatter.

"So far, so good," he said. "But I'm going to need more."

"Like what?"

"An alternative theory. More importantly, a name."

I didn't have to think it over—I knew what I was going to say as soon as I saw him sitting on the wrong side of the glass.

"The cook," I said.

"The cook? That's a bit close to home."

"Doesn't change the facts."

"Acting on her own, or at your behest?"

"On her own."

"See, now that's interesting. I heard that she was employed as the cook at your insistence, and that cooking was only half of her job. The other half involved reporting to you."

"That's a story," I said. "Nothing more than a story."

He pushed back in his chair, crossed his legs, and rested his hands on his top knee.

"Convince me," he said.

"My eyes aren't convincing enough?"

"In a word, no. So what proof do you have to offer?"

"Will an eight-hour confession do the trick?"

I told him about the long drive from Podunk, Texas, back to Tampa.

Hours of Sarah sniveling and saying she hadn't meant to kill him, that it had started as self-defense and ended in blind rage. He'd touched her one time too many. It was more than she could take. I said she kept going on and on about how sorry she was, about how a lifetime of good works would never make up for what she'd done.

I have to admit, I sounded damn convincing. Part of me hoped they *were* recording this conversation—it would give any jury a fat dose of reasonable doubt. The other part of me was imagining Sarah's first and final encounter with Vincent Costello.

"She was so sorry that she ran away?" Defoe asked.

"Even the guilt-ridden have survival instincts."

"What was she doing with your knife? The fact that she had it on her suggests premeditation. It suggests she picked her fall guy in advance."

I started to say something vague about self-protection, then dropped it. Sarah wanted to send me away for life—what did I care if Vincent took her for a cold-blooded killer?

"Maybe she did," I said. "Our marriage peaked with the honeymoon. Since then it's been nonstop combat. Maybe she saw her chance to kill two birds with one knife."

Defoe quit smiling, which did nothing to improve his looks.

"Your story rings true," he said. "The unfortunate victim had a reputation for being handsy, to say the least. And based on the little I know of you, it isn't hard to imagine that your wife would wish you ill."

"So what now?"

"I'll pass on your version of events. We'll see what the man on the throne has to say."

"Any predictions?"

"Depends on his mood. I'll try to catch him during his after-dinner cigar."

"I'd rather you didn't wait until after dinner."

"Sit tight, Detective Walsh. You'll have word soon enough."

I watched him walk away, then sat there until a guard tapped me on the shoulder. I'd like to say that I felt remorse or sadness, but that would be a lie. Back in my cell, I beat Marty at hangman for the first time. The word I guessed was *doomsday*.

CHAPTER 39
ANNA COSTELLO

I'M NOT sure what it says about me that I wasn't hungover. Probably nothing good. At almost 10:00 a.m., Sarah was bringing herself to life with a long, luxurious bath. I'd called down for our breakfast and, more importantly, coffee.

Meanwhile, I took the morning paper out onto the balcony. In my previous life, it was always Anthony who read the paper. He called it his morning quiet time. Now I was claiming my time, sliding back into the big, bad world I'd been locked out of for so long.

The sky was bright and clear, the air just warm enough for me to sit outside in my bathrobe. The smell of horse manure mixed with the softer odors of baking bread and frying eggs. I set the paper on the table, flipped past the first page, and went straight for the fluff: fashion and film, gossip and real estate. It felt like that kind of day—the kind where you linger and meander and keep the mood light.

But then there it was, in a slim sidebar on page seven: the story that would turn our lives upside down and give them a hard shake. The headline said it all: DISGRACED DETECTIVE SET FREE ON $5 MILLION BAIL. I waited until my breathing slowed to a seminormal rate, then read through to the end. There was a lot of speculation about who had such deep pockets. I could have solved that mystery. The question was, why? Why was Uncle Vincent backing a cop who'd been caught red-handed holding the weapon that murdered his nephew?

Best-case scenario, at least for us: Vincent wanted Sean outside, where he could snatch him up and take his time. I had no trouble believing that Vincent would pay five million dollars for the privilege of avenging Anthony's murder himself, mano a mano.

Worst-case scenario: Sean had powers of persuasion I'd never noticed.

He'd convinced Vincent that the knife was a plant. There was no way Vincent would let himself be convinced unless Sean sold him another killer, and Sean only had three options to choose from: Sarah, Serena, and me.

I was spinning back and forth, trying to figure out which scenario was most likely, when the French doors opened behind me and Sarah came strolling out with our breakfast tray balanced professionally on one palm.

"I don't think coffee ever smelled this good," she said. "You must not have heard the knocking."

The bath had done wonders for her. She'd woken up looking green around the gills and pale everywhere else. Now there was color in her cheeks again, a bounce to her step. She seemed weightless, ready to burst into song.

Then she saw my face.

"Oh, honey," she said, "I know I only just got here, but we both agreed: we can't be seen together until after the trial. Last night was risky enough."

"It isn't that," I said.

"Then what's the matter?"

She set the tray on the table, brushed her still-damp hair back behind her ears, and rested a hand on my shoulder.

"Don't tell me the drinking did you in," she said. "That isn't the Anna I know."

I just held up the paper and pointed. She hadn't made it past the headline before she dropped into her chair and let out a sharp whimper.

"Oh, my God," she said.

"I know."

"But who . . . ?"

"I'll give you one guess."

"Vincent?"

I nodded.

"But why?"

"That's the five-million-dollar question."

"Coffee," she said. "I need coffee."

I filled our cups while she read on, her face going from ruddy to crimson.

"You think Vincent will kill him?" she asked.

I was impressed: she seemed genuinely concerned, and not for herself.

Life in prison was bad enough for her soon-to-be ex: she drew the line at capital punishment. The cynical side of me thought, *That's reserved for other people's husbands.* But this wasn't the time for a catfight.

"Consider the alternative," I said. "My erstwhile uncle-in-law won't be satisfied until someone stops breathing. Sean was framed. We framed him. Maybe he figured it out and made Vincent a believer."

Sarah lifted the lid off her eggs Florentine and set it back down without so much as glancing at her plate. Then she took a little tour of the balcony, running her hand absentmindedly along the railing. She looked as though she'd lost her wits.

"It never ends," she said. "You turn what you think is the final bend, but the road just goes on and on and on."

"Oh, it'll end," I told her. "Everything does. The question is how it will end, and whether or not there'll be anything left for us afterward."

She sat back down, her eyes glassy, her mouth hanging open.

"What are we going to do?" she said. "What in the world are we going to do?"

Before I could answer, bells started going off somewhere in the room behind us—long, short, long, short. It was the ringtone on my burner phone. Only one person knew the number.

"That's Serena calling," I said, not sure yet whether I had the will to answer.

Sarah sprang up.

"I'll get it," she said. "I haven't talked to Serena in ages."

"The phone's on my nightstand."

I followed her inside, watched her lunge across my bed, grab at the phone, knock it to the floor, and then go scampering after it on hands and knees.

"Serena?" she said. "Serena, are you still there?"

"Put it on speaker," I said.

She fumbled for the button. The voice that filled the room wasn't Serena's.

"She's sitting right here," a man said. "Would you like to speak with her?"

Defoe. I recognized his nasal, wispy voice, remembered telling Vincent that his right-hand man sounded more like a librarian than a killer. "Sheep's clothing," Vincent said. It sounded like a warning. I thought now that maybe it was.

"Sarah," Serena said, "whatever you do, don't—"

Defoe snatched the phone back.

"Is it Sarah I'm speaking with?" Defoe said. "I thought this was Anna's line."

I started to answer, but Sarah beat me to it.

"It's Sarah," she said. "And if you hurt her, I swear to God I'll—"

"Feisty," Defoe cut her off. "Just like your beloved aunt. She's here, too. Want to say hello?"

Sarah clutched at her chest. I hoped to hell she'd remembered her insulin.

"Don't you listen to a word this cadaver says," Lindsey yelled. "He's using us as bait, and I won't—"

"As you can tell, the gang is all here," Defoe said. "I thought I'd invite you to the party."

Sarah looked up at me from where she sat slumped between the beds. It was clear she'd reached her limit.

"We wouldn't miss it for the world," I said. "You need us to bring anything?"

"Do my ears deceive me, or is that the Widow Costello?"

"Hello, Defoe. How's life as Vincent's trained monkey?"

"Always so brave," he said. "At least from a distance. Last time I saw you, you were fleeing the scene of an accident. You're lucky I didn't call the police."

"Thanks for that. Now about this little shindig…"

"Here's the deal: it's a kind of surprise party. At least, we want the location to be a surprise."

He told us to pull up outside Lindsey's house at 8:00 p.m. on the dot. There would be a black sedan parked at the curb. We were to follow it to what he called the "party house."

"Needless to say, any sign of an uninvited guest—or guests—and the evening will end very badly for your friends."

With that, he hung up. The room went as quiet as a crypt.

PART III

CHAPTER 40
SARAH ROBERTS-WALSH

"SLOW DOWN," Anna said. "We won't make the flight if you get pulled over."

I took my foot off the gas until the speedometer hit seventy— a compromise she'd have to live with.

"We need to call the police, Anna. This is way, way, way above our pay grade. We're dealing with professionals here."

"Anthony was a professional," she said.

"A professional accountant."

"That's what it said on his tax returns, but there was more to Anthony than numbers. We took him down, didn't we?"

Her sense of calm was only inflaming my panic. I wondered what kind of chill pill she'd taken. Probably a benzo or four. I thought maybe I should ask her to share.

"We had surprise on our side then," I argued. "Vincent's men know we're coming. They have Serena and Lindsey hostage. The police—"

"Will get them killed."

"And we won't?"

"No. Because we'll have surprise on our side again."

"What are you talking about?"

I wanted to scream, *It's not your aunt with a gun to her head!*

"I know where they are," she said, her voice neutral and detached, as if she was practicing to be a hypnotist.

"You're clairvoyant now, is that it?"

"No, ma'am. I just have a good memory for sounds. You didn't hear that chiming in the background? Defoe had to raise his voice to talk over it."

I tried replaying the call in my mind, but I'd been too frantic to pick up on anything past Defoe's instructions.

"Anthony hated that clock," Anna said.

"What clock?"

"The grandfather clock in his uncle's country getaway. It was so damn loud you could hear it two floors up, in the attic bedroom where we always slept. Kept Anthony awake all night long. There was something haunting about it, he said. I think he believed the place was literally haunted."

"You're saying that's where they have Aunt Lindsey and Serena? In Vincent's cabin?"

"I wouldn't call a four-thousand-square-foot home a cabin, but yeah—that's where they're holed up."

I thought it over while I darted in and out of traffic, one hand hovering above the horn. Maybe she was right, but I couldn't see how it changed anything.

"All the more reason to call the cops," I said. "They can swoop in there now. Vincent's men won't know what hit them. Hell, they're probably napping, saving their energy for the big night."

Anna sniggered.

"Hard to believe you were married to a cop for all those years," she said.

"One bad apple doesn't mean—"

"Oh, please. The whole damn tree is rotten. Any doubt I had was erased when Sean showed up at that seedy motel. Call 911 and Vincent will know about it before you hang up the phone."

Her energy was picking up now. She sounded a little less sedated, a lot more determined.

"So what do we do, storm the place?" I asked. "Just the two of us? Get ourselves killed along with Aunt Lindsey and Serena?"

I took my eyes off the road long enough to see that Anna was grinning.

"We don't need to storm the place," she said. "For once we can use Vincent's paranoia against him."

I was desperate for her to cut to the chase.

"Enough with the riddles," I said. "What do you have in mind?"

She let her head fall back against the headrest—a sure sign that she was about to take her time.

"Back in the day, Anthony wanted to impress me. He sent flowers to the shitty little bungalow where I still lived with my parents. He took me whale watching in a helicopter. He even cooked for me, if you can picture that. And he let me in on family secrets. I'm talking *family* with a capital *F*.

"We'd only been dating a month when he brought me to one of the infamous Costello retreats at Vincent's backwoods chalet. I was peacock proud. I couldn't believe it. Anthony Costello wanted to show *me* off to his family. Like I was a prize. Like he was sure this little bumpkin from Jackson would make their jaws drop—all these career criminals at the top of their game. People who owned baseball teams and yachts and penthouses around the globe."

I thought, *Enough with the rags-to-riches melodrama*. But trying to speed her up would only slow her down.

"Anthony and I got there early. He wanted to show me around 'the grounds.' By grounds he meant a thousand acres of Florida wilderness. Like I said, I grew up in the sticks, but I've never been much of a country girl. Especially not Florida country. Live oak and cypress swamps, alligators and indigo snakes—throw in a broken-down plantation house and you've got the set for a slasher movie.

"But now I had my man to protect me. He led me down this windy, overgrown trail for what felt like miles, though I don't think it could have been—I'm not sure how many acres are in a mile.

"Anyway, we got to a spot where the trail was blocked by an enormous, moss-covered log. I was ready to climb over it, but Anthony held up a hand. He said he wanted to show me something, told me to stand back. I watched him crouch down like a sumo wrestler and set both hands on that log. Then he pushed and heaved and grunted until he turned red in the face and there was spit flying out of his mouth.

"The thing didn't budge, but he kept on trying like nothing short of a hernia would stop him. I thought, *What the hell are you doing?* But since we weren't married yet I only said, 'Want some help?' He stepped back. 'Go on,' he said, 'give it a try. Maybe a woman's touch will do the trick.'

"Pushing solo wasn't what I'd had in mind, but I could tell something was up, so I played along. I crouched down just like he had, laid my hands where he'd laid his, and shoved with all my might.

"Well, the thing rolled right away, and I nearly did a face-plant. It couldn't have weighed more than a pound or two. Meanwhile, Mafia boy was laughing his tonsils out. I was mad as hell, but I laughed along with him, because that's what you do when you think you might be in love with someone you barely know. Then he stood up straight, stopped laughing, and pointed.

"There was a square of blue tarp on the ground where the log had been. He pulled it back and revealed a round steel door like the kind you'd see on the top of a submarine. He grabbed the handle, twisted, and pulled.

"'My uncle had this put in,' he said. 'In case the wrong people came visiting.'

"I stepped forward and took a look. There was a shiny metal ladder leading down into the dark. Anthony told me to think of it as a shortcut, then said, 'After you.' I damn near had a full-blown panic attack.

"'Are you crazy?' I said before I could stop myself. 'I'm not climbing down into that black spider pit.'

"He told me to relax. 'My uncle thinks of everything,' he said. He reached his hand down under the rungs and flipped a switch. The hole lit up like a runway. 'See?' he said. 'Uncle Vince even flees in style.'

"He told me the trail ended at the county road. Vincent had a car hidden in the brush—a BMW, which for him was slumming it.

"'So shall we?' he asked.

"We climbed down. The tunnel was made of poured concrete. It had track lighting, and I swear to God the thing was climate-controlled. Not a spider in sight.

"If we hadn't stopped to have a little fun, we'd have made it back to the house in ten minutes flat. I didn't understand how that was possible given the epic hike we'd taken aboveground, but there you have it—the Costellos are magical, in their way.

"The tunnel lets you out in the basement. From there you cross the rec room and take the stairs to the kitchen."

We were coming up on the airport. I gave Anna a sideways glance.

"Lets *me* out?" I said. "*I* cross the rec room?"

She flashed a big smile.

"I'll draw you a map on the plane," she said.

CHAPTER 41

ANNA COSTELLO

SO THERE I was, walking up a patented mile-long Costello driveway toward a place I never thought I'd see again, those spine-chilling live oak trees looming on either side. Apart from what moonlight made it through the branches, the place was pitch-dark. I'd have traded places with Sarah in a heartbeat.

I had a gym bag strapped to one shoulder, and inside it was the roughly one million dollars I'd raised for Sarah and Serena. I'd thought about holding back a few hundred thousand, but *million* has a ring to it. The kind of ring that would get Defoe salivating. As Anthony put it, "That's one greedy son of a bitch." And if anyone knew greedy sons of bitches, it was my dearly departed. Besides, if things went according to plan, Defoe wouldn't get to keep the cash. And if things didn't go according to plan, it wouldn't be of any use to Sarah or Serena.

I was glad I'd talked Sarah out of calling the cops. In my book, death—even a slow death—beats the hell out of life in prison, and there wasn't any way to send in the cavalry without putting ourselves on the most-wanted list. At the very least, Sean's old running buddies would want to know why Vincent saw fit to kidnap an unskilled worker and an aging nurse. The notion that we'd framed Sean would start to look more and more credible, the holes in our story—like the fact that we hadn't exactly given ourselves airtight alibis—more and more glaring.

I was glad we hadn't called the cops, but that didn't mean my knees weren't knocking as I turned a corner into the clearing that surrounded the house. It was just as I remembered: a log castle in the land of the alligator. Even back then, I should have known that I was headed for trouble.

I took out my phone and checked the time. Seven p.m.— an hour before we were supposed to turn up outside Lindsey's house. There were lights on in the house, a single sedan parked out front. I figured Defoe had sent an underling to play escort. No way he'd have gone himself on the off chance we had called the cops, and Broch was too valuable to risk over a car ride.

The sedan was the same car I'd run from in that alley. That meant Defoe was inside and had Broch with him. It was always possible they'd brought backup, but Costello's men generally work in pairs—just like the police.

Here goes nothing, I thought as I started across the clearing.

I watched for an eye at the window, a crack in the shades, but there wasn't any movement that I could see. Why bother keeping watch? This location was supposed to be secret. No point in dragging it out. I walked right up onto the porch and rang the bell, like a trick-or-treater or a Jehovah's Witness, then stepped back so that whoever answered would have a full view from the side window.

It was Defoe—first peeking from behind the curtain, then stepping through the open doorway with a handgun pointed at my dome.

"How...?"

"The grandfather clock," I said. "That was sloppy on your part."

"I suppose it was. But now here you are! As I said before, always so brave."

"A fistful of Xanax helps."

I held up the gym bag.

"I come bearing gifts," I said.

"How thoughtful. Of course, I'll need to give you a quick search before I allow you inside."

I put the bag down, assumed the position. He squinted into the clearing, then holstered his gun in his pants and gave me a very thorough search.

"Enjoying yourself?" I asked.

"Not yet," he said. "Later, I plan to have loads of fun."

"I'm sure you will: there's a million dollars in that bag. And more where that came from."

The second part was a lie, but I thought it might stop Defoe from shooting me in the head and taking the money. He picked the bag up by the straps, held it out in front of him.

"Feels about right," he said, handing it back to me. "We'll make sure once we're inside. Meanwhile, where is your cook? Don't tell me she declined our invitation."

"She ran," I said. "You scared her senseless. She's probably checking into a hotel in Oaxaca right about now."

"How unfortunate."

"I was hoping a bag full of cash might make it a little more fortunate."

"Let's see where the evening takes us."

I followed him inside, down a long entrance hallway, and into the dining room. Broch was there, leaning against the wall between twin portraits of Vincent and his long-dead father. Lindsey and Serena were there, sitting on opposite sides of the table. They each had one hand zip-tied to their chair and the other free. There were empty TV dinner containers sitting on place mats in front of them. I'd just missed feeding time.

The grandfather clock was there, too, ticking away as loud as ever. I gave it a mental wink: *Thanks for the tip, pal.*

"You guys all right?" I asked.

Serena nodded.

"Tell me Sarah's all right," Lindsey blurted out.

"She's fine," I said.

At least they looked healthy—for now. Defoe was probably waiting for a full house before he broke out the iron maiden.

"On the table," he said, meaning the bag.

I hoisted it up, set it down. You don't think of money as being heavy, but a million dollars has mass. I needed both hands.

"Now open it," he said.

Speaking of having mass, Broch abandoned his tough-guy lean and came lumbering over. He smelled like garlic and cheap tobacco. I glanced at Serena, then Lindsey. They looked numb, curious, and terrified all at once.

"Prepare to be a whole lot richer, gentlemen," I said. "Of course, how you split it is up to you. If you're not the sharing types, there's always pistols at dawn."

"Quit stalling," Broch said.

For a troglodyte, he was damn perceptive: I was stalling. According to Grandpa Time, it was almost seven twenty. My lone reinforcement should be arriving any minute. If we weren't in sync, the evening would end very badly.

"Patience," I said, stretching out over the table and tugging the zipper back. "You'll have the rest of your lives to spend this."

I spread the flaps apart, gave them a gander at their new fortune. Broch nearly spit out his gold caps. Defoe played it cool, but I caught a slight tremor in his lower lip.

"Now empty it," he said.

I started removing the bundles one at a time, stacking them in careful columns.

The clock's ticking seemed to grow louder and louder, as if the sound was coming from inside my head.

Any day now, Sarah, I thought.

The bag was just about empty. That hideous clock I'd hoped never to hear again struck the half hour. It was getting late early.

CHAPTER 42

SARAH ROBERTS-WALSH

FINDING THE trail in the dark was easier than I'd imagined, but Anna hadn't been kidding: this was the kind of dense and tangled forest that horror flicks are made of. My flashlight only lit up so much. Point it at the ground and I wound up getting hit in the face with a low-hanging branch; point it at the trees and I wound up tripping over a rock or a root or God knows what.

And then there was the soundtrack: there must have been a thousand brands of insect chirping and clicking and screeching. I tried not to think about all the creatures I couldn't hear. Were snakes nocturnal? Wild boars? Florida panthers? I wished I'd paid closer attention when Aunt Lindsey dragged me on her nature walks.

The rifle I was carrying didn't give me much comfort. It wasn't Doris's shotgun, but it had a similar heft and feel. Anna had tried to talk me into buying a handgun. We stood there debating the merits right in front of the pawnbroker.

It was true that a pistol would have been more practical, but I'd never fired one before. *Stick with what you know,* I thought. Especially when you had a rock star teacher.

I wished Doris was here with me now. She was exactly the

kind of person you wanted in your trench at the darkest hour. Loyal, fearless, willing to fight.

I wondered what she thought of me after my sudden and violent departure. Probably she thought I was weak. In my place, she'd have gone down swinging. Or firing. Me, I'd rolled on my back and played possum. At least in her eyes. Of course, I couldn't tell Doris the full story—for her sake more than mine.

I was starting to wonder if this log existed—if maybe Anna hadn't sent me on a wild-goose chase while she carried out some plan of her own—when I turned a corner and walked smack into it. If it had been a real log, I'd have bruised my knee something fierce, but because it was synthetic and lightweight all it did was startle me.

I pushed it aside, shone my flashlight on the blue tarp, and let out a scream I hoped afterward would blend with the insects' general din. There, in the center of the tarp, curled up and groggy, was the largest, fattest water moccasin I'd ever seen outside of a reptile house. Black and tan scales. Squat, wedge-like head. Easily three feet long. I jumped back, unslung the rifle from my shoulder, and took aim, dropping the flashlight in the process so that the snake disappeared in the dark and there was no longer anything to aim at.

"Goddamnit!" I yelled.

The fall didn't do the flashlight any good—it was flickering on and off now, acting like a strobe light. I knelt down, angled it at the tarp. The snake hadn't budged. Then it dawned on me: he wasn't just groggy; he was deceased. I moved a little closer, stomped my foot to be sure. Still no movement.

I slung the rifle back over my shoulder, inched forward, grabbed a corner of the tarp, and dragged it away until the submarine escape hatch Anna had described was clear. *Hope you don't have any friends,* I told the snake-corpse, folding the plastic over his body just in case he decided to play undead.

The door was heavier than I would have thought, or else it was stuck because no one had opened it in a long while—maybe since Anthony and Anna took their little tour. I groped around until I found the switch. It was right where Anna had said it would be. The problem was . . . it didn't work. I flipped it up and down a dozen times. Nothing. Not even a flicker.

A half hour into our rescue attempt and I had a dead snake, a half-broken flashlight, and a pitch-black tunnel to navigate. But there was no turning back now. It didn't matter how scared or discouraged I was—three lives depended on me following through with a plan I never should have agreed to in the first place.

So I sucked it up and started down, gun on my shoulder, flashlight between my teeth.

I felt like a cook playing action figure. Courage had never been my thing. I was the girl who crawled out to the edge of the diving board and then lay flat on her belly, clinging for dear life. I was the sixth grader who got bullied by third graders. Later, I became the woman who married a cop because she thought she needed protecting. I promised myself that if I got out of this alive, I'd play it safe until they buried me. No skydiving on my fiftieth birthday. No running naked into the ocean when the next winter solstice rolled around. I wouldn't even buy lottery tickets anymore.

Meanwhile, the misadventures just kept coming. After a slow and careful descent, I missed the last rung of the ladder and came down hard on my left ankle. Definitely twisted, possibly sprained. I hobbled forward a few steps, reached out to brace myself against the cold concrete wall. I hoped Anna's memory was solid: I hoped it really was just a ten-minute walk on a healthy pair of legs.

The malfunctioning flashlight made it seem as though there were shadows where there shouldn't be. Every few yards I'd jump back, land on my bad ankle, and stifle a scream. I tried turning the light off, feeling my way along the wall, but then I was struck with a fit of panic—a sensation that it was the wall touching me instead of me touching the wall, as if the ghosts of men the Costellos had killed and hid away in these concrete slabs were reaching out now to take revenge on anyone who passed by.

My breathing started to take on the rhythm of the flashlight—long gasps broken up by choppy wheezing. I was sweating all over. I felt light-headed.

I kept pushing away a thought that didn't help: if the lights in the tunnel weren't working, then neither were the vents. Maybe I wasn't panicking: maybe there really wasn't any air to breathe. And maybe I wasn't hallucinating: maybe the tunnel really was narrowing, the walls closing in.

Just as I'd done on the diving board all those years ago, I got on my hands and knees and crawled forward. Anybody watching would have thought I was chasing after the flashlight's spastic bursts, the way some cats will chase the beam of a penlight.

And then, when I thought I couldn't take any more, when I thought I really would pass out, I nearly smacked my head on a metal sliding door. I poked at it with my finger to be sure it was real. Yep, this was no mirage: I'd reached the end. I got to my feet, thinking, *Now's the time to be afraid. Now is when the real danger begins.*

But I wasn't scared. If anything, I felt a strange surge of confidence, as if I'd burned up all my fear in that tunnel and was ready to conquer whatever waited for me on the other side.

CHAPTER 43

SERENA FLORES

THE MONEY just kept coming. One bundle after another until the columns nearly reached the chandelier. More cash than I'd ever seen at one time. The kind of cash that does things to men—especially men who spend their lives looking for easy ways to get rich. Men who take and give nothing back. Men like Defoe and Broch, who'd snatched us off the street and tied us up and pointed guns at our heads.

I watched Anna, watched her hand moving in and out of that bag. She seemed steady, strong, unafraid. This was a new Anna Costello, different from the woman who skulked around that ridiculous castle, hiding from her marriage in plain sight. I didn't know what she was planning, but I knew there had to be a plan. And I didn't believe for a second that Sarah had run off. That she was scared, yes—but Sarah was the type to stare down her fears.

The stacks of bills kept climbing. Defoe was trying hard to look unimpressed, but Broch was another story. His mouth hung open as though he'd forgotten how to breathe, and he shifted his weight back and forth from one foot to the other. He looked like an inflated toddler who had to pee. Even Lindsey seemed mesmerized. There was more money on that table than a nurse could hope to make in a lifetime. Maybe two lifetimes.

"Almost there," Anna said. "Bet you boys are dreaming of a cabana in Barbados right about now."

Her voice rose as she spoke, as if she was calling to someone in another room, the way she used to call for me to bring her things—a glass of water, a bottle of aspirin, a pair of slippers she'd left downstairs. Broch was too busy salivating to notice the rise in volume. Defoe stuck by his blank expression.

"Last one, coming up," Anna said, her voice louder still.

But when she pulled her hand back out of the bag, it wasn't holding money; it was holding a silver handgun—the kind that's small enough to fit in the palm of a hand. In a single, smooth motion, she pivoted and pointed it at Defoe's head. But before she could say anything, I felt the barrel of Broch's cannonlike revolver pressing against the back of my skull.

And then the shot came. Not from Anna's gun or Broch's gun, but from somewhere close by. An explosion so loud it toppled the stacks of bills and had my ears ringing and buzzing as though I was trapped underwater. And then Sarah appeared in the doorway, looking out at us from behind the long barrel of a rifle.

I could sense Broch's head turning. I reached up, grabbed his wrist, yanked it forward, and bit until I tasted blood. He howled, stumbled backward. I looked down and saw his revolver lying at my feet. Forgetting I had one hand tied to the chair, I reached for it and went tumbling over, landing flat on my back with the chair beneath me.

But I had the gun now. I trained it on Broch. I had no doubt I'd shoot him if he took a single step forward. After what we'd done to Anthony, it would have been easy enough to pull that trigger. Broch must have seen it in me because he backed away with his hands held high.

Over the droning in my ears, I heard Lindsey scream "Anna!" I glanced sideways at my former boss, saw that Defoe had taken her gun and slipped behind her. He had the snub-nosed barrel against the small of her back and stood with his chin nearly resting on her shoulder, as if he was playing peekaboo.

Lowering his hands, Broch took a quick step forward, but stopped short when I swung my head back and cocked his revolver. The truth is, I wanted to shoot him. I was done being afraid of violent men. I didn't want to kill him: I wanted to cripple him in a way that would keep him from ever hurting anyone again. But the giant was afraid of me now. He threw his hands back up in the air, retreated until his shoulders hit the wall.

My ears popped as if I was on a plane that had just cleared twenty thousand feet, and I heard Sarah's aunt playing negotiator.

"No one needs to get hurt here," she said, "so how about you all just set your weapons on the table?"

"I've got a better idea," Defoe said. "Tell the cook and the maid to put their weapons down, and I won't kill the widow and the aunt."

I heard my voice before I knew it was me talking.

"How about you put your gun down or the maid kills your partner with his own gun? He makes a nice, big target."

Defoe laughed, and not for effect. He laughed as though the idea that he might care if his partner lived or died was his new favorite joke.

"Drop it, Sarah," he said.

"No," Anna said. "Don't. Take the shot."

Defoe's smile turned to a snarl.

"Don't play around, little girl," he said. "This is my world, not yours."

Lindsey, her voice shaking, said, "Please, do what he asks."

"Take the shot," Anna said.

"One," Defoe said.

"Shoot," Anna said.

"Two."

"Shoot, goddamnit."

"Three."

I felt the floor shake beneath me, saw the chandelier swinging above me, and then everything went quiet again.

CHAPTER 44

SARAH ROBERTS-WALSH

NOW I'D killed two men. I glanced around the room. Serena, lying on her back on the floor, held Broch at bay with the gun she'd taken from him. Anna sat at the head of the table, trembling, wiping Defoe's blood from her face and neck with a handkerchief. Defoe's corpse lay on the floor behind her. I wasn't ready to look at him. None of us were.

I couldn't look at Aunt Lindsey, either. Not after what she'd just seen me do. Me, her niece turned daughter. I remembered what she had said when I was caught cheating on a math quiz: "You can be anything you want in this life, except a disgrace." I thought she'd say a lot worse now, but she slipped right into take-charge emergency room mode.

"For God's sake, wake up, people," she said. "Sarah, go find a knife and cut us free. Serena, if that brain-dead Aryan so much as twitches, give him one right between the eyes. We'll just dig the grave a little deeper. Anna, stick the cash back in that bag. Come on, now. No time to waste."

The marching orders were a blessing, a chance for me to cruise on autopilot while the shock died down. I limped into the kitchen, set the rifle on a counter, and started opening drawers.

By the time I returned with a serrated steak knife, the cash was packed away and Serena was sitting upright.

It was Anna who asked, "So what now?"

"Now we end this," I told her.

"End it how?"

I turned to Broch.

"Let's ask him," I said. "What was supposed to happen next?"

He told me what I could do to myself in no uncertain terms. It wasn't that he was grieving Defoe: he just didn't like being bested by a handful of women.

"Shoot him," Aunt Lindsey said.

"Shoot him?" Anna asked.

"Aim for the kneecaps. That'll get him talking."

"Let me do it," Serena said.

She sounded like a kid on line for the Ferris wheel. Anna and I exchanged a quick glance: coming from Serena and my aunt, this bloodlust was something new. It made me wonder how Vincent's men had treated them.

"No, I'll do it," Aunt Lindsey said. "I'm old. My eyesight's bad. I might miss and hit him in the crotch."

"Ha, ha, ha," Broch said.

"They always have such snappy comebacks in the movies," my new aunt Lindsey said. "This one's a disappointer."

She took the oversize revolver from Serena, lifted it in both hands, and aimed for Broch's right knee.

"Go pee if you have to, honey," she said to Serena. "They weren't exactly generous with the bathroom breaks."

"I don't want to miss this," Serena said.

Broch growled. Aunt Lindsey ignored him.

"Now Sarah," she said, "you go ahead and ask your questions, and if you don't like his answers, say the word and I'll put him right."

I thought Aunt Lindsey and Doris would get along just fine.

"You ever fired one of those things, Granny?" Broch asked. "The recoil'll knock your head off."

"That's it! Show some spunk," Aunt Lindsey said.

"So tell us," I said to Broch. "What was the plan?"

He blew me a kiss. Aunt Lindsey fired. I think she meant to miss, to scare him, but she wasn't lying about her eyesight. She grazed Broch's thigh, sent him reeling and writhing around on the floor.

"You crazy bitch!" he shouted.

Meanwhile, he hadn't been lying about the recoil. Serena and I corralled Aunt Lindsey in our arms, kept her vertical. She was undaunted.

"Let me try again," she said, pulling back the hammer.

"All right, all right," Broch said. "We were supposed to hold you here overnight, get you good and scared."

"Then what?" I asked.

"Vincent was going to turn up in the morning, give you all a real grilling. After that, I don't know. No one knows but Vincent."

Anna stepped up behind us.

"Then I guess we pay Uncle Vinny a surprise visit," she said. "End this once and for all, like Sarah said."

"Amen," Serena said.

I looked around at my co-conspirators. My friends and family. Maybe this sounds strange or out of place, but I was proud of them. Proud to know them.

"What do we do with him?" I asked, pointing at Broch, who seemed to be teetering on the edge of consciousness.

"Oh, I can patch up that flesh wound, no problem," Aunt Lindsey said. "As long as he doesn't bite."

"We'll tie him up for you before we go," Anna said.

"Good. I'll keep an eye on him while you girls run your errand."

"What about the dead one?" Serena asked.

"I know where we can leave him," Anna said. "Though we should probably wrap him up first. There's a linen closet next to the downstairs bathroom."

"We're going back through that tunnel, aren't we?" I asked.

"I haven't set foot in there in over a decade."

"I think it's changed since then," I told her.

Serena pulled out her phone, snapped a photo of Broch with his eyes rolling back in his head.

"For Vincent," she said. "In case we need leverage."

"All right," Aunt Lindsey said. "Let's go, girls. Chop-chop."

CHAPTER 45
ANNA COSTELLO

GETTING DEFOE into that tunnel was no small task. We wrapped him in black satin sheets, tied his feet together with twine, made a kind of handle by hooking a bungee cord around his torso. For someone so bony, he was damn difficult to lift. Halfway down the basement stairs I felt my hernia coming on. Then it was across the rec room, through the false panel, and into the pitch dark.

"You think our lives will ever be normal again?" Sarah asked.

"They were never normal in the first place," I said.

Sarah, with her wounded ankle, limped ahead of us while holding up the gas lantern we'd found in Vincent's shed. I held Defoe by his feet and carried the gym bag strapped across my chest. Serena, walking backward, gripped the bungee cord in both hands.

I kept thinking Defoe would spring to life, tear away the sheets, and grab me by the throat. The tunnel would have been the right place for it. Sarah hadn't been kidding: without functioning lights and air vents, it had all the charm of a tomb—which worked out nicely, since that's what we were using it for. And to think Anthony and I used to sneak down here for our private rendezvous. Trying to remember that time was like watching an old movie starring two actors I'd never seen before.

"Where do we leave him?" Serena asked.

"I'm thinking the midway mark," I said. "Unless the house gets raided with Vincent in it, no one will ever find him."

We set Defoe's corpse down, rested, picked it up again. Vincent's tunnel must have been the driest spot in all of Florida, but my blouse was drenched and I couldn't blink fast enough to keep the sweat out of my eyes. Serena suffered the way she'd always worked: in silence. It wasn't until later that I saw the deep imprints across her swollen palms.

"All right," I said, "this is far enough."

We counted to three and let go. The thud resounded like concrete landing on concrete. We kept going and didn't look back. Without a dead man weighing us down, we might have been walking on air.

At a little before midnight we pulled up to the security gates outside Vincent's McCastle, me behind the wheel, Serena in the passenger seat, and Sarah nursing her bum ankle in the back. Not one of us had said a word during the drive.

"Hello?" I shouted into the little black box. "Anybody home?"

Two stocky guards hit Pause on their card game and came sauntering out of their little cabin to look us over. I didn't recognize either of them.

"You sure we shouldn't have brought the guns?" Serena asked.

"Listen to Annie Oakley," I said. "You think we'd win a shoot-out with Vincent's army?"

Huey and Dewey wore black slacks and navy-blue windbreakers with the initials v. c. stitched across the chest. They each carried a gun on one hip and what looked like a Playskool walkie-talkie on the other. The one sporting a knit cap leaned in while his cohort walked the periphery of the car.

"Good evening," Knit Cap said. "You ladies lost or something?"

He looked more like a camp counselor than a first line of defense, but then the guys out front were mostly for show. Whatever they knew about Vincent's business they'd read in the papers. Vincent kept the heavy hitters inside, circled around their master.

"Nope, we're in the right place," I said. "I'm Vincent's niece. Or niece-in-law, if that's a word. Anthony was my husband."

He mumbled something about being sorry for my loss, then backed out of earshot and spoke into his handset. Meanwhile, his partner kept walking in circles around our car.

"We could take them," Serena whispered. "I mean, if we had to."

My onetime maid hadn't just busted out of her shell: she'd shattered it. I only hoped she wouldn't get us killed.

Knit Cap finished up his conversation and came padding back.

"Mr. Costello says he knows you, but not your friends. We'll have to do a quick search if you want to go in. Your persons and your vehicle. Sorry about that, but it's standard—"

"Oh, no worries." I smiled. "We're used to it."

They frisked us, pored over the car's interior, then spent a long time digging around inside the trunk.

"What's this?" Knit Cap asked, holding up the gym bag. Of course he'd already discovered what was inside.

"A repayment," I told him. "To Vincent. He'll be very un-happy if any of it goes missing."

"And this?" his partner asked. He'd found Sarah's insulin kit.

"I'm diabetic," she said.

Guard number two looked confused. I couldn't tell if he'd never heard of diabetes before, or if he thought Sarah was lying, trying to smuggle heroin *into* Vincent's mansion, which would have been a first.

"I'll prove it to you," she said. "I'm due a dose. It's been a busy day. I forgot to inject myself, and I'm starting to feel a little woozy."

She took the kit from him. He stepped back, as if maybe she was La Femme Nikita and would drive that needle into his neck. Up close, you could see he was just a kid. A kid who'd watched too many movies.

Sarah gave herself a fifteen-unit shot.

"Now watch closely," she said. "If I nod off, feel free to shoot me."

That seemed to satisfy him. Meanwhile, Sarah's cheeks looked a little rosier than they had before.

At long last, we piled back into the car and waited for the gates to part.

"You ladies have a nice evening," Knit Cap called, waving us through.

I steered the rental down yet another ridiculously long and meticulously landscaped Costello driveway, then parked under the very modern glass and steel porte cochere Vincent had stuck on the front of his Tudor mansion. A half dozen more men stood in line to greet us. These guys weren't in uniform because they didn't need to be: they were the real deal.

"You think they're planning to kill us?" Serena asked.

"Not yet," I said. "Vincent will want to talk to us first."

"Talk, or torture?" Sarah asked.

The leader of our welcome party signaled for us to get out. His name was Nigel. He was Defoe's cousin. I'd forgotten all about the family tie until he stepped into the light and the re-semblance became glaring: same razor-thin lips, same sunken, pockmarked cheeks, same walleyed gaze. I hoped he wouldn't ask us how our evening had been so far.

"Hello again, Anna," he said. "I'll take you to see him."

He showed no interest in Sarah or Serena, probably because

he figured he wouldn't know them for long. We followed him in-side. The rest of his crew stayed behind as if maybe their owner hadn't gotten around to house-training them yet.

"It's been a while," Nigel said.

He said it with a smile, but really he was rubbing salt in the wound. I'd been unofficially barred on account of the fact that Vincent couldn't stand me. I'd almost forgotten how tacky it all was. A sea of marble and gold. Gold chairs, gold hope chests, gold picture frames. Gold side tables and vases and lamps and light fixtures. Vincent would have gilded his children if he had any. I wondered what Sarah and Serena thought of the place but didn't dare ask. Probably they were too anxious to notice much of anything.

"Here we are," Nigel said.

He pulled up short in front of a pair of thick mahogany doors. I knew what was on the other side: Vincent's lair. The room he prized above all others. A room that reminded me of banquet halls in old movies about English kings and the knights who betrayed them. Stuffed animal heads mounted on the walls. Candelabra chandeliers. Bloodred curtains to block out the light by day and prying eyes by night. This was where he conducted business, where he received guests, where he ate his three squares. He treated the rest of the house like an extension he regretted having built.

Nigel swung the doors open and I found myself staring across a long and elegant oak table at the man I knew wanted me dead, the man who'd tried to kill me once already and would no doubt try again. His smile was warm and gracious and inviting, and that scared me more than anything. Vincent was always at his most ruthless when he had a smile on his face.

CHAPTER 46
SARAH ROBERTS-WALSH

HE HAD three glasses of pinot noir waiting for us.

"Please," he said, gesturing to the empty chairs on either side of him, "join me. I'm having a bit of a late-night snack. Or maybe I should say an early-morning snack."

His *snack* was a heaping bowl of coq au vin. I could smell the red burgundy wine simmering off the top. Under different circumstances I'd have asked to meet his chef.

"I wasn't expecting you so soon," he said, "but this is a lovely surprise. It's lucky for me that I've always been a night owl."

I have to hand it to him: Vincent was damn robust for a man north of eighty. His merino sweater clung to pecs and biceps that would have been at home on a much younger man. Still, I didn't look at him and see the legend who once beat the head of a rival family to death with his bare hands. That Vincent had faded away. Now he let his offshore accounts do the talking, kept his bare hands clean.

Anna shot me a glance that said, *Don't be fooled.* I wasn't. I wouldn't be, ever again.

I sat to Vincent's left, Serena to his right, Anna to Serena's right. I guessed she wanted a body between her and her onetime uncle. The muscleheads stationed at either end of the room stood so still they blended in with the decor.

"Happy as I am to see you all," Vincent said, "I was anticipating a larger party. Tell me: what happened to your escorts?"

Serena pulled out her phone, clicked to the photo of Broch, and held it up for our host to see. Vincent made a show of squinting.

"Well, he seems a bit worse for wear."

"He'll be fine," Anna said. "We left him in the care of a very capable nurse. I'm afraid there's not much she can do for Defoe."

Vincent set down his fork and knife, appeared suddenly peevish. I thought he'd snap his fingers and have the twin henchmen open fire. Instead, he burst out laughing. His long, rolling guffaws hurt my ears.

"Well played, ladies," he said. "Very well played. Maybe I'll put you on the payroll. First, though, there's a more pressing matter we must attend to. You'll find I have a few surprises of my own."

He picked up a little bell I hadn't noticed before and rang it three times. The sound reminded me of the Diner Things in Life.

"I imagine you'll enjoy this most of all," Vincent said, staring straight at me. Just then I'd have given anything to be back in Doris's kitchen.

The double doors swung open and Nigel came striding in. At his heels was the man I'd hoped I'd never see again outside of a courtroom: my husband, Detective Sean Walsh. Vincent looked around at our slack jaws, nodded approvingly.

"No need for introductions, I see. Please do have a seat, Detective. Or should I say 'Former detective'?"

Nigel guided Sean to the throne-like chair opposite Vincent, then turned and left the room. Sean sat down. He glared at me with pure hatred but didn't say a word. Neither did I. His hair was slicked back and he wore an all-black tracksuit. Classic thug attire. No one who didn't know better would have guessed he was the cop in the room. To my surprise, I felt more repulsed than afraid. The features I once thought of as chiseled now only looked hard. The eyes I thought of as piercing had turned ice-cold.

"Sean, I believe there's a burden you'd like to get off your chest," Vincent said. "A rumor you'd like to set straight involving you and my departed nephew."

"Yes, sir, there is. But before I begin, I want to thank you again for posting bail. Five million is more than—"

"Don't mention it, son. A man of your caliber has no place behind bars."

Vincent's manner was paternal, even affectionate. But he didn't offer Sean a glass of wine. That might sound small, but when you're a chef you notice these things. You understand what they mean—better than you understand words.

"First and foremost, Mr. Costello," Sean said, "I didn't kill your nephew. Anthony and I were friends. We were partners. Hell, we were like brothers."

"Brothers kill each other all the time," Vincent pointed out. "So do friends. As a homicide detective, you must know this."

"Yes, but there's usually a reason. A contested will. A woman. Some long-standing grudge. None of that was true with me and Anthony. I don't have any family of my own. No siblings. My mother died when I was young, and my father's a drunk. I haven't seen him in twenty years. Anthony was an orphan, too, except he had you looking out for him. He took me in the way you took him in. We went out fishing on his boat. We played golf together. We talked. We grew to trust each other, and that was rare for both of us.

"Then he introduced me to you, invited me into the family business. He even gave my wife a job. It's not easy making it on a cop's salary. I owed—I owe—everything I have to your nephew. To you. I'm telling you, Mr. Costello, I wept when I heard he was dead. I had to run out of the squad room."

He was getting teary now. I watched the whites of his eyes turn red. It was a damn fine performance, and I could sense exactly where it was going.

"As for how Anthony died and who killed him, I told it all to your man Defoe. Anthony and I both had our vices. We both paid the wrong kind of attention to the women in our lives. I have a temper. Sarah bore the brunt of my temper, even when it wasn't her I was mad at. I was quick with a slap. Sometimes a punch. I'll admit that. I see myself more clearly now than I ever have before. I deserve to be punished, but only for the crimes I did commit.

"And Anthony? Anthony was all appetite. Food, money, and especially women—he couldn't get enough, and he wouldn't take no for an answer. That isn't news to anyone at this table. I didn't know that my wife was one of the women who said no until it was too late. It never occurred to me that Anthony would cross that line. Maybe that seems hard to believe given my years as a cop—given all the things I've seen people do to each other—but like I said, Anthony and I were close. I thought of him as a brother."

Here he paused to wipe away tears with the heels of both palms. The waterworks were real even if the sentiment behind them was fake. I don't know how Sean did it. He hadn't trusted Anthony. He hadn't loved him. He hadn't thought of him as a friend, let alone a brother. He looked at Anthony and saw opportunity knocking—period. From day one it was a contest to determine who could remain useful the longest. Whoever won that contest would see the other buried or jailed. There was no third way for their relationship to end.

"Sarah had a violent husband and—I'm sorry to say it—a

sexual predator for a boss," Sean continued. "Maybe it was only natural that she'd find a violent solution."

I rose halfway out of my chair, started to protest. Vincent held up a hand.

"You'll have your turn," he said. "For now, the floor belongs to your husband."

I sneered at that last word but did as I was told. Sean finished making his case.

"Murdering Anthony and framing me for it was like killing two birds with one stone. Anthony would never lay hands on another woman, and she'd have her vengeance on me. Everybody knows that being a cop in prison is a fate worse than death. She'd wake up every morning with a smile on her face, thinking about the day that was in store for me.

"And it couldn't have been the other way around. She couldn't have killed me and framed Anthony for it. A Costello would have a brigade of lawyers behind him. They'd keep digging until the truth came out, and when it did, there'd be nowhere she could run to, nowhere she'd be safe. But me? A trial would eat through my resources in under a week.

"Like I told Defoe, I'm not just speculating here. It all came spilling out during the long drive from Texas to Tampa. The only thing she wouldn't tell me was what role the other two played. She claimed it was self-defense, but once my knife turned up with Anthony's blood on it, I knew that couldn't be true. The three of them fled for a reason. It was all choreographed down to the last detail."

He pushed back in his chair, let his head drop. All eyes turned to me. This was a Costello-style trial, and it was the defense's turn to speak. Only I couldn't think of a thing to say. Defoe had been right: this wasn't my world.

But it was Sean's. The parade of career criminals he'd interrogated over the years had taught him how to lie convincingly. The trick, it seemed, was to ground your lies in partial truths. My husband was violent. Anthony was a sexual predator. The three of us had killed Anthony and framed Sean. All that was true. But I hadn't confessed. Sean hadn't wept for Anthony, and he wasn't an orphan: his mother was alive and well and teaching kindergarten in Boca Raton. She just didn't want anything to do with her son anymore.

"Well?" Vincent asked.

I was that little girl on talent night all over again—struck dumb, unable to walk out onstage. I was sweating and breathing hard. My lower lip began to tremble. And all I could think to do was confess. Come clean and face my executioner.

Lucky for me there was a budding lawyer among us.

CHAPTER 47
SERENA FLORES

SARAH LOOKED as though someone was about to push her out of an airplane at thirty thousand feet. She needed help. I'd led Haagen and her sidekick by the nose—I figured I could do the same to Vincent. I took a long gulp of wine, then stood and stared him right in the eyes.

"It's me you want to talk to," I said. "I can tell you things about your nephew that not even Anna knows."

"Oh, really?" he said, looking one part doubtful and two parts amused. "What kinds of things?"

"The kinds of things you might not want to hear. Tony was free and easy around the foreigner. Half the time he forgot I was there, and the other half he figured my English was only good for taking orders. Clean the toilet, scrub the floor, change the sheets. When he talked to me, he ended every sentence with *comprende*."

"And yet you seem to speak English very well," Vincent said.

"Yes, but never in front of him. I thought I'd be safer if he believed I couldn't understand."

"You were afraid of my nephew?"

"I was raped by your nephew. Let's not dance around that

word anymore. Tony might have been your blood, but he was an animal. I'm not afraid to say it. He hunted women the way animals hunt in the wild—he looked for the easiest, most vulnerable prey."

I watched Vincent's face very carefully. His expression told me I was reading him right. He valued plain speech. Sugarcoating to him was worse than lying.

He turned to Anna.

"Is this true?" he asked.

Anna shut her eyes hard and nodded.

"And did you know about it at the time?"

She nodded again.

"That's a shame," he said. "If you'd come to me, I might have set him straight. If reason didn't work, I would have killed him myself. Some indiscretions I'll tolerate, but violence against the fairer sex isn't one of them."

There was no pity or compassion in his voice. He didn't care about what had happened to me—he only cared that his nephew had done it.

"What about Sean's indiscretions?" I asked. "He was the one who cleaned up after Anthony. He was the one who let us know exactly what would happen if we talked."

I stared straight at Sean when I said this. I wanted him to see just how much I hated him. I wanted Vincent to see, too. Sean gritted his teeth and hissed at me.

"You lying little bitch," he said. "You'll be lucky if you—"

Vincent cut him off. He turned to one of his guards and said, "Tommy, the next time Detective Walsh speaks out of turn, kindly see to it that he never speaks again."

Tommy nodded. Sean bit his lip. His face went red all the way up to the hairline.

"So what is it you know that I don't?" Vincent asked.

"Sean and your nephew were robbing you blind," I told him.

"Skimming off the top, were they?"

"Yes, but not only that. They were using your name to extort money."

"Extort money from whom?"

I looked at Sarah. She nodded for me to keep going. The truth is, most of what I knew, I knew from her. Tony talked in front of me as if I wasn't there, but it was Sarah who did the snooping, Sarah who opened drawers and looked in filing cabinets and stood in hallways with a hand cupped around her ear. She was the one who wanted to know, who had to know, what kind of business her husband was doing with a man like Tony. But she couldn't be the one to tell Vincent what she'd learned. She couldn't say out loud that she'd been spying on a member of the Costello family—not even a disgraced member.

"Anyone with power and a secret," I said. "Cops on the take. Prosecutors who threw cases. Judges who overruled verdicts. Sean would hear rumors at work. He'd look into slam dunk convictions where the defendant went free on a technicality. He'd investigate drug dealers who were arrested once and then never again. He used his contacts. He used the police database. Once he was sure, once he had proof nobody could deny, he'd pass the intel on to Tony. Tony would use the proof to make threats. He'd say it was you who sent him. He'd demand a percentage: *Pay up or go to jail.* And while they were in jail, their families would be *taken care of*."

"And not in the good way, I presume," Vincent said.

Sean was struggling to control himself. Blood trickled from his bottom lip, and his right knee kept banging the table. Vincent, on the other hand, remained perfectly still, his expression neutral.

"Sean, is this true?" he asked.

"Not a word."

"I can prove it," I said.

"How?" Vincent asked.

"Tony kept a ledger. A handwritten ledger. Computers can be hacked or seized. Tony didn't trust them. But it's easy enough to hide a ledger where no one will ever find it. No one except maybe the maid. Like I said, Tony was careless in front of me. I saw where he put it."

Vincent swallowed the last of his meal, then patted the corners of his mouth with a cloth napkin.

"I'd like very much to see this ledger," he said.

I started to tell him where it was. He held a finger to his lips.

"It's best if that information stays between you and me," he said. "Come whisper it in my ear."

Until then I'd kept my voice steady, but now I was scared. I thought maybe I'd gone too far. Maybe Vincent couldn't accept the things I'd said about his nephew. I saw him cutting my throat as I leaned in, making an example of me for the others.

But stealth attacks weren't Vincent's style. Instead, he patted my shoulder and called me a good girl.

I cupped both hands around his ear, said in the lowest voice he could possibly hear, "The fireplace in his den. The mantel is hollow."

"Understood," he said. Vincent's eyes darted back and forth between me and Sean.

Then, loud enough for everyone to hear, he said, "I'm not easily impressed, young lady, but believe me when I say I wish I had a hundred like you."

CHAPTER 48
SARAH ROBERTS-WALSH

WHAT HAPPENED next was so matter-of-fact, so casual, that it almost didn't seem to be happening at all.

"Where are my manners?" Vincent asked. "Tommy, please bring ex-detective Walsh a glass."

That was it. That was the signal. Tommy stepped over to a ceiling-high liquor cabinet, took a long-stemmed glass from the bottom shelf, and carried it to Sean. Then, in a single, smooth motion he pulled a bright blue nylon cord from his pocket and wrapped it around Sean's neck.

Sean kicked, spat, flailed his arms. Tommy dragged him backward out of his chair and onto the floor. I felt myself screaming but couldn't hear my own voice. Without knowing I would, I sprung up and flung my body at the man who was murdering my husband. Tommy's understudy caught me in midair, spun me around, pinned my arms in a bear hug, and held me so that I couldn't watch Sean's last moments.

But I heard. I heard the half-formed words catching in Sean's throat. I heard his heels knocking against the floor. I heard Tommy grunting. Worst of all, I heard the silence afterward.

Those mammoth arms let me go. I dropped to my knees,

rocking back and forth and sobbing. I had no right. I knew I had no right. Not after what I'd done to Anthony. To Defoe. I shut my eyes, saw the blade cutting through Anthony's shirt and sinking deep into his flesh, saw Defoe's head reel back, saw the blood fly. I saw what I hadn't really seen: my husband's eyes rolling back, then falling shut for the last time. Things I'd done. Things I'd caused to happen. The images flew at me in 3-D, and I knew right then that I'd never be rid of them.

Anna and Serena came running over to me. I couldn't tell them apart, couldn't tell who was cradling me in her arms and who was stroking my hair. By the time they'd helped me to my feet, Sean's body was gone.

It was just the three of us and Vincent in the room now. Vincent stood at the liquor cabinet, pouring two large snifters of brandy. He crossed the room, offered me one, waited patiently until I took it in both hands.

"Down in one," he said. "Believe me, it helps."

Then he went back to his seat at the head of the table. He was right about the brandy. I felt it moving through me, numbing me inch by inch. The trembling slowed, then stopped. Anna pulled out my chair. Serena held my arm while I lowered myself into it. Vincent sipped his drink while they took their seats. After what felt like eternity and a day, he cleared his throat.

"I suppose I didn't have to do that in front of you," he said, "but this is a world you chose for yourselves. All of you. There were other men to marry, other jobs to take. There were other ways to deal with my nephew. I see no reason to treat you with kid gloves."

In other words, he knew. He knew it was us, and not Sean, who'd stabbed Anthony to death. He paused long enough for the weight of what he was saying to sink in.

"I didn't post Sean's bail out of the goodness of my heart," he said. "I did it to end our partnership. You are absolutely right, Serena: he and my nephew were robbing me blind. I've known this for quite a while. I only played the doddering old man to buy time, get the facts in order. Some of those facts you've provided yourselves. Of course, Sean didn't kill Anthony. I never believed that he did. I don't know who wielded the knife, whether it was one of you or all of you, and to be blunt, I don't care. The truth is, I should be grateful. Anthony's murder saved me the hefty sum that comes with a contract killing. When I was younger, I handled these things myself. Now, I can't afford the exposure."

He swirled the brandy around in his glass, sniffed at it, took a careful sip.

"This may sound strange given that I break the law for a living, but I didn't get where I am today without being a man of principle. Anthony, like his father before him, was not a man of principle. Sean had no moral character whatsoever. Both deserved to die. Your actions, on the other hand, are not so ethically cut-and-dried. As someone who thrives on vengeance, it would be hypocritical of me to condemn you for killing the man who caused you such great pain. Then again, he was, as you say, my blood. If I fail to retaliate in any way, my enemies will think I'm weak. I've already taxed their patience by living this long.

"Of course, there's also the matter of Defoe. I don't look forward to telling Nigel, but to be honest that killing doesn't bother me so much. Defoe was a liability. He was a pure mercenary, and every mercenary is a turncoat in the making. No, I'm inclined to think you did me a favor there, too.

"So here is what I propose, and it very well may be the fairest proposition I've ever made. You can go on with your lives. You can prosper, fall in love, repeat your mistakes or make new ones. But you can't do it near me. In other words, I'm banishing you, much as kings banished their subjects in the days of yore. Florida is off-limits. Georgia and Alabama are ill-advised. Seattle, Los Angeles, San Francisco—these are real possibilities. If you're feeling frugal, I hear Portland has its charms.

"Wherever you choose to go, you have twenty-four hours to get there. I won't pursue you so long as I don't know where you are, but if our paths happen to cross after the allotted time has passed, well...I doubt I need to finish the sentence. If you're die-hard Floridians, at least you can take solace in this: I'm even older than I look. I doubt your exile will last a decade."

He took another slow look around the room. Anna was staring down into her still-full glass. Serena was rubbing at a spot on the table with her thumb. They weren't upset: they were trying to hide their relief. I'd be lying if I said I didn't feel relieved, too. The whole sordid chapter was coming to a close. We'd made it. It had been ugly—uglier even than we'd imagined. The scars might fade with time, but they'd never heal. Still, we'd gone to war and won our freedom. Tomorrow would be day one of a brand-new life.

Vincent picked up his little bell and rang it three times. Seconds later, Nigel appeared.

"Show them out, will you?" Vincent said.

Nigel gave a little bow, then turned on his heels. We stood and followed him. Not one of us dared to look back.

CHAPTER 49
ANNA COSTELLO

BUT UNCLE Vincent had one more card to play.

"Except for you, Anna," he said. "You and I have other matters to discuss."

Sarah and Serena looked at each other, then at me. I thought I could hear their hearts pounding along with mine.

"It's all right," I said. "You girls go on. I'll be fine. Won't I, Vincent?"

"I'll see she gets to her destination."

My destination? A mud pit? An alligator's gut? As threats go, that one was vague, but not so veiled. Vincent looked at his watch.

"The clock is ticking, ladies," he said.

It was clear they weren't going to budge.

"We still have Broch," Serena said.

Now I was sure her brave streak would get us all killed.

"And you can keep him," Vincent said, grinning. "Men like Broch are a dime a dozen. They're meant to be disposable."

I locked eyes with Sarah.

"Would you get her out of here, please?" I said. "I'd like some private time with Uncle."

She took Serena's arm, nudged her away. Nigel shut the doors behind them.

"Please, sit down," Vincent said. "It's a shame how seldom we've found ourselves with an opportunity to really talk."

I eyed the dinner knife lying idle beside his plate. I figured it wouldn't be idle much longer.

"I'll pay you," I said as I took a seat. "The house, the cars, the yacht—you can have all of it."

"Do I look like a man who needs money?"

"I'll disappear, I promise."

"Oh, yes, you will. But on my terms. It's true what I said: I can't afford to look weak. Disposing of the cook and the maid wouldn't exactly be a show of strength, now would it? But you? Anthony's widow? The woman who infiltrated our family and then did her level best to destroy it? I might be merciful, but my mercy has its limits. You're a cancer. I have no choice but to cut you out."

He'd stood to watch Sarah and Serena go. Now he sat back down, comfy and casual as though we really were going to have a nice little chat. I took up my glass and drained it. Then I took up Serena's and drained hers, too.

"That's right," Vincent said. "A little anesthetic never hurt. You can swig straight from the bottle if you like. I seem to remember your relations passing one around at the wedding."

He leaned forward, reached behind him, and pulled a gun from his waistband. Then he took a long, cylindrical object from his pocket. A suppressor.

"This is for me," he said. "My ears aren't what they used to be. Anything louder than a low roar and I hear ringing for days."

He kept talking to me while he screwed the cylinder in place. He told me I wouldn't escape Anthony so easily. He said any two people who managed to screw up such a good thing ought to find themselves bound together in this life and the next. He sounded as though he was scolding a puppy.

"Do you know who you're avenging?" I asked. "Anthony was laughing at you. He said stealing from Uncle Vince was like stealing from a senile baby. 'Big tough guy,' he said. 'You have to hold his hand so he doesn't wander off.' He joked about getting you one of those toddler leashes."

Vincent was savoring the moment, taking his sweet time assembling that gun. Something in me had changed tracks. I was more angry than afraid. Maybe Sarah and Serena had felt something similar that morning in the kitchen.

"My mind is as firm as it ever was," he said.

"That's what I told Anthony. I told him he was playing a dangerous game, but he didn't care. He wanted to hurt you. It was more about the hurt than the money."

"Why on earth would the boy have wanted to hurt me? He owed me everything."

"Because he couldn't bring himself to kill you. He wanted you to make the first move."

Vincent let out a big, theatrical guffaw.

"You're talking nonsense," he said.

But he knew that I wasn't. Beneath the smooth facade, a crack was beginning to open. His fingers had stopped working the suppressor. He was listening. He wanted to hear more. Certain truths would be lost to him forever once I was dead.

"Anthony hated your guts," I said. "He knew better than to let it show, but he couldn't remember a time when he didn't hate you."

"Absurd," he said.

He turned back to the task at hand, but his fingers wouldn't cooperate. The suppressor fell onto the table. He picked it up, started over. He was seething now, struggling to keep the anger down. I decided to go for the jugular. There was something I hadn't known for sure until tonight—until Vincent said that Anthony was just like his father.

"Actually, it makes perfect sense," I said. "I mean, you did kill his old man."

Now I had his full attention.

"I did no such thing," he said. "And Anthony never believed that I did."

The second part might have been true. Anthony never talked about his father. He didn't have much to talk about: William Costello died when his son was only three.

"Then where's his portrait?" I asked.

"What?"

"At the country house. There's a great big painting of you. There's one of your father. But where's Bill?"

He shook his head as if he was dealing with a lunatic.

"I'm going to enjoy this," he said. "I'm going to enjoy it very much."

"Is that why those veins are bulging on your forehead? I always thought Anthony was paranoid, but it's true, isn't it? Bill Costello was the real brains. He set it all up. He just wasn't ruthless enough to keep it going. That was your special talent."

"I'm warning you," he said. "There are slower ways to die."

"So one day Billy just disappeared, his body never to be found. You cried so convincingly the cops skipped right over you. They looked at cartels, rival families, even a serial killer who'd been racking up bodies. But never at you."

"They had no reason to look at me."

I ignored him.

"You call yourself a man of principle? You're a fake. A fraud. A con man. You stole your brother's life."

"Shut your mouth."

"'Brothers kill each other all the time.' Isn't that what you said? How'd you do it? A bullet to the back of the head? Quick and painless? Then again, I guess we can never really know about the pain part."

"Enough!" he screamed, rearing up out of his seat. "I'm going to—"

But as he rose the suppressor went flying, and the gun slipped from his hand. He looked around, confused, blistering with hatred—for me, for Anthony, for himself. I lunged forward, grabbed the dinner knife, and drove it into his chest.

CHAPTER 50
SARAH ROBERTS-WALSH

VINCENT'S OUTDOOR militia milled around under the porte cochere, smoking and laughing and shuffling their feet. Now and again one of them would glance in our direction. They'd probably never seen an economy car parked outside Vincent's castle before. Either that or they wondered why we were sticking close by when their boss had so kindly spared our lives.

"We can't just sit here while he murders her," Serena said.

"What are we supposed to do?"

"I'm calling the police."

"Even if you found a cop who wasn't in Vincent's pocket, he'd never get here in time."

But she already had her phone out and was punching in the access code. That brought the militia running. They surrounded the car, drew their guns but didn't point them at us. Their foreman banged a flat palm on the hood right above my head. I cracked my window. Serena stuck the phone back in her pocket.

"This is a no-loitering zone," he said.

"We're just waiting for our friend," I told him.

"No need to worry about her—Mr. Costello will see she gets where she's going."

His grin was more than Serena could bear. She dove across my body, tried to gouge his eyes out through the glass. The ape laughed. His buddies joined in. Their laughter made them look grotesque, like gargoyles come to life. Serena cursed at them in Spanish. I clapped a hand over her mouth, wrestled her back into her seat.

"All right," I said. "We're going."

I turned the key in the ignition. They backed away to let us pass.

"You're serious?" Serena hissed.

"We won't go far," I said. "But we can't stay here."

I shifted into Drive, had my foot hovering above the gas pedal when Serena grabbed my arm.

"Look," she said.

I turned my head, saw Anna through the house's open double doors. I nearly screamed with relief. Then I saw Nigel on her heels, holding the barrel of a revolver against the small of her back.

"Mierda," Serena said.

"Just stay calm," I told her.

Vincent's goons tucked their guns away and scrambled back to their station. You'd have thought they'd seen a dead woman walking. I shifted back into Park, kept the engine running.

Anna wasn't saying anything, and neither was Nigel. They headed straight toward us, Anna keeping the pace at a crawl, careful not to give Nigel a reason to pull that trigger.

"Come on, come on, come on," I whispered.

Serena was gripping my leg. I felt her nails digging in. We couldn't have been more than a dozen yards from the doors, but it felt as though we were watching them cross the Sahara. When they were close enough, Anna gestured for me to roll my window all the way down. She put her hands on the hood where Nigel could see them, bent her knees, and leaned in.

"You mind popping the trunk?" she said.

This was a rental: by the time I found the button with the right icon, Anna and Nigel were already standing behind the car, waiting. I watched them in the rearview mirror until they disappeared behind the raised hatch. My mind was racing, trying to keep ahead of whatever might happen next. I thought Nigel would shoot her, push her in, have us drive her body to the Everglades.

But then Anna shut the trunk, and I saw Nigel walking back toward the house, the gym bag dangling from one shoulder. Anna climbed into the back seat.

"Sorry, girls," she said. "I promise I'll make it up to you."

CHAPTER 51

One Month Later

WE WERE gathered in the kitchen for a kind of farewell dinner party. Aunt Lindsey had a fresh batch of her triple threat simmering on the stove—the high-end kind, made with heirloom beans and chunks of tenderloin.

"Seems like the right dish to serve given the company," she said. "God help anyone who trifles with you three."

The smell reminded me of my childhood, seemed to erase all the ugliness of the past few months. At least for a short while.

"Us?" Anna said. "What about you? You kept Goliath at bay all by your lonesome."

"Weren't you scared being alone with him in that house in the woods?" Serena asked.

"Nah. You should see some of the characters who end up in my ER. Anyway, between fixing his leg and cleaning up after his playmate, I had plenty to keep me busy. I can still smell the bleach."

"Where do you think Broch is now?" I asked.

"Probably staring out the window of a Greyhound bus on his way to Timbuktu. You know, I still can't believe I shot a man. In all my years, I never—"

She stopped short, turned a shade darker than crimson. I understood why: grazing a man's leg was small change compared to what Anna, Serena, and I had done. I decided to launch the conversation down a new path.

"I'm thinking that stew's warm enough by now," I said.

"I swear I've never smelled anything this good," Serena said.

"Just wait till you taste it," I told her.

Aunt Linds lifted the pot from the stove, set it back down on a trivet at the center of the table.

"You might want to let that cool a bit," she said.

Meanwhile, I poured the wine.

"We should toast," Anna said. "To our friendship."

"To our freedom," I said.

"To the rest of our lives," Serena said.

We clinked and drank and filled our glasses back up to the brim.

"What promising lives they are," Aunt Lindsey added. "Especially now that there's no trial hanging over your heads."

After Sean missed his first court date, police assumed he'd skipped bail. They questioned me daily, stationed an unmarked car outside Aunt Lindsey's house, then gave up and turned the search over to Interpol. When it became public knowledge that Vincent Costello was missing, too, every paper in town assumed that Sean had killed him and either fled or been killed in turn. The police didn't disagree, though Detective Haagen was awfully disappointed that she didn't get to arrest anyone. I guess she had a right to be: she'd put in a ton of work and had nothing to show for it. Of course, for a homicide detective, the next opportunity is never far off.

"There's something I've been wanting to ask you, Sarah," Anna said. "Were you really a double agent, spying on my husband for Sean?"

The question caught me off guard. I wondered if she'd come

up with it on her own or if Haagen had planted it. Either way, I was done lying.

"At first," I said. "Sean called it important work, said I'd be saving lives by helping him bring down the Costellos. To be honest, that was never my real motivation: I thought collaborating with Sean might bring us closer together, save our marriage. But it became obvious pretty early on that he had no interest in arresting Anthony—he just wanted me to keep an eye on his business partner. Can you forgive me?"

"For what? We didn't know each other from Adam back then. Besides, I used to pray that Anthony would get locked up. Would have left me with all of the perks and none of the headaches."

"Amen to that," I said.

"I just wish we weren't all heading in different directions," Anna continued. "I never thought of myself as a team player before you guys came along."

She already had an eight-figure offer on Anthony's estate. Her plan was to do a bit of traveling, then start over in New Orleans.

"I want to see how much trouble I can get into on my own, without a husband pushing me along," she said.

Serena had big plans, too. With a financial assist from Anna, she'd be attending Emory's law school in the fall. It wasn't hard to picture her prosecuting the Vincent Costellos of Tecomán, making her hometown safer for future generations—maybe even for her own children.

"What about you, Sarah?" Aunt Lindsey asked. "Where are you headed?"

She'd caught me with a mouth full of triple threat. I shrugged, then swallowed hard.

"I really don't know," I said. "Wherever my work takes me, I guess."

"Maybe you could cook for one of those cruise ships," Serena offered. "See the world."

"A sailor in every port," Anna said.

"Isn't it sailors who have a girl in every port?" Aunt Lindsey asked.

"That, too," Anna said.

I laughed. I'd miss them. I really would. But we were three very different people when all was said and done. Unlike Anna, I'd had enough excitement for one lifetime; unlike Serena, I wanted nothing more to do with dangerous men. All I wanted was to shut my eyes at night feeling certain that when I opened them again in the morning I'd be facing a gentle and predictable world.

EPILOGUE
MICHELLE BROWN

The sound of the miniature Liberty Bell ringing above my head startled me even though I knew it was coming. Doris poked her head out through the kitchen's double doors, yelled "Anywhere ya'd like," then disappeared back inside.

I took a seat at the counter. It was the same time of day on the same day of the week as my first visit. The same elderly customer sat two stools over, wearing the same filthy John Deere cap.

"Peaceful in here," I told him.

He kept his head buried in his paper, same as before.

I ran my eyes over the Great Wall. I'd never asked Doris how she came by all those license plates. Maybe her customers donated them. Maybe her late husband picked them up on the road.

Late husband.

We were both widows now.

"Coffee's free with the waffles," Doris said, setting a menu on the counter in front of me. "Only special we got today is pea soup."

She looked a little more frazzled and a lot more tired than

the last time I'd seen her—so tired and frazzled that she hadn't recognized me yet. I wasn't surprised: those bustling dinner shifts would have run a full staff ragged, which explained why the help-wanted ad was back up on the Great Wall.

"I'll take the waffles," I said. "I'm dying for a cup of coffee."

Something clicked when she heard my voice. She stepped back, gave me a long, hard scan.

"Well, I'll be," she said. "Never thought I'd see you again. Not here, anyway. Maybe on the news, dressed in orange."

I'd hoped for a warmer reception, but I knew damn well I had no right to one.

"I came to apologize," I said.

"Apologize for what?"

I stole a quick glance at the old man in the John Deere cap. Nothing short of sixty thousand dollars spilled across the floor would get him to look up from that paper. Still, I figured I'd err on the side of discretion.

"For the way I left," I told her. "For the situation I put you in. And for not reaching out to you since then."

She scratched at a mustard stain on her apron while she considered whether or not to let me off the hook.

"And that fella you left with?" she asked. "How's he doing?"

I started to answer, then stopped myself, then started and stopped again. I couldn't find a way to say it that didn't sound cold-blooded. Doris understood.

"Natural causes, was it?"

"Natural enough, given the life he led."

"And that thing he drove you back for?"

"Settled. I have no more commitments in Tampa."

She worked on that mustard stain some more.

"Problem is," she told me, "anyone can say sorry. It's a fairly easy word to pronounce, even for a Texan. A little labor, on the other hand—now that shows genuine remorse."

"What kind of labor did you have in mind?"

"Well, my life would get a whole lot easier if I had someone back there minding the grill. Would free me up to work the floor, charm the clientele."

"It so happens I'm a pretty good cook."

"Is that right?"

"I went to school for it and everything."

"You willing to roll up your sleeves? Show me how sorry you really are?"

I nodded until I thought my neck might break.

"There's nothing I'd like more," I said.

"Well, I guess I can give you a trial run, Mich...Wait a minute, that's not right. What is it I should call you again?"

I thought it over. "Sarah" would sound all wrong coming out of Doris's mouth. I'd never been Sarah Roberts-Walsh here, and I didn't see any reason to start now.

"Let's stick with Michelle," I said. "Michelle Brown. That's what it says on my driver's license."

Doris reached a hand across the counter.

"Welcome home, Michelle," she said.

COME AND GET US

Turn the page for a bonus story from James Patterson
and Shan Serafin

CHAPTER 1

I HAD NO way of knowing it at the time, but when Aaron told his joke, I was thirty-nine seconds away from driving our mini-van through a guardrail over a cliff and into a river. I would be steering us down a canyon, bringing the two people in this world I care about most to the brink of death.

And somehow, that wasn't the worst thing that happened that afternoon.

This is what happened.

We were driving down a desolate stretch of highway. Three of us. Me, my husband, Aaron, and my daughter, Sierra. We were in the gorgeous no-man's-land between Utah and Arizona, a few canyons north of the "grand" one. Normally, I'm chatty behind the wheel, trading terrible jokes and bad puns with Aaron, but roads like these leave no margin for error.

"What do you say if you meet a talking duck and an honest lawyer?" he asked.

When a car is speeding along a curvy highway and starts to lose traction near the edge of a cliff, the solution, believe it or not, is to turn *toward* the direction of the skid. This means toward the cliff, toward the unthinkable. It sounds logical from a physics perspective. Turning into a skid. It sounds like the sort of level-headed action that everyone at a cocktail party would nod in agreement about. *Yes, do that. Steer toward the tragedy. We'd all do that obvious, logical thing.*

Thirty-one seconds.

But what if the reason you're skidding in the first place isn't simply because you lost focus but because a three-ton black SUV has intentionally sent you into it?

There was an SUV behind us.

Inches behind us. Its menacing grill was flooding my rearview mirror, looking like Darth Vader's helmet on wheels. The driver—fat, bearded, and ugly—was coming as close as possible to touching my minivan's rear.

"Let him think he's winning," said Aaron, calmly backseat-driving me.

He was next to our four-year-old, helping her command the galactic kangaroos in her video game.

"Let him think he's winning?" I replied. *"Why?"*

Sierra had recently reached what many parents herald as the new milestone in child development: how to complain about the Wi-Fi signal she needed to upgrade the game. But Aaron was her voice of reason. And mine.

I knew what he was getting at—I should calmly drift over and give the tailgater enough room to split our lane, so that he could pass us and be on his angry little way.

"I don't want to pull over for him," I said. "I don't want to reward that kind of behavior."

"He's a grown man, not a Labrador."

I took a breath, a yogic breath. "Fine. What *do* you say if you meet a talking duck and an honest lawyer?"

"Holy crap, an honest lawyer!" said Aaron, which made him laugh.

I slowed down and drifted. He was right. I was letting a trivial situation get the best of me. Time to be the adult and let it go.

I took my foot off the gas a smidgen and sure enough, my new friend came up alongside my left fender, trading his monopoly of my rearview mirror for a monopoly of the side one. I'd already prepared the perfect facial expression for him, a mix of disdain and tranquility.

But he kept that satisfaction from me.

He hovered in my blind spot, then decisively faded back into his original position.

Seventeen seconds. I immediately glanced ahead on the highway, thinking he'd seen something in front of us. Construction cones? A bridge? Trucks? But we were the only two cars out here, traveling together through the desolate desert cliffs. Before he pulled up behind us moments ago, we hadn't seen another car for an hour.

"He's not passing us," I informed Aaron.

"Good. See? Zen," he replied. "Let him *think* he has the power and, presto, the guy retreats."

Mr. SUV had indeed faded back to my rear but he was still following close behind. Close, until three seconds later he was trying to pass me again but on the opposite side now, on the shoulder side of the road. This put him on the inner path of a very blind turn. Let him fly by, I mused to myself. Good riddance.

Eight seconds.

The healthy thought didn't dispel the rising tension I was feeling.

"Sierra, hold my paw," said Aaron to our daughter. That was their little code for assurance—whenever there was a goblin in the house or a clap of thunder in the distance, the two koalas in the family held tight.

"Daddy, hold my paw," she immediately echoed back. Five seconds.

Sensing the tension in the car, they were now entwined. Just in time. The SUV was *so* close to us—when it happened.

He clipped the far corner of my rear bumper, a solid enough strike but not nearly hard enough to seem like anything other than an accident. I lost control of our car. Four seconds.

We began to skid clockwise, toward the guardrail.

Two-point-five seconds.

And instead of flashing on the cocktail party in Manhattan when we'd joked about how to react in a high-speed car chase—three years ago, when Aaron got hired for his first big job as a lawyer, for a nice corporation called Drake Oil—I instead flashed on the general concept of my husband and Sierra in my back seat, innocently playing together in the kangaroo galaxy.

And I hesitated at the wheel.

There was no time anyway.

Seventy-three miles per hour.

We were going to go over the edge.

Zero.

CHAPTER 2

I HIT THE guardrail at over seventy miles an hour, exploding the metal post from its anchor in the rock and shattering the metal outward as if it were the fringes of a ribbon, at the end of a marathon.

My heart froze, not just for what was happening in the moment, but for what was looming ahead on my disturbingly clear horizon.

There was no ground in sight.

We were going over a cliff.

It was just air meeting dashboard. There was no ground in this picture.

"Miranda!" my husband screamed, the involuntary expulsion of your wife's name when terror takes hold of your vocal cords.

The front of the minivan flew forward as my stomach sank about ten miles below my seat. All four tires went airborne as 99 percent of the ambient noise abruptly vanished, like someone clicked off the master volume on life, which, in turn, ushered in the horrific sound of my four-year-old daughter screaming at the top of her lungs. The most bloodcurdling, most agonized shriek imaginable.

"Mmmmaaaaammmmaaa*aaaa!*"

My entire body went rigid as my inner organs twisted in a knot. I stomped my foot down on the brake pedal, crushing it into the floor, as if brakes mattered while our minivan did what minivans were not supposed to do.

We were airborne, and then we were not. We rejoined the planet without slowing down at all. The front of the van hit the dirt, a massive grade leading toward the abyss. We flipped over, for a second on all four wheels, and I felt the traction of the tires bite for just a second as I had a chance to correct the careening vehicle ever-so-slightly forward again.

It was a brief moment of hope, but there was no control. Our minivan kept flipping, vertically and horizontally.

As the world spun in front of me, I caught a glimpse in the rearview mirror of my treasures—screaming and crying just as I must have been. We bounced horrendously along the spine of the hillside with its rocky dirt hammering our tires and our chassis, until we finally smashed into the bottom of the canyon.

Upside down.

Where everything then became eerily still. Everyone's cries had stopped.

Only the river murmured. It was getting in somehow, trickling across our ceiling. We were partially on the rapids, partially on the shallow end of the bank.

Only later would I appreciate that while bad luck had delivered me an SUV to contend with, good luck had delivered me the one spot by the river that would hold us. A dozen feet farther and we'd be submerged.

I turned to look behind me. I saw my husband, seemingly drifting in and out of consciousness.

"You good?" I asked him.

He didn't look good. It took him a long moment to answer. "Mmmmm…"

"Sierra?" I said to my daughter, a one-word query.

She was wide-eyed but alert, apparently intact.

I instantly activated myself. Sleeves rolled up. Time to move. All of us. My husband, though sluggish, started fiddling with the straps on Sierra's car seat. I took off my seat belt, trying to land as gracefully as possible onto the wet ceiling. It wasn't very graceful. I looked back to Aaron to make sure he and Sierra could both wiggle free. His forehead had a nasty gash across it. Long, thick, deep. But he was present enough to help Sierra down.

"I'm gonna climb back up to the main road," I announced to him.

"'Kay," he replied.

I'd fully expected him to debate me, to tell me he should be the one to go, to tell me I should stay here with Sierra, but he didn't protest. I wasn't sure if that was a good thing or a bad thing.

I didn't dwell on it. I got moving. The shock neutralized any hesitation I might have had, maybe should have. I was numbly executing a series of actions I wasn't even sure would work. We needed help, serious help. An ambulance. A medical helicopter. We hadn't had reception for a long time, and I couldn't see either of our phones, which must have bounced around the van.

Water was really starting to get in, now—I realized that most of the windows were shattered. Of course they were.

One thing went right, though: I had no idea what inconvenient place we decided to cram our emergency kit when we packed the car, but there it was, in the middle of all our other belongings, on the ceiling, getting wet. I grabbed it and slung it on my shoulder like a purse.

I kicked out the shattered glass of the passenger window—luckily the van was at an angle, and the passenger's side was slightly above the water.

Even though the SUV driver had just shoved me off the road,

I somehow expected him to be yelling down to us right now, to have realized what he'd done, pulled over, and formulated a plan for getting help down here to us.

But I'd seen enough cop shows that I realized what had happened up on the road wasn't accidental. It was called the PIT maneuver.

And he'd run us off intentionally.

CHAPTER 3

WHEN I GOT out I looked up and saw that the rock face was much steeper than I anticipated. A vintage Grand Canyon-y type of cliff face. The whole region looked like a slice of Mars with an extra sprinkling of jagged cliffs. I wasn't really sure how Sierra was going to get up there, let alone my injured husband. Frankly, I wasn't even sure how *I* was going to get up.

It would be a grueling climb—maybe better described as a scramble, though the more I considered the angle, it looked like a downright free climb. This wasn't totally daunting: I was once a strong climber, even competitive; but that was years ago. My exercise regimen these days was mainly chasing a toddler around the house.

Nowhere to go but up, though, if I were going to flag down help on the road. I hoped for muscle memory when the time came. Is climbing a rock face like riding a bike?

I was snapped out of my assessment of the rock face when I heard a groan. The minivan was moving. The river was *moving* the minivan!

It should have been safe in the shallows. It wasn't.

"Aaron, the van's moving!" I shouted.

I ducked back into the passenger window I had kicked out to find Aaron stuck in the back seat, pinned by the vehicle's journey into the silt. The passenger seat had broken and had buckled onto his thigh.

He tried to hand me Sierra, but she refused to leave him. She was huddled behind the driver's seat, now halfway deep in river water.

Despite her panic and his head wound, he remained calm and managed to pick her up and tried to hand her to me.

But there was nowhere to go. The path I'd waded through the current was a one-way street too turbulent to retreat against. We coaxed her out through the front passenger window, but there was nowhere to set her down—I wasn't going to put my four-year-old in running river water.

I managed to open the sliding rear door enough for him to fit through, and began to pull on him, one arm holding Sierra, one arm pulling Aaron. He was using one free hand to push himself and the other to push on the broken seat pinning him. The car was tilting toward the river now. I didn't realize how precariously we were balanced but we didn't have much time. Aaron was frantically trying to extricate his leg.

"On the count of three," I said. "One . . . two . . ."

"Three," we both grunted. And pried him free.

We were waist-deep when the van flipped into the water, submerging the top half. We stared for a moment at what would have been our family coffin. We'd gotten out on the far side of the river, on the wrong side to go back to the road. Aaron started moving across it, his head bleeding. I didn't know how he was functioning. I followed, clutching our daughter. The current quickly became brutal, but the three of us kept trudging along. We were now chest-deep in the rapids, water gushing past us at a relentless velocity. But we could see the direct route to the nearest bank, and it didn't seem to be getting any deeper. The hard part was over.

And then I lost my grip on Sierra.

"Aaron!" I screamed. She was already six feet away from my outstretched hand. *"Aaron!"* I needed him to turn around and outstretch his.

He looked back and instantly lunged to grab her—thank God—by the arm. And held tight. But he'd lunged downstream and lost his balance. And they were now being carried away. Fast. All I could see was the top of her purple Kangaroo Commander hat bobbing downstream.

I got to the bank of dirt and rocks and ran helplessly alongside the buoyant duo. Everything in the world I cared about was floating twenty feet away from me amid raging rapids, soon to be squirted between the jagged rock-teeth of the river.

If I could get ahead, I could start thinking about sliding down the bank to water level and extending myself across the rocks to grab them. But the current was increasing—*where is it taking them?* I ran along the bank and began to see and hear what had seemed faraway before: there was a waterfall ahead. Of course.

CHAPTER 4

I'D BEEN RUNNING blind. I hadn't paid attention to the horizon. Sierra and Aaron were about to go over the edge. *Haven't we had enough edges today?* I lost my footing for a step as I opened up my stride, but managed to stay on pace, sprinting along with them.

"The branches!" yelled my husband.

"What?" I yelled back.

It took me a moment to realize he meant the lone tree growing out of the rocky bank, way up on the left side, imprisoned by the relentless current. My mind raced. Okay, all I have to do is race ahead, hop down along the wet, slippery stones, grab at the trunk, break off a branch, hope it was the right length, hope it was the right sturdiness, then dangle it out across Aaron's path.

Sierra looked too shocked to be scared. She was clamping onto his neck while he was trying to hold her up and protect her from the hidden rocks. He was on his back, traveling legs first so his feet could absorb a blow if a rock or tree trunk surfaced; cupping her on his torso like an otter might shield its treasure.

"Hold a branch across," he shouted.

I knew what to do and had very little time to do it. I was racing down toward the tree.

I'd finally surpassed them in the race. Now, with a little bit of a lead, I'd have a moment to turn toward the water and hustle over to the tree and break off the best possible—

I was too late.

They went over the falls before I could even complete my yell. "Aaron!" I cried. The involuntary expulsion of your husband's name.

I thought I could get to them in time but I didn't anticipate just how much the current would accelerate near the drop. They simply disappeared over the edge. Followed by my useless shouts.

"Aaron!"

It was as if they had been yanked below a horizontal line of existence. I was so shocked by what I saw that I halted in my tracks, struggling to maintain any rational grasp on the situation.

Within a moment, I snapped back into awareness and resumed the chase to see where they had landed. I arrived at the edge on the left bank and searched the river below. It was as large a waterfall as I'd feared, with one factor in our favor: the plunge pool wasn't rocky. There was enough clear depth down there to accommodate a full drop. Within several torturous seconds I saw them, two heads bobbing along. They'd survived.

In a wider section of the river, with only slow rapids, they were floating in a froth that lasted maybe five seconds before pushing its fresh contents downstream. I scurried down the wet crags and was soon keeping up with them along the gentle current. They were thankfully moving much slower now.

"She's okay," Aaron shouted to me.

I skidded on my butt down a rocky, dirty incline. He pulled himself onto the bank just as I arrived. Sierra was wide-eyed, frozen in fear. She wasn't speaking.

He handed her to me so that he could finally collapse. I hugged them both, embracing their icy skin. He looked ready to pass out, but I didn't feel good about him surrendering consciousness.

"Not here, babe," I said.

He was ghostly pale from a loss of blood and from the water. The air was warm, but the water was cold. And he'd pushed himself through the entire ordeal running on fumes, on adrenaline.

"Let's get over to those crags," I said to him. "See? Down by that first boulder?"

He didn't answer.

"Babe?" I said to him, waiting for him to find the strength to speak.

"Crags," he finally replied, deflating.

I looked at Sierra. She still seemed shell-shocked, but physically unscathed. "You okay?" I asked her.

"Crags," she agreed. My cooperative tag team.

I grabbed my husband by the hand and helped him up. We thus began the four-legged, three-person limp toward the boulders looming nearby. I'd also spotted some cavelike openings, amid the spill of giant rock fragments. We could hide in one of those. This would be important—to keep us out of the direct sun, away from animals, away from wind, and away from the cold of night, if we were still here then.

It's important, when taking refuge, to make sure someone knows your chosen locale. We did have a signal flare in the emergency kit I had grabbed. It had a granola bar, a magnifying glass, a first aid kit, a canteen, and the flare. And I'd glimpsed what I thought was a small town in the distance while running along the river. It was far away, but I had to assume it would have a few residents who might be looking in our direction.

"I think we should send up the flare," I said to him.

He could barely keep his eyes open.

"Or should we wait?" I asked.

He was too weary but found enough determination to give me a meek thumbs-up before fading again. I had no idea if that thumb meant *yes, wait,* or *yes, send it.*

"Uh," I said. "Did...?"

So I sent it.

PFFFFFaaaaffff! The colorful firework popped in the sky about five hundred feet above us. Sierra was in awe. Aaron barely noticed. I hated to do this in broad daylight, but nightfall might be longer than we could wait.

Once inside the cave, my husband collapsed on the dirt. I'd intended to find a good spot for him, but gravity had made that decision for us and I didn't have the heart to move him.

"This'll work," I said.

I started to lecture him about the importance of elevating the wound. He had a gash on his forehead, and its flow needed stanching. But after five sentences of lecturing, I realized he was out cold. Sierra was the real surprise. I'd assumed this catastrophic situation would render her a stuttering wreck, but she was calm, serene. It's a trait I'd love to say she inherits from her mother, but Aaron is the eye of the hurricane in our lives.

"You're my rock, babe," I said to him. "You know that?"

Which brought me to a bleak conundrum. He needed help. It wasn't just the blood loss or the bad leg, but the prospect of head trauma. His eyes were rolling back in his head. His blackouts were coming without warning. His speech was slurred. This man needed medical attention soon or he might die.

And the monstrously harsh reality was that to save him, I might have to leave him there.

It wasn't even midmorning yet.

CHAPTER 5

SHOULD I STAY or go find help on my own, back to that damn rock face? I was in a foreign landscape, unsure how to navigate its terrain.

But what if Aaron's skull was fractured?

I'm terrible when it comes to first aid. All I could reference in my head were flashes of random TV shows. Any instance of a chiseled ambulance driver pushing on the chest of an injured pedestrian. What did they do with the head? What did they *say* to the head?

"Sierra, I need you to do something brave for Mommy," I said to her.

She came over right away, with a generally stunned look on her face. She stood in front of me, patiently waiting for me to tell her about the next calamity.

"Sierra, I need you to press on Daddy's head."

She stood there for a moment, then said gravely, "But Daddy has a bad head."

"Yes, and that's why you have to press. Like this. See?"

I showed her. His plaid button-down shirt had enough fluff to absorb some wetness without getting soggy. I could tie it, but I didn't want to move his head any more than necessary.

I made a map in my head and did some calculations, before turning to my husband. "Aaron, honey, listen to me if you can. I'm going to leave you for about three hours. Ninety minutes out. Ninety back. That gets me five miles. Sierra will be here. I need to find help and get a helicopter for you."

I waited for a response from him. I got silence.

"Daddy wants a helicopter?" asked Sierra.

"I'm going to hike toward the junction at 89," I said to my blank husband. "That gives us the best chance of seeing traffic. Because the road we were on was pretty dead." Dead is a bad word. "I mean...I have hope...that I might see a few cars and flag one down. Maybe the SUV that hit us."

He didn't stir. Nothing.

"Aaron?" I put my hand on his shoulder.

He was still. Disturbingly still. I could barely detect any breath; he did have a pulse, but it was weak.

I took a deep breath. I turned to Sierra. I summoned my best Solemn Mom face, making sure not to enter Scary Mom face–zone, and said, "Okay, Sierra, I need you to do something very important."

"Is Daddy sick?"

"Yes. He needs a doctor. I'm going to find one." I was ready for her to freak out that I'd be leaving. She stayed still as I continued. "The important thing is Daddy will need to rest as much as possible, so even though—"

"I can watch him," she said.

She stood there like a brave little soldier, perfectly at attention.

"You can?" I asked.

"Yeah," she nodded slowly. "I can hold Daddy Koala's paw."

"He might wake up and say strange things but don't worry, he's being silly. Just tell him that Mommy went to get a doctor, and he needs to stay still."

"Okay. Don't worry, Mommy."

"I love you, Sierra." I kissed her on the forehead and grabbed the hiking pack.

We had one granola bar left. It was murder trying to think of how to divvy this measly thing up. Some for Sierra? Some for Aaron, who probably wouldn't even eat it? Some for me, the one who might have to sprint for two hours straight? How do you divide the lone granola bars of life?

We had planned to stop for lunch in Chasm before heading to Jed's house. Despite everything, I could hear her stomach already rumbling.

I put the whole thing in his jeans pocket and smiled at Sierra, relying on her to decide to eat it if she needed to, or sacrifice it if Daddy needed it more. Me? I was fine. I could run on pure anxiety juice. I was already overdosing on it.

I began to head out and was close to the mouth of the cave when I heard Aaron's voice behind me. He was starting to talk!

I spun around just as he was already slipping back into a deep sleep. He'd summoned every last ounce of his energy to utter a sentence that would occupy my mind for the rest of the day.

"Be careful who you trust."

CHAPTER 6

I WAS ALONE now. Not in the spiritual sense. Not in the romantic sense. But in the imperiled sense. The survival game. I was now hiking away from everything that mattered to me.

How does a small child survive in a cave? She would never leave her dad's side, but what if her dad's side left *her?* What if the unthinkable happened while I was gone? What if my husband died? What if tiny Sierra ended up there alone?

I was walking across incredibly jagged crags. Rocks sharp enough to cut flesh, rocks that could severely hurt me if I twisted my ankle. But worse than the pain if I was crippled—Sierra would be alone. No one would know where we were, where my husband was. She'd be stranded.

With that in mind, I crossed the rubble painfully slowly. The hesitation felt necessary, but it was a risk in itself; hesitation breeds bad decisions.

Be careful who you trust.

Why would Aaron tell me that, out here in the land of zero population? Nobody lives here. Nobody camps here. Nobody *was* here. I'd started to truly see it on this hike. We'd be lucky to find anyone at all.

But I had to maintain hope. *Maybe today is the day there is a nurse convention in the desert crags.* I was heading for elevation, to the closest viable ridge. From there, I figured I'd be afforded at least a twenty-mile vantage point. There was a fairly clean path up the rock face on my left that looked like a few miles of gradual slope, before zigzagging back up the hillside for another stretch of gradual slope to the top of my target ridge.

Or I could climb.

Climbing would be risky—possibly deadly—but I'd be saving myself hours of walking, a tough economization to resist. I could be up that ridge in half an hour. It wasn't steep, and limestone is a safe rock. I'd climbed tougher routes. My instincts said I could handle it.

And yet my mind kept arguing with the numbers.

This particular hill offered a decently high chance of success. Let's say 80 percent. The problem was that I'd be facing that sort of choice more than once. And every time I chose the riskier option, I'd be multiplying the risk factor times all the future risk factors. That's 80 percent times 80 percent times—

"Oh, my God, Miranda," I said out loud, "just make a decision."

I'd just wasted minutes trying to figure out how to avoid wasting minutes. So I chose to climb. I started walking toward the cliff face and was soon monkeying up it. There were handholds to grip. And the footholds I found felt solid. My confidence increased as I looked straight up and had a clear visual of most of my route.

It really didn't take long to reach the top, and I had an immediate task scheduled for myself. Research.

I'd sent up the signal flare thinking I saw sunlight glinting on a town, like maybe Red Bluff.

But I was wrong, I was now seeing a harsh reality. There was no city, no town. From this mercilessly clear vantage point I could see that what I thought was a town was...just a mirage. A desert mirage. The oldest cliché in the book.

I was flooded with regret. I'd sent up our only signal flare with no purpose.

With that bad news suddenly came good news—

Crack!

What sounded like a rifle shot was startlingly loud in the quiet landscape, and echoed. I didn't think it could be more than a half mile away, though I had no idea which direction.

I instantly rejoiced at the prospect of hearing hunters in the distance. My first thought was, *Humans. Salvation.* Sure, it was dangerous to have bullets flying around. Most people would rightfully cringe and take cover. But in this case, bullets were music to my ears.

Crack! The next shot echoed around me. Even closer.

I don't know what you would hunt in the desert, though.... Maybe it was a search party?

I stood tall and shouted, "Hey! Help! I need help!" I was waving my arms like crazy. "Whoever you are, please help me!"

I scanned the area, waiting for a response that didn't come.

"I'm right here!" I said even louder. "Help!"

And the valley said nothing.

"Here on this ridge!" I yelled.

I kept repeating this routine for a half minute. Until I saw something that changed my mind about how the rest of my life might unfold.

The shooter—not very far away, maybe a hundred feet at most—well, he could see me. He was looking right at me, that was clear. He was on the ridge too, on higher ground. And he was aiming at me. Directly at me. *Crack!* Another shot was fired in my direction. From him. At me.

"Hey! What the hell is wrong with you!?" I screamed.

As I recognized who he was.
Fat.
Bearded.
Ugly.
The SUV driver.

CHAPTER 7

THIS WAS AN attack. This wasn't an accident. This man was trying to shoot me.

I froze for longer than I care to admit. I always imagined that in a situation like this a thousand thoughts would race through my mind—some emotional, some practical, some an inventory of my life—but I was mentally blank. I eventually spun around and clumsily fled down the nearest slope.

I only had one viable thought in my head, not a very impressive one: to duck behind a bush.

My laughable instinct was quickly vetoed by my legs anyway, because my legs said run.

So I ran.

Movement became autonomous. I sprinted down the slope, creating a flurry of dust behind me. *Crack,* he fired another shot through the air at my back. Was this his third or fourth? Maybe his tenth, for all I knew. I'd never been shot at before. I felt irrationally insulted.

"You're shooting at me!" I yelled, turning.

Is that all I can come up with?

"Stop!" I added.

I was crouching down again, my back to the dirt slope, taking cover, trying to figure out what to do. I wasn't in charge of my voice.

The man with the gun said nothing but kept coming. He stormed across the patches of loose shale, relentlessly focused.

I knew I had to keep moving, but I couldn't see anywhere to go. I looked back and yelled again. "My name is Miranda Cooper! I'm not whoever you think I am! I don't even know you!"

If I had to identify him in a police sketch I'd say: bearded, fat, ugly. But I could add: mean, with hate in his eyes. Was this guy actually trying to ram us off the road? He seemed absolutely oblivious to what I was saying now.

Was he trying to ram my *husband* off the road?

Crack, another shot. Another miss.

Was he himself a husband? A jealous one? Did Aaron sleep with somebody? An affair?

Where *were* we headed in our minivan? To hide? In the midst of mortal peril, my crazed brain was now conjuring up all the grotesque situations that my husband could've entangled himself in. I was picturing a hotel in something like Atlanta or St. Louis. A nice one. Two hundred dollars a night. The hotel bartender announcing last call and Aaron looking at his voluptuous business partner, whoever she was, someone with a sexy neck, while they both giggled about whose room to go up to.

No.

It's not possible. Not Aaron. He was taking us on a trip to meet a new friend he'd met on the job. Some guy named Jed. My husband doesn't cheat.

And I know every wife thinks the "not him" thing, that hers is the one prince in the world who wouldn't roam; but infidelity is beneath Aaron.

The man was now close enough that I could hear his breathing and grunting over his footsteps. He was closing the gap between us, scuffling himself down the hillside across the shale.

I looked around for places to hide or for a covered path to run along. He had a rifle with a scope. I started wishing I knew enough about guns to discern if his was a hunting rifle or a cop rifle. Useless speculation.

Something else occurred to me. My first possibly non-useless idea. Go back uphill.

If he's silly enough to choose the shale-side of a hill over the limestone-side of a hill *once,* he might be silly enough to choose it a second time. A choice with consequences. Because when a rockslide happens, even if it's just a small area that collapses— you're going to go down, hard.

The trick would be to get him to chase me up the south face. I'd be unprotected if I baited him. I looked up at the potential routes, searching for safety zones. Nope. It was all exposed.

I didn't have much longer to stew on it. I just needed to gather enough confidence to traverse the steepest part of the slope. From where I was standing, it looked incredibly intimidating. *Make a decision, Miranda.* If I took a curved path, the shape of a question mark. . . .

Crack, another shot sailed over my crouched position. I looked down. I wasn't in the best shoes: some cross-trainers I bought for the Hip Hop Cardio class I never took.

They were going to have to outperform their mission statement, though. They needed to give me traction up the only road out of hell.

CHAPTER 8

I SPRINTED UP the gravel incline just as, *crack,* another gunshot exploded in the air behind me, instantly followed by the sound of dirt puffing up by my feet. He was getting closer. I kept climbing. This was only going to work if I managed to do one particular thing—not get hit by a bullet.

I hadn't realized how insane my plan was until I was fully exposed on the rock face. I'm sure I looked like the biggest target this wacko had ever seen. Yet there I was, heading up the cliff as fast as I could, in the strategic path of a question mark.

He started running up behind me. He really did. Straight upward, the cheat. And I began to believe this entire ploy might just work.

If he would enter the slide zone, I'd gain about five minutes on him. The rocks would tangle him up. He might sprain an ankle. At the *very* least, he'd slide all the way back down and be bewildered. I'd be free to make a mad dash. I might even manage to separate him from his gun.

Crack—another shot. Missed, but splattered the dust directly near my hand.

I could see him fiddle with the gun. Because it was broken?—no, to reload it. He was coming up a lot faster than I anticipated. I was just nearing the top and he was already nearing the end of the loose shale, a patch of hillside about the size of a grocery store aisle. He'd already traversed most of it fast, surprisingly without incident. What was motivating this idiot?

The footing beneath him was holding up agonizingly well, and I'd stopped to *watch* all this, letting him gain on me, assuming I'd have already achieved the desired landslide by now. No such luck.

I'm not sure what I did to give him road rage but now he'd taken it off the road. Was life so bad in the Wild West that people chased after fellow motorists on foot?

"I'm just a mother!" I yelled at him.

He was nearly across the band of "helpful" geology. I was nearly at the end of my safety zone. The rest of my climb was going to put me in a long corridor of easiest targeting. *Crack*, he fired another shot at me.

And then his foot plunged.

Downward. Deep. I didn't see it at first but I heard it. I'd ducked down after the last bullet whizzed by my head (note, Miranda, the best time to duck is *before* the deadly projectile arrives, not after), but I heard something like miniature thunder down below me. I heard, yes, a rockslide. It was like thunder, or a bowling alley.

I looked, and not only was he sliding down the slope, as I'd hoped, but the entire diagonal section of rocks cascaded with him. He was riding a magic carpet of sharp, jagged stones. The avalanche knocked him off his feet—the point a guardian angel should step in—and, dumbfounded, I watched him plummet all the way down to the hard ground of the ravine. *Didn't see that coming*.

The only sign of the disturbance was an elongated cloud of

dust rising below. But he was down there. In bad shape. He had to have fallen a hundred feet.

I strained to see through the dust and detected a crumpled heap of errantly strewn limbs, lying motionless. His leg was rotated awkwardly outward, probably broken.

Okay, what now? The only route down was to march back past him. But what if he was faking it? What if he was waiting until I got close to shoot me, up close and personal?

I picked up the sharpest piece of shale I could find. It felt heavy enough to do damage, but light enough to throw. Maybe I could spin it at him like a Frisbee.

I started scooting down the hillside, trying and failing to be quiet. He hadn't yet looked up or moved. *Spinning a rock like a Frisbee is ridiculous. What is wrong with you, Miranda?* I could see him more clearly as I got closer. He was sprawled, facedown. It felt very likely that I would tumble forward to plummet as he had, and land right on top of him, dead.

I held my rock-weapon up, like a quarterback ready to throw.

"You almost killed my daughter!" I shouted.

I wanted to just throw my projectile at him, but I had some more choice words. "My daughter...she's four! And you were shooting at me! Why?!"

He really was quite still. I knew I should walk away, continue on to get help for Aaron—every moment counted. But I felt drawn to see him up close—to know what we were dealing with.

"Hey!" I said. "Hey, I'm right here with a sharp rock! You don't have to pretend to be out! You don't have to fake it."

I started to wonder if he was still breathing. I moved between him and his rifle, lying in the dirt about ten feet away. I kept my shale-football-Frisbee-rock-spear held high above me and felt the clichés bubbling to my mouth.

"One false move, buster, and you're going down in flames!"

Flames? I knelt by his side. I needed to flip him over. *Buster?*

I steeled myself. He might lunge at me. He might turn out to be someone I knew. He might be someone whose identity made sense and somehow proved to me that Aaron wasn't a good husband. Every part of my brain started whirling. I pushed at his shoulder and stomach and managed to flip him over.

It was horrible. His face was torn open.

"Are you okay?" I asked in a nice, maternal tone of voice. "Can you breathe?"

This man was certainly no friend of mine. But faced with a dying human, I couldn't just walk away. I had to do something.

There are so many times I've told myself I need to take CPR. So many times Aaron and I decided that to be good parents, we had to be experts in resuscitation. Who knew when we might need to revive Sierra? Or each other? Or our dog? I had read the steps—but here I was, feeling helpless. I knew there was pressing, and counting. . . .

"Hey, man, wake up!"

In the heat of the moment, I was panicking. I was increasing my anxiety by the minute. *I killed this man.* I put my hands on his chest. To press.

Step one. Ask, "Hey, are you okay?"

Step two. Check for breathing and pulse. Not breathing. But he had a pulse, though it was weak.

Step three. Chest compressions. I vaguely remembered some trick with the song "Another One Bites the Dust," which sets the cadence for the chest compressions. Ironic, given the circumstances. Did he even need chest compressions? *I killed him. It was my plan to trip him down the mountain.*

Step four. Call for help.

If I yelled out for help, out here approximately one billion miles from the nearest anything, no one would come. But if I were to *call. . . .*

That's when the obvious dawned on me. I didn't have a

phone, but he did. He must. More important than his gun, I could take his phone.

Save him first, Miranda.

I would revive him, then find the phone, call 911, and request an ambulance for him and helicopter for my husband. The new plan. I leaned over to start the compressions.

But before I could even touch his chest, he coughed.

He was awake.

"Hey!" I yelled. "Hey, you're up! You're okay? Are you? Can you breathe?"

No words came out, just a terrible sound.

"My name is Miranda. You just fell down a mountain."

He coughed and up came blood. Lots of blood. It was in his lungs. Whatever the problem was, he had ruptured something vital, deep within him. He burbled up a crimson stream that trickled down his chin and cheeks.

"Tellth ..." he said to me.

"What?"

"Tell ..." he said. He stopped. Then he continued. "Them."

"Them? Who? Okay, I will. Tell what?"

It took a moment, but he finally answered. "My team ... to save me."

"What team?"

Team? Did he say team?

"Was there someone else in the car with you?" I asked. "Did you ram me off the road?"

I needed to give this man time to respond.

"Why did your team ram me off the road?"

He was dying. Now. Here.

"T-tray ..." he said weakly. Was this his dying breath? He looked over at me.

"No," I said. I would not let him quit. "No way. Stay awake, buddy. Please."

"Kiss," he said.

"Don't give up, man!" How had I gone from a road trip with my family to watching a man I didn't know die?

"Tray," he gasped, then started again. "Tray ... Kiss ... Kilt ..." and then a big exhale ...

And he was gone.

CHAPTER 9

HE DIED. RIGHT there in front of me. I watched a human being leave this world. At thirty years of age, I was lucky—this was the first time I'd ever seen someone go.

I stood up, feeling heavy and sick to my stomach. My head was swirling. My face was sweating cold droplets down my brow. Before I knew what was happening, I gave way to my nausea, sending my upper body folding forward with hands braced against my thighs. *I did this to him.* I sent him up the loose shale. I ended a man's life. No matter what kind of idiotic warfare he had waged on me, I'm not in the business of ending lives. And I'd just ended one.

"Damn it, Mandy."

I took a few breaths, got my bearings, and knelt by him again.

I began a prayer. A silent one, not words but more feelings. Putting aside the guilt that threatened to overwhelm me, I prayed for him to be forgiven, to see a better place than whatever chaotic evil had led him to a life of chasing innocent women through the desert with a rifle.

Or was he chasing Aaron?

"Tray. Kiss. Kilt," I said to myself. What in God's name could that mean?

I unpressed my palms and stood back up.

I had to be careful. This man mentioned others. The rest of his "team," so I could assume that there were other fine gentlemen in the car that ran us off the road. If he was now in my canyon, shooting at me, what were these "others" doing?

I drew a little map in the dirt with a stick. The river. The highway. The cliff we tumbled over. The spot where our van was sprawled out like a turtle on its back. The waterfall. The crags. The cave containing my husband and child.

As far as I could tell, this guy, this corpse next to me, got lucky finding me out here on the south end of the canyon. Unless he had tracked me in a more sophisticated way than I was aware of, he wasn't expecting me to be right here. The safer place to look—where I was betting his team was right now—was the area very close to the highway where we were run off.

So my new goal was to get to the main highway we were headed toward. A big eight-lane behemoth of glory.

Tray. Kiss. Kilt. I picked up Mr. SUV Driver's rifle. It was scratched but didn't look broken. I tried to cock it, but the gun didn't cooperate.

Then I remembered—*the phone!*

I quickly turned back to him. I'd completely forgotten. I dug for his phone in his pocket, found it, and tried to turn it on. It was locked, as expected, but I should at least be able to dial 911, which I did…but got nothing. We were so far away from any signal, even a priority call wouldn't get through.

I put it in my pocket, to try again later.

Tray. Kiss. Kilt.

I stood up and erased my map in the dirt with my shoe.

Kiss. Maybe I'd been onto something before, and Aaron really had kissed this guy's wife. That made sense. No. No, it didn't.

Why would Mr. SUV Driver bring all his friends? His driving maneuver seemed too premeditated for a crime of passion.

Who exactly was this "Jed" we were visiting? He supposedly had a ranch and lovely horses, fine, but why suddenly visit a guy we barely knew? Why had I agreed to this visit I knew nothing about?

Maybe he kissed some girl at work? But no, I didn't think there were many single mingling types at Drake Oil.

I noticed my shadow on the ground. There was my silhouette, unchanged but for the gun in my hand. I was that woman. The gun woman.

My shadow seemed to belong to a different person.

Armed with a gun, a phone, and a new sense of purpose, I hiked over to the crest of the ridge. *Tray Kiss.* Maybe it's actually *Drake Is.* I was replaying the audio in my head, not just the words. I was scrutinizing the nuances. Tray Kiss. *Drake Is.* The dead SUV driver was saying *Drake Is* Something.

"Drake is . . ." I said to myself, imitating his voice.

The more I thought about it, the more I couldn't imagine any other possibility.

What I was hoping to achieve was a good view of the back canyon. This was about a two-mile corridor. If Mr. SUV Driver had hiked through here, maybe his teammates were nearby. Fine. As bad as it sounded, I preferred this possibility to its catastrophic alternative: enemies might be heading toward my *family*, toward my injured husband and my tiny daughter. If they were willing to shoot at me—I mean, no questions asked, just shoot at me—what would they do to my daughter?

No way, not letting that happen. I needed to survey the terrain as fast as possible and plot a countermeasure. I sped up to a run, now among the top crags.

Drake. Is. Kilt. This was about my husband. This was about something he did. Said. I was replaying every aspect of Mr. SUV Driver's voice in my head. *Drake. Is. Kilt. Exhale.* And I was now starting to hear the end of his speech a little differently. There was more of a word tucked in there. Drake. Is. Kilt. Something.

I was on the crest now, viewing the expanse of the valley. I could see the arroyo where Mr. SUV Driver first greeted me with his bullets.

Drake is *guilty*.

I finally heard it for what it was. Guilty. *Drake*, the oil company, *is guilty*.

But I couldn't let the mental gyrations distract me from the puzzle in front of me. If there were other men out there, and Mr. SUV Driver came from the top of the far crest…they probably split up right before the crest. There—tracing his trail upward with my eyes I could see the other path, the one they might have followed. It led back to the crags. And that meant that they were already on their way back toward Aaron and Sierra.

Unacceptable. I needed them to go anywhere but into my nest.

Panic set in, flooding me with nervous, hand-wringing energy. But I already knew what I had to do.

There was no more time to waste.

I raised the rifle upward. I committed myself to a plan that would spur this cat-and-mouse game to its inevitable conclusion. I held it with both hands. Straight upward. Like I've seen on TV.

I fired, once. *Bam*. The recoil nearly knocked me to the ground, and the sound was startling, tearing into the soft silence.

You hear that, gentlemen? Bring it.

CHAPTER 10

DRAKE OIL IS a fine, fine oil institution. A group of nice people who just want to help America and kittens.

That's what the ads would have you believe.

And that's what the press would have you believe. The articles. The billboards. The way the cute logo was cutely designed. And, most of all, the way the quiet legal disagreements were quietly settled. Thanks to my husband.

This I knew. He is, after all, one of their lawyers.

I was running as fast as I could. Sure, I was trying to get them to follow me; but I couldn't let them actually *get* me. I was going as fast as I could for as long as I could.

Without wind, this was the quietest space you can imagine. It was so still you could actually hear the silence. This was helpful. I should be able to hear anyone coming from behind me. When I stopped, every so often, I could listen.

There was nothing.

"Keep moving," I whispered to myself.

My mind raced. Jesus, did my husband piss off somebody who settled a suit with Drake Oil? Who then needed vengeance on my family?

I continued this way, running as fast as my burning legs would allow, for what seemed like an hour. There were no footstep sounds behind me yet, but plodding along like the opposite of a ninja, I suddenly, faintly, heard someone yell something in the distance.

I stopped, trying to muffle my own panting. I needed to examine the silence, searching the air for the distinct sound of what I thought was a man's shout.

Heart slamming against my breastbone, even my pulse became deafening.

I scanned the horizon behind me, the outline of the red columns of rock, searching for traces of a human shape. Probably one aiming a gun at me.

What in the world did Aaron do to get people to *coordinate* an attack against him? Did he stumble into something dangerous? The silence and stillness held no answers.

I got moving again. My legs were cramping, the stopping and starting becoming harder for my body to execute.

Aaron hadn't said anything to me, but I imagined that his daily access to the entire legal landscape of Drake must have given him a glimpse of something insidious. He would've kept it secret from me, for fear that my unstoppable lungs would have bellowed it to anyone who'd listen. I couldn't blame him. He was right.

I worked my way back up to a full sprint, capitalizing on the downhill grade, ignoring the cramps and the strains. I was nearing a huge area of boulders nestled near the river, coming around a blind corner, top speed, when the following disaster happened faster than I could process:

1. I heard a pop.
2. I crashed into an obstacle I didn't think would be there and bounced off.
3. I realized it was a man.
4. He and I locked eyes in a moment of mutual shock.
5. We agreed not to be friends.

CHAPTER 11

HE WAS A mercenary. In what felt like one millisecond after our collision, he decked me across the jaw, *hard.* I recoiled backward. If Mr. SUV Driver was a dangerous man, this second guy was a nuclear war.

You could see it in his eyes: this wasn't a person, this was a professional killer. He was dressed for attacking things—soldier pants, Kevlar vest, handgun, hiking boots.

I was on my back. I'd never been hit before. Not even my older sister, Valentina, would punch me. We were slappers and that ended at age nine.

I had surprised him, but well-trained instinct enabled him to regain the upper hand. I would've assumed, prior to this moment of my life, that it would hurt to get hit; but it actually was too shocking. I hadn't read the "So You're About to Be Punched in the Jaw" orientation brochure, but it might explain that with the hit, your grasp on reality vaporizes. You get stupider.

So there I was, on the dirt, catching up with my current reality. He was slowly approaching me but I was too cloudy to even scoot myself backward. I just stayed there. Done.

And then my enemy noticed something, at the same moment that I did.

He stopped in his tracks, a bewildered expression now on his face, replacing the steel of a moment before. He was looking down at his left hand, palm-up as if checking for raindrops. The raindrop was red, and it had come from his shoulder.

He had been shot. By me.

CHAPTER 12

I VAGUELY REMEMBERED hearing a pop. That was the sound of my gun going off, though I hadn't realized it way back seven seconds ago. I'd been carrying my rifle, running along rather blithely with my hand loosely on the trigger, when I slammed into the back of him. A car rear-ending another car. Thrown to the ground when he punched me, I must've pulled the trigger.

The whole transaction had taken place in the blink of an eye. The bullet must have entered him in the shoulder and exited in the upper part of his back. I'd been quite certain I'd walked into my own execution just now. Yet here we were, both motionless, both in shock.

He began to inspect himself beyond his palm, noting the expanding circle of blood on his shirt. His injury looked severe.

But not crippling.

"Now" flashed in my mind. I scrambled for the gun (who is this new Miranda, operating my body?), which had fallen to my side. I fumbled, grabbed it, and spun to take aim. He dove forward, right at me. I got lucky once, but rifles are not effective close-range weapons, which he proved by diving on me.

Our fight wasn't over. Our fight had just begun.

Thank God there was a bullet in him, or through him, because this was the strongest living organism I had ever put my hands on. I used to playfight with Aaron in bed, knew his contours and weaknesses. These muscles here, from Mr. Kevlar, were unbelievable. Hard as rock. Huge. And trying to kill me.

I desperately curled into a fetal position and received a hit in the ribs that took my breath away. *Oh, God.* I caught his wrist and clung to it, in a weak attempt to disable one of those bionic arms. This would be painfully fast—I'd be knocked out with two more punches. But I dimly realized we had begun rolling.

Toward the river.

He pulled me into him, trying to bring my head down to knee my face like it was a martial arts fight on TV, but I used all my strength to turn away from his right side. I was, in effect, cranking the two of us in a sideways tango downhill, toward the river.

We rolled at first slowly, quarter turn by quarter turn, as he battered me with his fist. Before, I'd been too shocked for his hits to register. Well, now, I was exquisitely feeling them. Every single one. The head, the neck, the head again, the ribs, trying to get me to release my grip.

My grip?

I somehow had my hands gripped around his throat now.

My fingers clutched as hard as they could, a relentless hold on his nape, with my thumbs pushing into his voice box. My own strength surprised me. Call it rage, call it maternal instinct, call it whatever you want—I was operating under the influence of pure adrenaline. I was much smaller than this man, but he was now up against a climber's hands. My grip was life or death.

"Who are you?" I said through gritted teeth. Our faces were close enough that I could see the vessels around his pupils.

Then the horizon began to flip over behind him. We were rolling. But I didn't care. I was peering deep into his eyes.

"Who are you?!" I repeated as the horizon continued to turn, as we tumbled toward the last ledge on the cliff.

He didn't blink, even more of an automaton than Mr. SUV Driver.

He hit me again. I withstood it. I don't know how. Simply adrenaline? I knew that my gun was on the ground, back up where we started rolling. If he would just be so kind as to cooperate by letting go of me, I could go get it and shoot him again.

"Are you Drake?" I asked him, grunting as we grappled. I asked again, "Are you Drake Oil?"

It felt like I'd been on the ground with this man for a full year of my life, yet there I was—still alive, still a contender. In my favor was the fact that his bullet wound wasn't just one hole, it was two. I knew because I was covered in his blood from rolling in the dirt. I was beginning to see I had hope.

Until we splashed in the river.

I didn't register being midair, but I definitely noticed when the free fall finished and we plunged into turbulent, cascading water. My world went cold as we were dunked under and instantly swept along.

His grip softened just a bit; it was all I'd hoped for in these interminable minutes. Let that be printed on my tombstone: SHE GOT HIM TO SOFTEN HIS GRIP.

But he was on top still, his formidable body weight shoving me deeper down. We banged limbs for what seemed like the entire month of June. I suppose I should've been worried about upcoming rocks, but he'd introduced a new variable into the equation—not sure when that was exactly. He had a knife.

Underwater, amid murky eddies, I didn't have his throat anymore. I had both of my hands on his wrist. My instincts had rerouted all my physical focus from his esophagus to the jagged, murderous blade in his fist.

One swipe, one cut, and I would've been done.

With rocks on all sides, we were getting up close and personal with the unforgiving wrecking balls of the rapids. My one goal was to try to swim upward, break free of his iron grip, and get to the surface. I could engage instead, try some kung fu moves on his face—but I'm not the fastest thinker when it comes to underwater close-quarters death-match combat.

Didn't matter. The game ended on its own.

His size was his advantage on land, but it became his Achilles' heel in the rapids. He was too big to make it safely through the rocks unscathed. The riverbed did its job.

Poonk. A muffled thud. I could hear the blow his head took from a cluster of granite. He swung his last two punches at me in a halfhearted, half-conscious motion.

His grip on me faded.

The surface seemed to rush down toward my face, and my body emerged like a clumsy rocket. I had been treading so hard, I actually got my full torso up above the waterline before being beaten back down by the current. I was floating. I tried to glance behind me to see if he'd surface, too. We'd both been under for what felt like a decade. I scanned the surface behind me but he'd been consumed. I assumed, given the gunshot and blood loss, that he was dead.

And I was adrift.

I slowly took inventory of the situation: where I was heading, where I'd been, and what I now had in my possession.

I had nothing. The river gave me victory but it stripped me of all else. In addition to the gun I'd already lost, I'd lost my jacket. I'd lost my phone. The only thing I didn't lose was pants, and a clear sense that things were going to get worse before they got better.

CHAPTER 13

I MANAGED TO drift over to the riverbank and crawl up onto dry land, dragging my torso above the waterline. It was a Herculean effort, though pathetic. To an onlooker, I'd appear to be a major drama queen. One hand slowly clawing after another. Pulling in slow motion. Gasping.

I'd kill to see anyone out here . . . of course, I've killed the two people I've run into so far.

But I was alone, having led myself a million miles away from hope. All I had were wet clothes and unanswered questions. Why Drake Oil? Why my husband? Where's a phone?

I needed physically proficient help. I needed a cop. Better yet, an FBI task force.

Where to go now? The crags were south. The freeway north.

My husband, in the crags, might need me. I could give him an update on my trials out here in the wild. And he could tell me whatever he might have to tell me. Like, y'know: *Miranda, funny thing I should've mentioned; here's why an army of men might try to kill you on your stroll through the western United States.*

The possibility of actual help, though, was north. A busy

highway. The bigger highway gave me the best chance of finding a good Samaritan, and then law enforcement.

Yet what would I even say? Even if I managed to flag down a speeding motorist by the side of a highway at night, what if he or she didn't believe me? Even if I managed to find the nearest police force, how would that story go?

"Officer, I need your help," I said aloud, rehearsing. "I . . . uh . . . I . . ." Talking things out always helps me when I'm overwhelmed; it comes naturally to me. And right now, exhausted, starving, battered, half drowned, I felt half insane. Why not make an imaginary friend while I was at it? Anything to keep me going.

I took a few gradual steps along the higher slope. I would, again, hike to the nearest vista point, so I could make an informed decision.

"Excuse me, Officer," I repeated to the imaginary cop.

"What seems to be the trouble, miss?" I said back to myself. Slight southern accent.

"Well . . . you see . . . Drake Oil."

"Reckon I don't follow," I said, tilting up my imaginary cowboy hat. I decided I had on boots and spurs. A female deputy detective.

"For a bite of your éclair," I said to her, "I'll tell you."

I took a bite out of the phantom detective's phantom éclair. And noted that my hunger level was starting to get to me.

"He started working for Drake Oil three years ago," I said.

"Who?" said the detective.

"My husband."

"I thought you said you were the one in oil."

"We both—"

"Skip the foo foo," said the detective. "Tell me facts. Just the facts. Three sentences. Go."

I was already a mile through the canyon, by my reckoning.

The clock was spinning unforgivingly in my head. My imaginary detective had no patience. So I got to the point.

"Once upon a time this really awesome chick with a sharp wit and tendency to say exactly what she thinks met a man named Aaron Cooper, who made her heart glow. Like E.T.'s finger would glow. We both had...*have*...a love of the great outdoors. I was doing geological survey work for oil drilling and he was doing legal work out in the field. We had noble aspirations to help make the world a better..."

"Ma'am."

"Sorry. The point is that soon I became a full-time mom. And my husband got promoted at Drake Oil. And I never thought I'd be up against murderers." I started to lose my train of thought. "What could my husband mean about trust?"

"What?" said the detective.

"Trust. Who I'd trust. What did he mean?"

More important than answers is keeping my family safe. The only assurance of that was to keep the wolves as far away from the front yard as possible.

"You can trust whoever earns it," said the detective.

* * *

As badly as I wanted to go back to Sierra and Aaron, interrogate him about what he'd meant by his cryptic warnings, I decided to steer my enemies in the other direction. If I'd identified the voices correctly, there had to be at least one left. And if he, or they, were following me, tracking me, listening to me, then I was now devoted to keeping them up north.

I turned immediately to march in that direction. I didn't walk to stay hidden. I walked to move fast. *Find the highway. Find the cop.* I guessed that it would be three miles, but took shortcuts wherever the topography would allow it. Cutting across the rock face. Occasionally jogging. And with that determination I wound up all the way on the north rim of the canyon.

Daylight was waning. Ugly things were happening all around me and I was pretending I was fine with that. I was pretending I could chitchat with imaginary cops and that I hadn't killed two people. Most of all, I was pretending I wasn't terrified out of my mind. The truth was if I let reality hit me, I would crumple.

So I had to lie to myself, had to think that I could make things work out. When darkness had undeniably fallen, I found some scrub that I could sleep in that would hide me well enough. It wouldn't hide me from the cold, but I was less worried about the cold than the bullets. I was worried about Aaron and Sierra, of course, but I had to assume they were safe in the cave. I didn't think there was any way that I would sleep— but the events of the day had taken their toll, and I was soon dreaming of food and water and big koala hugs.

CHAPTER 14

AFTER SOME AMOUNT of time I awoke. Maybe it had all been a dream! But no, here I was in a maze of tall, slender rock formations, short coffee-less minutes after waking. It was dangerous to be up here, a treacherous jungle gym of limestone, but it was worth it. I'd found a vantage point to finally behold: the Grail.

Up ahead in the distance was Highway 89, strewn gloriously across the desert like an umbilical cord to salvation.

I'd never been so happy to see concrete. Cars zipped by in the distance—happy families on their happy ways. It was a giddy feeling of hope I hadn't experienced in quite some time. It was intoxicating, mental bliss. And it was precisely what got me in trouble.

There were voices around me. Men. Nearby. I hadn't noticed until it was too late. Two men. Getting louder. Getting closer. Even from my vantage point, I couldn't see where they were but I could hear one shouting directions to the other. And I soon caught his name.

"Clay! Down this way?"

"No, go uphill from where you are," shouted Clay. "Can't you see the one stack that's in shadow?"

Clay was the man in charge. They must've gotten lost, or sep-arated.

"Where?" shouted the guy who wasn't Clay. "I can't see it."

They were practically on top of me. There'd be no turning around without getting caught. Thankfully, they couldn't see each other or me, although I did manage to catch a glimpse of Clay. He was clean-cut, corporate, athletic, matching the smart rasp in his voice. Seemingly not a mercenary like the first two I'd met . . . but still paralyzed me with fear.

They had guns. And I didn't.

But they didn't *know* I didn't.

I had an opportunity, albeit a scary one. I took a deep breath. I needed my voice to reverberate throughout the cathedral of rocks and throughout their souls. I would need those men to tremble. I would need them to believe I was pointing a rifle at them.

So I cleared my throat, steeled my voice, and bellowed my opening gambit. *"Move and I'll kill you."*

CHAPTER 15

THEY BOTH STOPPED talking. After an eternity I heard some quick, quiet scrambling. Then total silence.

My heart was pounding so loud I was sure they would echolocate me by its beat. I couldn't see Clay, but I knew he was across the rock colony, about thirty feet away from me. Eventually I could hear him again. He was quietly guiding his partner around the maze with shrill whispers.

All three of us were now blindly situated in a deadly game of Marco Polo.

I kept track of their chatter and managed to intercept some of his hushed commands, thereby piecing together my own plan of attack: how to move, where to move, when to move. I had the upper hand. From my hidden perch, I would give them enough phony clues to convince them I was watching the whole time. Then, with clever wording, I could get them to put their guns on the ground and back away.

Brilliant, right?

Wrong.

Suddenly, I looked around to realize that *I* was the one being gamed. Clay was baiting *me,* knowing that I could hear his last round of whispering. He was just loud enough that I could catch his details, not loud enough that it was obvious.

He'd lured me to crawl into what I now saw was a central cluster of the rock formation. He'd orchestrated our rendezvous.

I was in serious trouble.

I expected him to get quiet now that he had me where he wanted, but he talked directly to me.

"Miranda," he said. Not shouting but projecting. Like a Greek orator. Saying my name like a dad would say it, like he was addressing his teenage kid who was caught sneaking back into the house at 2 a.m.

"Miranda," he repeated.

I didn't answer.

"My name is Clay Hobson."

He couldn't see me. Though he ensnared me, he still didn't know exactly where I was or whether I was armed. It was a miracle he and his pet thug hadn't stormed my nook. If they did, both of them at once, I'd be cornered in broad daylight. It'd be over.

But they weren't coming.

"I'm not here to hurt you," said Clay.

Yeah, right, you can fertilize the lawn with that one.

"I'm not here to hurt your family, Miranda."

He was playing verbal chess.

"I'm here to help," he added. "We both are."

I was too scared to retort but I couldn't afford to stay quiet. I needed to assert some kind of competitive quality. My silence was a giant white flag, being waved like a sheet of Kleenex, indicating I was weak.

"I'm Clay and my partner's name is Terrence Unger. We're worried about your husband."

"You can fertilize the lawn!" I yelled.

He went quiet. The lawn? That was *not* what I wanted to

say. That was the worst phrase possible. I strained to listen for them trading more instructions, but I could only hear the nearby rapids, which certainly didn't help. Every splash and babble seemed to have Clay's communications hidden within it.

"Miranda." He finally spoke up again. "I'm sorry about the other two gentlemen you met. They were hostile to you. And that's inexcusable. The truth is—"

"If you touch my daughter, I'll kill you!" I shouted.

"Not everyone in our little group is agreeing on how to proceed," he finished. "Yes, absolutely, if I touch your daughter, please kill me. I'm not here to do anything but help you and help your daughter. And especially help Aaron. Where is Aaron?"

Directly north.

That's what I wanted to say—the opposite of where he really was. But I knew this statement would be too elementary. Clay would have to assume I'm suggesting the opposite direction. He would go south. And he would find my family.

"Miranda?" shouted Clay.

Then he stopped talking. The other guy—his partner, or goon, or rent-a-thug—was quietly asking about something that almost sounded like the word *dynamite*.

"Wish we had some of that dynamite here," he murmured.

Dynamite?

"It's at the ranch," Clay murmured back. "With Branch. Wish we could use it on that strike."

Dynamite for what? And what's the branch he mentioned? What kind of strike were they planning?

"Miranda, do you need food?" said Clay loudly.

I didn't have a wristwatch but I could tell our standoff had been going on for a while.

"We have food," he added. "Do you need some?"

The stalemate was seductive. Simply the opportunity to eat something felt irresistible. Yet as we kept talking in circles, I was beginning to realize Clay's game was deadlier than I thought. It was only after the third round of silence that I pinpointed it but I could hear him mumbling very quietly again, which I'd assumed was to his partner, but he wasn't talking to him.

Clay was on the phone. Clay had *been* on the phone.

"Where is Aaron?" he randomly said aloud to me again, this time in an even nicer tone than before. Then he resumed murmuring.

A phone call. He must have been using a satellite phone, like we used when doing survey work in remote locations.

Clay wasn't playing mind games to get me to move, he was manipulating me to keep me still.

CHAPTER 16

I PROBABLY SHOULD'VE been more strategic. I could have waited a moment and at least calculated some defensive geometry. But I jumped up and left, with no plan or preparation. I jumped up and sprinted.

My new friend Clay Hobson had been summoning his extra troops. He'd pinned me down and held me at bay while he gathered his forces. I cursed myself for being so gullible.

But now I was sprinting full speed in the opposite direction. Away from the highway.

The game had changed. The call had changed everything. I had to get to Aaron and Sierra.

Call it willpower. Call it fear. Call it ovaries. The point is I ran so hard that I stopped caring about things like pain and air. My leg muscles were scalding, my lungs were screaming, but I didn't care. I ignored it.

I came stumbling up the crags, stumbling toward the cave entrance, and nearly collapsed. Only now did I notice that my leg was bleeding. So was my mouth, actually. I'd dry-heaved so hard—gasping for breath, failing to swallow, failing to dampen the palate—that I scorched the back of my throat. I spat blood. I was far from caring.

I was 100 percent preoccupied with the cave I'd finally reached, worried—no, terrified—that I'd be walking into a tomb. They'd spent a night in here and I was ready to find a mortified child huddled over a stiff corpse with a single, diagonal beam of sunlight cracking through the darkness from above, illuminating them like a medieval painting.

And that's exactly what I saw. Minus the sunbeam. Minus the corpse.

"Mommy!" said Sierra from the far corner of the darkness. She jumped up, dissolving into tears.

We embraced for what must've been a three-week hug. She clamped onto my chest and I looked across the cave to find Aaron looking back at me. He'd been asleep until Sierra's joy had roused him, energized him. I can only imagine the fear they'd felt since I'd left.

As I gathered Sierra in my arms and approached my husband, I could see that his cheerful disposition was a facade. He was in bad shape. His skin was ghostly pale and there was a hollow quality to his eyes. I'd been the one fistfighting all day, but it seemed like he took every one of the blows. He looked a decade older than he did yesterday. The happy man who was in the back seat of the minivan with my daughter, navigating the kangaroo galaxy, was barely in the same cave with us now. He was a stranger.

"M . . . randa," he said.

The whole run back I'd been tallying up a million questions for him that, under normal circumstances, I would've launched into with guns blazing. As if anything about any of this was normal.

"I'm here for you," I said to him. No questions. Just love.

"You found . . . ?" he struggled to speak. "You found them?"

It took a moment for me to understand what he meant.

"Yes," I replied.

"They tried..."

"To kill me? Yes."

"Then we ha...Then we have some...talking...to do." Every syllable a struggle.

"No."

"Cases..."

"Not now, babe."

"I can...explain." He gathered himself. "Drake. I saw...I've been trying...to find a way to..."

"Aaron, not now." I had to interrupt this. I couldn't let him drain his precious resources. "Listen. If you love me..." Yes, I was pulling the *if you love me* card. "If you love me...then you'll do what I'm about to tell you. No questions asked."

He answered without hesitation. "Anything."

My true ally.

"You want me to wear leather chaps?" said Aaron. "And a cowboy hat?"

"No," I replied.

"I'll do it. If that's your thing."

Oh, suddenly now he has perfect speech?

"My thing is brains," I said. "You know that."

"Brains and a leather hat." He was trying to crack a smile.

Men.

Sierra hadn't left my arms since I'd returned.

"Sierra, help me lift Daddy's legs," I said as I shot Aaron a single-upturned-eyebrow glare. "You know our very impressionable four-year-old daughter is listening."

It was reassuring to know that even in the worst of circumstances, we were still the biggest flirts of all time.

"Save your strength," I whispered.

"Don't yell at a dying man," he said, his smile just shy of a grimace.

"You are *not* dying."

We all went still. I'd raised my voice for the first time perhaps in years. Before I could go on, he mustered all his strength and spoke clearly.

"I know this doesn't make any sense. And these guys are . . . no joke. But I trust that you . . . can protect Sierra."

I didn't want him to keep going.

But he had more. "You're smarter than them, Miranda. You're the smartest person I know."

I hate compliments like that, praise from blind faith. I hate them and love them.

He added, "You just tend to doubt yourself."

"Yeah," said Sierra.

"Now," said Aaron, shifting gears. "What is this horrible thing you're about to ask me to do? Eat broccoli?"

I took a deep breath and looked over at our daughter. She had her hair in a loose, half-finished side-braid. She learned it on the internet last month. This would not be easy for them. It wasn't even easy for me to think.

"I need you to climb," I said. "I need you to climb."

CHAPTER 17

THEY WERE COMING, I explained to Aaron and Sierra. The bad men were preparing to converge on our little sanctuary. The cave was no longer safe.

I knew it was now or never.

"Okay. We can do this," said Aaron.

"Me, too," said Sierra.

Within minutes I'd gathered up my two ambassadors to begin the hobble. We each drank from the canteen. Getting Aaron to his feet was more about courage than muscle. He seemed about ten terrifying pounds lighter than when I last saw him. He barely stood upright, even with my support. Sierra could topple him just by tugging on his sleeve.

"We have only one shot at this," I began my speech. "We have to get their car."

He didn't respond.

I continued. "Clay Hobson. We have to get the SUV he was in. I'm guessing they parked somewhere on the stretch of road above our wreck. If it's still there, it's our one chance."

I glanced at his face. I had already composed the rebuttal to his upcoming rebuttal.

"Believe me, I looked," I said. "I looked for a random car, for a cop, a hiker, pay phone, a wad of promising trash. Anything. Any hope. I tried the roads. I tried to get to 89, but Clay blocked the way."

Aaron's face was unmoved. I don't know if it was stoicism or loss of blood, but his reaction was as calm as could be expected.

"You've gotta get to the SUV. If you follow the river upstream past where we crashed, there's a steep grade leading up to where we went off the highway. It's going to be a tough climb, but it's our only chance."

"If my wife wants me to climb..." he said with a smile, "then, ladies and gentlemen, I'm climbing."

Sierra was walking alongside us. She would normally get carried by him across terrain like this. But Aaron wouldn't have enough strength. So I crouched down to be eye level with my new lieutenant.

"Hey little koala, how are you and your cute paws?"

"Okay," said Sierra.

"Thank you for being a good nurse. Now I'm going to promote you to Minister of Security and Transportation. Can you handle that job?"

"Okay."

I looked up at Aaron and smiled at him.

His voice was undeniably grim. "You're not coming with us, are you?" I could hear him trying to hide his concern.

I felt so sorry for them.

"I've mulled it over a thousand ways," I replied. "This is the only one that has a chance."

"Your Transport Minister doesn't approve," he joked. Half joking.

Sierra looked up at him and then over at me. She's the world's feistiest four-year-old, but you'd never guess it here. She seemed to sense the intensity of the situation even through our veiled updates.

I kissed her and stood up. As much as I hated to part ways, I turned around and started my journey.

"Wait," said Aaron. "Why head to the SUV if we can't even unlock the door?"

I knew my answer would lead to more questions and none of us had the time, nor the blood sugar for it, so I replied without turning back. "Because I'm gonna go get the keys."

CHAPTER 18

THEY WENT ONE way. I went the other. If you drew it in the dirt, you'd have a diagram that looked like a badly written V. Actually, a curvy V. Like a bird, sort of.

I didn't want to turn around to look. I was denying finality, and looking back meant capturing a mental image that I couldn't afford to fixate on.

But several minutes later I couldn't stop myself.

They were a half mile away from me, my poor, slow-moving duo.

I teared up. I knew I would.

They put their entire trust in me and were doing the impossible. Against medical wisdom, and self-preserving instinct, they limped along.

I watched them disappear. And then I started bawling. Hard.

Suck up the tears, babe. No jeopardizing the mission now. I had my agenda and my work cut out for me.

The plan was to get to the SUV driver's body. Hopefully they hadn't moved it, hopefully his keys were still in his pocket. Get the keys and run like I have never run to get back.

It was still lying where he died, at the bottom of the grade,

313

surrounded by the rocks that had ended his life. I felt horrible all over again, but was relieved to see that animals hadn't found him—yet.

I had a tremendous, unintentional shiver as I patted his pockets, doing everything I could not to look at him, not to breathe in.

"Looking for these?"

My heart stopped.

Clay Hobson stood there, keys held out, jingling slightly.

I had to think. Fast. I stood up, held my hands up to show I meant no harm. "I'm just trying to get my daughter and get out of here. I know my husband did things! I know that now! I wanted the keys to drive me and my daughter to the police station!"

They stayed still. I expected more smooth talking from Clay, but he was simply standing there, staring at me.

It was the other guy who spoke first. Which was odd. *He* was odd. Agitated.

He turned to Clay and said, "She's lying." Then he turned to me and said, "You're lying!" He aimed his rifle right at me.

But Clay chimed in. "Terrence!" I hoped, his way of saying *don't*.

"Get on your knees!" he shouted at me, his rifle emphasizing his fury. He was thrusting it toward me, like a jab with an invisible bayonet. "On! Your! Knees!"

While Terrence kept his gun aimed, Clay made a show of slinging his rifle onto his back. I kept my hands halfway up. I absolutely did not want to provoke unnecessary bullets in my direction. No, thank you. My hands were going to remain very visible.

"Don't shoot her, Terrence," said Clay, calmly, authoritatively.

"Then tell her not to move."

"Miranda?" said Clay. "Nice to meet you face-to-face. Please don't move."

"I won't," I said, beginning to kneel. "My husband is mortally wounded. I'm here to negotiate. In fact…" I cleared my throat. "I already have a proposition that you won't want to refuse."

"Liar!" said Terrence, who was clearly on edge.

"Relax, Terrence," said Clay.

"I'm on your team, Miranda," he said. "I'm willing to compromise in every way possible. But I need you to take me to Aaron first. That's the only condition on my end.

"The reason is timing. We don't have time," Clay continued. "No, wait, let me rephrase that. Your husband doesn't have time. As you said, he's mortally wounded. I need him to be alive to fight the good fight. And you need him alive because he's the father of your child."

There was no way I could take Clay with me to Aaron. I'd be powerless if something went wrong.

"He needs a doctor," I said.

"She doesn't trust you, Clayton," murmured Terrence.

"She's a wise woman," said Clay, looking directly at me. Talking about me while talking *to* me. "She needs me to convince her."

He held his knife outward for me to see it. It looked like he was going to lay it down as a peace offering.

He raised his knife. He was behind Terrence, so it almost looked like he was going to poke him with it. For just a half second, I wondered if he would, a delirious thought. Because that would make no sense at all.

Yet that is exactly what he did.

Clay Hobson plunged his knife into the neck of his partner.

CHAPTER 19

TERRENCE SLUMPED FORWARD onto his knees. I didn't move. I didn't scream. All I could do was stare as a large stream of dark red liquid began to cascade down his chest, shining in the sunlight.

I was still down, so now the two of us were kneeling mere yards away, facing each other, like some sort of bizarre warrior ritual. The blade was lodged. As Terrence reached back to grab the handle, he found that he couldn't even raise his arms. All he could do was look at me. Toward me.

Why?

Clay must have seen it on my face. *Why did you stab your friend?*

"To protect you," answered Clay without my asking.

He stepped forward and withdrew the blade from Terrence's neck. I was watching close, petrified. He looked up and held my gaze. Then he seemed to recognize my fear and tossed it on the ground, seemingly in demonstration of a truce.

"I never wanted it to come to this," he said. He was about to bare his soul. I could feel it. "Sadly, these are the forces we're up against."

Exhibit A. He gestured toward Terrence's body. Exhibit B. The body of the SUV driver. Exhibit C. The body floating down the river.

"Aaron and I..." he said. "We're facing powers well beyond our control. I had to find the right moment. Terrence wanted to kill you, and I desperately needed to protect Aaron."

I was trembling. "W-what is this?" I asked, referring to the entirety of the debacle. The company. The men. My husband. The history. Everything.

"There isn't time," he replied. "We have to hurry."

Terrence was on the ground, facedown. It was over for him.

I felt sick, despite the fact that this wasn't even the first dead body I'd seen on this wonderful vacation. Clay used a booted foot to push him over, and it rolled with a strange limpness. There's something rather vacant about a corpse, the way the shoulder flops over. The feet surrender. The expressionless face.

Clay kneeled, inspecting the body. I doubted it was easy for him to do what he did, but it was hard to detect telltale signs of a conscience in Clay. He seemed fine.

He looked over to tell me the heavy words I knew were eventually coming.

"Aaron's not innocent."

I didn't have a response.

"But he's a good man," he continued. "And you'll need my help if you want to bring him to a doctor."

He let that sit for a second. He stood up. *Need his help? His help?* I was suspicious but I knew I had no choice.

"A doctor?" I questioned.

"The clock's ticking."

I had to oblige him. In all these outlandish happenings, it made sense that the only way out was an outlandish offer.

"All right," I said. "But on one condition."

"Name it."

317

"The keys to the SUV...I carry them."

He dug in his pocket and tossed them to me. No hesitation. He was willing to do whatever I wanted.

I had more to say, more to demand. "The rifle...I hold it."

There was a natural pause here but I hit him with a third condition before he could object.

"And you..." I said. "You keep in front of me."

He weighed his options, looking across the canyon and the river, with so many nooks and crannies where one might hide. He stepped forward, closer to me but not intrusively so. I nodded to the river. He seemed to know immediately what I meant. We'd be hiking upstream.

I slung the rifle over my shoulder. The upper hand was mine now. It was tangible. Not because of the weapon, but because of the map in my head.

"Let's go," I said to him.

"Let's go save lives," he said back.

CHAPTER 20

I GUIDED CLAY through the canyon without saying anything other than where to turn. Dark thoughts were swarming around my soul like flies on a carcass. Aaron isn't innocent. Aaron may have hurt people. Aaron hid something.

"Veer toward the crest," I said to Clay.

You start a marriage with two eyes open, you stay in it with one eye closed. This is the standard advice. Yet had I proceeded along with *both* eyes closed? Was I also wearing earplugs? And a sensory deprivation suit? Did I know my husband at all?

I finally spoke up about a half hour into our hike. "Okay, fine, let's hear it," I said. "What sort of cataclysmic thing could you and Aaron be involved in?" I had a thousand questions, but needed to ask him things without *telling* him things.

"Oil," replied Clay.

We were hiking across the eastern vista, in the midst of the most spectacular sedimentary erosion I'd ever seen. Everything out here looked like a beautiful forgery of the Grand Canyon. If only I were in a place to enjoy it.

"Oil," I scoffed.

"The answer to ninety-nine out of a hundred questions."

"Is money."

"Is oil," he insisted.

My rifle was pointed at his back. I know there's safety proto-col to weapons and triggers and where you aim, but I was done being safe. If I accidentally tripped on a pebble and shot him in the spinal cord, so be it. I'd apologize in the eulogy.

"Did your husband ever tell you about the case of *Drake v. Llorenzo*?"

"No."

"That family?"

"No."

"From the town of Chasm? *Drake v. Llorenzo?* He really never told you?"

"Keep facing forward."

I was lying. Aaron had told me, but I wasn't intending to trust Clay yet. I needed to keep my guard up. Both verbally and phys-ically.

"Llorenzo's family got long-term illnesses from a water supply polluted by fracking," he said. "Drake Oil's fracking lines."

It was a legendary litigious nightmare spanning years. Clay knew every nuance of it and retold the chronology well enough for me to believe he was at least *part* of Aaron's legal department, or had been well briefed. The trial controversially ended when the Llorenzo family was exposed for taking bribes from a rival corporation. Another oil company was bribing Llorenzo to fabri-cate the entire lawsuit. The whole case was exposed as a lie. That was the brilliant Drake defense team at work. That's what won.

"I don't see how this is news," I replied when he finished.

"Ah, okay, good. So you're up to date," said Clay. "So what you probably *don't* know . . . what Aaron probably *hasn't* told you . . . is that those bribes never happened."

"You mean Drake fabricated the bribes?"

"Drake fabricated the *family*."

He was no longer the requisite twelve feet ahead of me on the trail. I'd dropped my guard. I'd completely lost focus on our spacing.

Fabricated the family?

"I don't get it," I said to him.

"Our legal team found a father of three who was willing to say he was sick."

"Even though he wasn't? Sick?" This made no sense. "So Drake invented its own fake case? Against itself?"

He was walking alongside me. My gun was no longer safely defending my personal bubble. He could've easily done something to me during this time. He could've strangled me, pushed me down, and disarmed me. I'd been completely distracted by his claim.

"It's a con game," he said. "We called it a false god. You control your enemy by controlling their hero: you *create* their hero . . . then you humiliate their hero."

"Why?"

"So you can make sure one big case, just one, will lose exactly the way you need it to. And when that case loses, it sets a precedent for all other cases to lose. It sways public opinion. It sways juries. It's unstoppable."

"How would you pull that off?"

"Pay everyone. Pay opposing lawyers. Pay the clerks. The cops. Judges. The hardest judge is the first one. But once a few are in, the pressure to conform is enormous. And contagious." Then he looked over at my face to mention something he knew would jar it. "Like the bonus Aaron got last year. The $145,000."

He saw me react. I tried to stay unperturbed. But the mention of that $145,000 wasn't easy to hide.

"Then what does that make *us*?" I said, half rhetorically. "What does that make you?"

"Drake is a monster. I work for them. So . . ." Then came an honest, grave, uninflected admission. "I'm a monster. Aaron isn't."

He talked a good game. Too good. His spin was so potent I didn't even care if he was conning me anymore.

"But I'm trying to makes amends," he added. "I'm here to help him. I was lucky to be recruited on this hunt but not lucky enough to be put in charge of it. So I had to be patient before making a move."

I decided to take a risk. "Who's Jed?"

He scrutinized me again. The gears turning in his head.

"You mean Jedediah," he said. "He's a retired judge. Drake has leases on his property for some of our fracking sites."

"So Jed is helping," I concluded.

"No, Miranda." He stopped to look me deep in the eye. "Let me make this crystal clear: you can't trust Jed."

I didn't respond. I didn't tell him to keep moving. I didn't need to. We had arrived.

We could now see the site where our minivan had crashed. All four wheels were belly-up, facing the sky. The vehicle had been drenched, jostled, twisted ten degrees, carried, scraped, then dumped back on the silt of the same bank several yards downstream.

It definitely looked like a crime scene, though.

"They were at the wreck?" asked Clay, scanning the area in front of us. "They were at the wreck the whole time?"

I kept him in front of me for the final few steps. I wanted to monitor his reactions. I wanted to see if he licked his lips with a thirst for vengeance, or was genuine in wanting to talk to Aaron.

"Here?" he asked again, almost squeaking the word. His incredulity mirrored a growing, nagging, terrifying fear that was welling up within me.

I was about to find out if they made it. If they had an accident. Or worse.

Or if they made it to the SUV, but someone was waiting for them when they got there.

CHAPTER 21

I STARTED SHOUTING for them. "Aaron! Aaaaaaarrrrron!" I repeated the refrain as I stood looking up the cliff face, hoping for any signs of life.

"I thought you said he was here," said Clay.

I continued to scan the cliff, and that's when I saw it: a small purple smudge about halfway up.

"What...is...?" I muttered to myself.

Her little kangaroo hat, lodged up in the rock. Which could only be up there if—

"Sierra!" I shouted.

Clay turned around and saw me looking up.

"Aaron!" I shouted.

"So they climbed up," said Clay. He brushed past me, leaving me in his dust.

He was already on his way.

I ran after him. Soon I was ahead of him. He chose one route. I chose the other. Within minutes we were vertical. I tried to peer downward, directly along the vertical face to inspect the long, thin pocket space that ran along the foothills.

"Aaron!" I shouted upward, past Clay, into the elongated void.

No response.

Clay didn't stop, and soon our two routes began to converge. They started out parallel but around the halfway point they angled into each other. He wouldn't look at me. You'd think it was the shame of knowing he'd betrayed me, but I caught sight of a cocky smile.

Without even glancing over he said, "You're not gonna get there before me, Miranda," he said.

He was a genuine climber, too. Perhaps better than I was.

"If you were *really* an ally," I replied, "you'd call out for him."

I started to outpace my rival. I was taking more chances than he was, reaching for holds beyond my normal span. But Clay kept up.

"You're not calling out to him," I continued, "because you don't want him to know that you're with me."

I was gradually forming a new theory. I didn't think Mr. Clay Hobson was simply ordered to do the job of attacking my husband. I didn't think this entire day was merely an assignment. The truth was that my nemesis, hovering twenty feet to my seven o'clock, was directly implicated in whatever ugly history they all shared. This wasn't a job—it was personal.

"Aaron!" I again shouted upward. "Run!"

CHAPTER 22

I WAS ABOUT fifteen feet ahead of Clay. I would have to use that advantage as soon as I reached the top. If only I had some hot water or oil.

He wasn't taking any chances. He freed up his right hand, pried loose a small rock, and threw it at me. I thought there was no way it'd actually—

"Ow!" I screamed, as the rock hissed into my hand.

He'd tagged me directly on the knuckles. A one-in-a-hundred shot. The pain was instant, loosening my grip, but it was a miss for my opponent. He was aiming for my head.

I looked down toward him. Thirty feet behind me now—but he'd chosen his route badly and had hit a dead end. He'd have to go down and over to my route and, maybe in a few minutes, catch up with me. But he readied another rock to throw.

I had the rifle on my back. I remembered when I fired it into the air, the recoil. My shoulder was still sore. If I tried shooting it now, it would knock me off the wall. Thinking about the gun, I lost concentration, promptly losing the foothold under my left toe.

I started to fall.

I swung half a pendulum arc, my body anchored only by my middle three fingers on my right hand as I lost three of my four holds. Pebbles crumbled from where my feet were, a hundred feet down to the crevasse below me. My rifle strap slid off my shoulder, down my torso, past my legs, and sailed toward the abyss, ricocheting off the cliff face, past where Clay might have caught it midair—no chance, although he did try—before spinning into the trench below.

We both paused for a moment.

He broke the silence. "Let's stop and think, Miranda. I believe we may have a misunderstanding."

I could see the look in his eyes. There was no misunderstanding. He was a demonic tarantula crawling up from below relentlessly. I'd originally thought we were evenly matched. I was wrong. He was immensely better at this. He had chosen a bad route, but was now rushing up behind me with a violent focus.

Bloodlust.

Then he made a move I didn't see coming.

"Aaron!" he yelled upward.

What is he doing?

"*Aaron Cooper!*" he yelled again.

I kept climbing.

"Your wife is coming to kill you, Aaron!"

What?!

"She thinks you betrayed her!"

He's insane. Did he actually think this would work? I started accelerating my climb even faster than its already uncomfortable speed. I took risks that required not looking down. "Don't listen to him!" I shouted upward.

"She's lost her mind, Aaron!" he yelled. "Protect Sierra! Because Miranda is coming to kill you!"

My husband would never believe this. Though, in his delirious state...I scrambled over the edge in an ungraceful lunge, then stood by the road getting my bearings. I grabbed the purple kangaroo hat. My predator was no more than thirty seconds behind me on the trek. I'd need every nanosecond of that margin.

Go!

The black SUV was parked down the road. I vaulted the guardrail and sprinted directly for it. I was of course profoundly relieved to see it there, but also instantly reminded that this vehicle was the source of my misery.

No matter, it was a sight for sore eyes. This model came with all the options I ever wanted: Aaron and Sierra!

As I got closer, stumbling my last few steps, I could see the two of them lying against the rear wheel. When I sent them up here, it had seemed impossible. I don't know if I actually believed they could make it. But there they were, delivered as promised. One napping daughter and one still-intact husband.

"Get inside!" I shouted at them. *"Get inside!"*

Clay was just making his way over the guardrail, only ten seconds behind me. I fumbled for the keys and the unlock button. Aaron and Sierra started to stir, roused by my voice, but gradually, too gradually for my liking. I arrived like a train wreck, my own momentum slamming me against the rear door on the driver's side. I yanked it open to shove (as gently as I could) the wobbling Aaron into the interior, throwing Sierra in his lap. I flung open the driver's door and jumped in, cranking the ignition just as the rear window was shattered.

Clay had found a rock—probably forged from his own kidney stones—to smash the window. He was already thrusting his arms into the back seat, attempting to grab my husband by the collar.

"Daddy!" cried Sierra, seeing her father about to get yanked into the clutches of pure evil.

I stomped on the gas and gunned it. Clay's arms retreated

as the SUV rocketed forward, and we finally hit the road at full speed. I wanted to make Clay appear in my rearview mirror and shrink.

And he did. Just as two white vans emerged in the distance behind him. His reinforcements.

CHAPTER 23

THE SPEED LIMIT was fifty on this treacherous desert road. I was doing eighty-five. Barely paying attention to handling the turns, I only cared about making the little white dots in my rearview mirror shrink.

Both vans had stopped to pick up their overlord, then quickly regained their cruising speed. I was mesmerized by the rearview mirror. I lost focus on the road before I corrected my swerve, fishtailed a bit, and steadied. *Miranda, you've officially been issued a second chance to get this right.*

To steer into the skid.

I banked hard on the next turn. It was a tight enough curve that it was marked with a road sign in cautionary yellow. SPEED LIMIT 45 MPH.

I took it at a hundred.

The back tires squealed as our entire SUV tilted toward the cliff. Not decisively so, but enough for me to dig my fingernails into the supple, calfskin, optional leather-covered steering wheel.

The white vans weren't slowing down at all. In fact, the closer one was a turn behind me as we slalomed along the S-curves.

"Hold on tight, please," I said to my cargo.

I lowered my glance at the rearview mirror to peek into the back seat at Aaron. He looked sickly pale, his skin was a blank, white canvas for a wife's deepest fears.

"I'm gonna find us a hospital," I said to him.

I started fumbling for the air-conditioning switch. These brand-new SUVs have monstrously elaborate control panels. It looked like NASA in there. Temperature. Humidity. Angle. Dual. Custom.

"Babe, there's gotta be a bottle of water somewhere."

He didn't answer. There was an orange backpack on the seat next to me, which I started to dig through, filled with hard paper rods. No water.

"Babe?" I said.

"I can find it, Mommy," Sierra spoke up.

Before I could caution her not to roam the interior of a vehicle that's careening around cliff roads, she was up and about, crawling over the headrest, so that her tiny bottom filled my rearview mirror for a moment. And just behind her, flying out of the previous turn we just finished, I could see something terrifying.

The first white van. Directly behind us. With passengers. With guns.

My hand fumbled across the air-conditioning panel, inadvertently scraping the radio volume knob upward. I grabbed the wheel with both hands and floored it, as music started blaring— Johnny Cash's "Ring of Fire"—while our SUV roared down the road at one hundred five miles per hour.

We thoroughly skidded at *every* turn. The back of the vehicle fishtailed and I'd correct it by guiding the front wheels toward the potential danger. It worked. We stayed in control.

But so did the white vans, which apparently had less to lose than we did, because they both dared every law of physics. Every maneuver, every curve—they were gaining on us.

And soon they were on either side.

"Mommy!"

Out came those guns. On my left, a man leaned out of the passenger window, wielding a nasty-looking contraption that fired more bullets than I ever wanted to know about.

BRATATATATAT! Either it was a warning shot or his aim was bad, but I could see the bullets whiz by in front of my windshield, and I didn't want to find out.

I'm sure the best move would've been to slam on my brakes and have him magically end up shooting the other van. That's how it works in cartoons, but I'm just not that kind of animated rabbit. Instead I jolted the steering wheel sharply to the left and slammed our SUV against the passenger door he was shooting from.

We bounced into the van and would've lost control had I not escalated the maneuver by swerving back across the road into the other guy for stabilization.

Wham!

Our SUV thus corrected its course and remained centered down the stretch of road, as the vehicles on either side of me lost traction. The first van wiggled, slowing him down so he was now slightly behind us; the other scraped the rock face and, to my shock and delight, careened back into the first one.

Now the two vans were meeting in my rearview mirror. And at a hundred miles per hour, that wasn't a simple collision.

This would buy us at least five minutes.

I sped up to one hundred twenty-five miles per hour. I had to assume they'd resume the chase, if they could, when they could. I didn't know what the capacity of my engine was but I knew my tires were shaking. Big, oafish SUVs are not meant to go *triple* the speed limit. Yet, miraculously, within a few minutes we were emerging out of the canyons, beginning the hundred-mile downslope back toward civilization. I still shook with adrenaline, constantly checking my rearview mirror as the mountains gave way to hills and landscape broadened to wide-open space.

Finally arriving at the closest intersection with the highway, I saw a flimsy barricade shutting down access to the opposite lane. No wonder! This was already a desolate highway, but Clay had ensured total privacy.

"Mommy, this is water," said Sierra. She'd found a bottle, half full with its lovely, clear contents.

"Thanks, honey. Back in your seat. We're safe."

We weren't safe, yet. We still had to encounter our first normal human. The road ahead remained sparse, mile after mile. Empty. But I needed her to hear those words. And I needed to say them.

We needed a doctor, but also needed protection. Clay said not to trust Jed, and we obviously could not trust Clay, and Aaron said be careful who you trust, so I had no idea what else was in store.

As the land opened up I could finally see my way ahead. There were roadside stores, gas stations, signs of civilization, and finally a sign for a town: Chasm, Arizona. I knew it had a population of maybe a couple thousand people, seemingly spread throughout the hills on either side of the highway.

I was driving us to the only location I knew of. Our original destination before all this started. Jed's ranch.

CHAPTER 24

"SALVATION," I SAID to Aaron in the back seat.

He stirred.

We pulled into Jed's ranch, which was easy to find because it was the only settlement for miles. I remember how isolated it had looked on our map when we started the drive—what seemed like ten years ago.

There were two small oil derricks just inside the front gate. We drove in with a flurry of dust behind us, barely slowing down for the turn.

"Plant," he murmured.

"That's right, babe. We found it."

"I'm...I'm..." he said with slurred speech. "Plant."

He must've been delusional at this point. Sweaty. Dehydrated. He was incoherently pointing at the oil wells.

The ranch property was massive, deep enough that the front drive alone ran a half mile. Once in the main roundabout, there was a barn, a shed, a small industrial-looking building, a house, and five or six different oil derricks strewn across the hillside.

I drove straight for the house and screeched to a stop by the porch. I grabbed Sierra and clutched her to my chest.

"Aaron, I need to go find a phone. Or a human being. You're allowed to pass out once you're in an ambulance, okay? No passing out before that, okay?"

"Plant," he said. Again.

I kissed his knee, the closest thing I could access while holding our child and trying not to waste precious seconds. Then I hurried toward the main house. There was a pickup truck parked out front. Shiny, new. Even in my hurry, I couldn't help but notice how nice the porch was.

"Hello?" I hollered. I walked up to the front door and rang the bell.

"My name is Miranda. Hello?! Jedediah? Can you call 911?"

I rang it again. I waited an agonizing five seconds. Then I tried the knob, felt it turn, thank God, and opened the door.

"Hello! Jed?" I said again. I walked in. I could apologize later.

The house was big and pleasant. And devoid of people. No radio playing. No pasta steaming on the stove in the back.

"Anybody home?"

"Anybody home?" echoed Sierra, my assistant.

We crept in and wandered all the way to the back without seeing a single soul. We crossed a long hallway leading to the rear of the house. The place was immaculate. More like a museum than a residence. Everything was untouched.

In what looked like a sitting room, I saw a phone. A landline.

I rushed the last few steps to snatch it up. I must have dialed 911 about five times in a row before I truly listened to the receiver. It was dead. No hiss. No tone.

"Dead?" I exclaimed, turning to look around. *What's up with this place?* Panic began to set in.

Then I heard a clunk.

It came from the far end of the house. Some shuffling, then

another clunk. Somebody was opening drawers in a desk. Opening and slamming. Somebody was in a hurry.

"Hello?" I said again. "Jedediah?" I went toward the shuffling noise.

From the hallway, I saw him. He was standing right there. A big, grizzly man, with white hair. His back was to me. He didn't turn around.

None of this felt right. None of this looked right, smelled right, sounded right. He'd have to have heard me yelling in his house a moment ago, but seemed unaware of my presence.

I was far enough away to do the following. Based on pure instinct, I quietly turned to Sierra and I gestured *shhh*. She complied, seeing the look on my face. I nudged her gently toward the side room right beside me, a hiding spot.

Then the homeowner turned around and looked squarely at me. His expression was not friendly. Neither was the shotgun he was holding down by his side.

I was tired of meeting men in this way. That *this town ain't big enough for the two of us* macho manure. We should've hugged each other and danced around the living room in circles—that's how I'd pictured this meeting. But he was silent.

"Are you Jed?" I asked. "I'm Aaron Cooper's wife. I'm Miranda."

He was just watching me. Cold.

"C-can…" I stuttered. "Can I use your phone?"

He muttered, "Don't have one."

He doesn't have a phone?

"Look," I said. "I'm sorry to intrude. There's no need for a gun. Do you have a cell phone I could use? Aaron is hurt. Badly. Can you help me find Jed?"

He kept looking down at me. He stood six foot three, easily. Viking big. An older man, but one who could torque a lug nut with his bare hands.

What was he doing? My husband was going to die. We didn't have another house we could get to soon enough. We didn't have anyone else we could trust.

And then I looked behind him and noticed a phone line on the wall.

The line was cut. Severed. A fresh incision that wasn't made last year or last month; it was made two minutes ago. He saw me see it. He now knew that I knew that he wasn't a nice person.

He said, "I *am* Jed."

CHAPTER 25

JED HEADED FOR the front door. With his shotgun. Toward the SUV. Toward Aaron. "No!" I shouted. "Wait!"

He didn't stop. I knew he would figure out where Aaron was, if he hadn't already.

I felt helpless. I needed a gun. For someone who'd never even *held* a gun prior to yesterday, I certainly got addicted fast.

I picked up Sierra, moving her to safety and looking for the gun rack I knew had to be in the house somewhere. None in this room. None in the hallway.

"Can you wait for me here?" I said to Sierra.

"Yes, Mommy."

No weapons in the living room. My panic tripled. "Are you my little angel?"

"I'm your Mister."

"My...?" I asked, kicking open a back room door.

"Mister," she repeated. "Of Transportation."

She made me want to weep like a spigot. "Yes! I'll be right back, okay? I need to help Daddy."

Running to the kitchen for a knife, I looked out through the living room window and saw that Jed was already at the SUV.

"*Aaron!*" I screamed. It was like a TV screen whose channel couldn't be changed. I froze.

Jed had his shotgun aimed as he crept forward the last few steps to the car. The tinted window was up on this side of the vehicle, meaning he couldn't see inside, but he held his gun aimed directly at the back seat.

With no warning, *blam blam!*, he blasted two shots through the window.

"*No!*" I screamed.

He yanked open the door. I could see directly into the back seat where Aaron would be.

Where Aaron wasn't.

Jed was looking at an empty back seat. He leaned in to check the rear compartment, came back out and looked around. The structures on the ranch were spread out, with not many places to hide.

Where was my husband?! That was the pertinent question.

And then we got our answer.

Boom!

What sounded like a building being *thrown* into another building was actually a fiery explosion big and bright enough that even in the middle of the Arizona daylight, you could see the flash, toward the main gate. A fireball the size of a warehouse had just plumed. The derrick underneath it was now a geyser of fire.

Aaron apparently knows his way around an oil well.

CHAPTER 26

JED STOOD THERE gawking at the spectacle. It was nice to see someone else caught off guard for a change.

Then he started heading toward the mayhem, a man on a mission.

To whatever degree he'd previously wanted Aaron dead, it was imperative now. I saw him cock his shotgun as he stomped toward the flaming derrick. I frantically ran back through the house. If I hurried, I could intercept Jed.

I imagined Aaron would've set off the explosion, then hobbled over to some bush to collapse. I sprinted through the house and burst through the back door.

And that was as far as I'd have to go to collide with the love of my life.

Aaron and I banged into each other headfirst and both grunted.

"You . . . But . . . Which . . . Did . . . ?"

"How . . . ? I . . . If . . ."

Then I kissed him.

Passionately. Both of my hands gripping his collar. My body pressed against his. Which felt way better than I'll ever admit in a court of law.

Then we got down to business. He had the orange backpack from the SUV. Those rods I saw earlier—*duh, Miranda*—were sticks of dynamite. Should've known.

"Fear is an amazing motivator," he said.

"I thought that guy was a friend. That's Jed. Jed Branch. But we need to get out of here as fast as—"

He took a step forward then lurched and lowered himself to the ground. I crouched beside him immediately. "Aaron!"

"I'm . . . I'm so sorry," he said, the adrenaline wearing off, barely able to speak. "Last year I found . . . puzzle pieces . . . people getting sick, families asking questions. By the time this . . . this . . . awful picture emerged . . . they were killing anyone who knew even one percent of it. I couldn't risk . . . letting anyone know that I knew. Which meant . . . trying to protect you by . . ." He started to tear up. "By keeping it from you."

I had to get him out of here. But how?

"Babe, *babe,* listen." I had to keep him rational. "I know you did right by us. You're a good soul. You don't have to prove anything to me."

"No, that's my point," he said. He pulled me close enough to whisper urgently, which we didn't have time for and he knew it. "What I'm telling you is, I'm truly sorry."

"Aaron."

"For keeping you in the dark." His tears were streaming hard, nearly re-energizing him. "I was too scared . . . of how many people were tied to it. But that's no excuse. I was getting set to blow the whistle. I was. Today, in fact. At a labor strike here on the ranch. But I needed to hide you and Sierra. And Jed was the only ally. But Jed's actually . . . Jed's actually . . ."

An evil, backstabbing worm? I knew what he wanted to call Jed. I'd already met several members of his species this morning.

"Babe," I said, pulling him up to his feet. "You did something I could never hold against you. . . . You tried to keep our family safe. So now...if I get us through this day...we'll be even."

He hugged me. I was about to bawl. The hurricane of emotions was finally catching up to me. And he felt so good to hold. But this wasn't the moment.

"Now, we need to get out of here." I grabbed his hand and hurried him to the back. We burst in on Sierra, who instantly perked up. "Mommy! Daddy!" I already knew what must be done, and there wasn't a moment to spare. I grabbed his orange backpack.

"Wha...?" he said.

"Where is that labor strike?" I asked.

I loved his move of lighting up the derrick. It was a gargantuan middle finger to Jedediah. It was a brilliant way to create chaos. And, most of all, it was a beacon. Of hope. That fireball and its smoke, and now its continual fountain of flames, would be visible for miles around—in particular, for whoever was at the rally.

"Not far—on the other side of the canyon. Behind the ranch."

There were other derricks on this ranch, just up the hillside. While Jed would be dousing the rig that was on fire, I could ignite another, and then another, one by one, making my way toward the strike. Help was sure to come. It might not be an ambulance at first, but it would be somebody.

Bag in hand, I started heading out.

"Where are you going?" asked Aaron.

"To finish what you started."

CHAPTER 27

IF I COULD avoid the wide-open stretch between the main house and the barn, somehow dart between the trees or sneak behind the random tractors parked along the road, I could survive the trip.

But Jedediah was already returning with his shotgun.

I ran to the first outer corner of the house, then peered around the edge to monitor him. The hope was for my dear husband to find a new hiding place so that Jedediah, or whoever came next, wouldn't get to him so fast.

Uh-oh. Down the long drive, the white vans were roaring onto the ranch, dust rising behind them. Both battered vehicles came to a halt in the middle of the courtyard. "Whoever came next" was here.

Jedediah arrived as men jumped out—six, by my count—including Clay.

That was my cue. While they were distracted, I sprinted up the back area, up into the hillside toward the cluster of derricks.

These two days had taken their toll on my legs: they were now Jell-O, buckling beneath every step. But I didn't have the luxury of indulging in weakness. *Push, Mandy.*

Too many minutes later, I tumbled forward into a helpful ditch, then turned around to spy on the activity. Far below, the group had begun to disperse. I'd glanced backward midway through my run, catching glimpses of the men arming themselves with rifles and pistols, Jedediah in charge. He and Clay were gesturing around, probably cataloging all the places I could be hiding. But they deployed their legion of thugs toward the main house.

Where Aaron and Sierra were.

"Do not go in there," I muttered quietly through clenched teeth.

Time to move. I hustled over to the first derrick, twice as big as it looked from afar. A colossal robot arm angrily punching Mother Earth. I was only too happy to fish out my first stick of dynamite. I drew on years of fieldwork to calculate the most vulnerable spot.

Ten seconds later—*boom!*

I'd gotten clear but it was deafening. The blast knocked me over, flat on my face, welcoming me to the earth I was avenging. I rose to my hands and knees to look down the slope into the heart of the ranch. All seven gentlemen were now looking back up toward my handiwork. Good.

There were some shouts and gesticulations, then they started coming my way.

Bring it.

I wanted them to march up the hill. All of them at once. I could just run like a rabbit, deeper into the property, toward the derricks, toward the labor strike itself. The first explosion was several minutes ago. Whoever was over at the factory had to have heard something by now, and seen the smoke.

The thug team was getting its fresh orders from Jed. Jed was indeed in charge. Which meant Clay had played me well. *Don't trust Jed, Miranda.* He knew that if he lost my confidence, I'd run to whomever he'd told me *not* to trust. And I did just that. Right into his crystal-clear trap.

But Jed and Clay seemed to be arguing. Then, abruptly, most of the men were sent in the other direction, back into the ranch—all, in fact, except Clay.

Clay was coming toward me. *Alone*. Which meant he took this personally.

That made two of us.

CHAPTER 28

CLAY CAME HUSTLING up the hill, frothing at the mouth. There was no question he fueled the vengeance in this troop. If Jedediah was the brain, Clay was the bile duct.

"You're dead!" he shouted outward.

He didn't know exactly where I was. I'd been squatting behind a clump of brush and cacti. He was trying to flush me out.

"Miranda!" he roared.

Another game of Marco Polo, hoping I'd bite the worm on the hook. I didn't. He had his own explosives now. Two sticks from Jed. The one way to extinguish oil fires is to blow them up.

The next derrick on my demolition list was way up the ridge, making for a long sprint along a trench in the hillside. I waited for the right moment, then ran for it.

Crack, crack, crack! Gunshots chased right after me. Clay wasn't fooling around anymore. He wanted me erased.

I kept going, running and running, eventually and unexpectedly reaching a barbed-wire fence. Was this it? Was this the rally? I could see a number of industrial derricks and a factory.

This wasn't Jedediah's property anymore. This was the edge of Drake's northernmost fracking plant.

And now the closest well was a fracking rig. A big, metallic mosquito of human engineering, sticking its snout deep and horizontal into its victim to slurp a mile sideways.

There was indeed a crowd in the distance. The labor strike! My first glimpse of normal people. Maybe a hundred of them.

"Help!" I shouted toward them. *"Help!"*

But they were too far away to hear me and were all gazing about ninety degrees in another direction, toward the last explosion I made, which was an understandably enticing thing to gaze at.

I'd have to lure them with another boom.

I ran for the closest well. *Crack,* another bullet ripped through the air, close enough that I actually heard it swish by my head. I arrived at the rig and dove for cover under the web of its piping. I soon had the dynamite sticks nestled in the crook of the main tube.

And that's when I was hit from behind.

Jed. The butt of his shotgun.

I'd been spared the bullets because he didn't want to aim toward explosives and high-pressure flammable gas.

But Jed didn't factor in how hard I'd hit him back. This gal had grown with the fight. Nothing could faze me at this point.

I spun around and rammed him headfirst, nailing him square in the midsection. He was a big guy, but his age had caught up to him. Chugging up the hillside left him vulnerable.

He went down hard and I quickly straddled his oily torso and started punching him with all my might. Over and over. Left, right, left.

Which is when a few members of the crowd emerged over the crest of the hill. And the first thing they saw was me beating up an old, gray-haired man. Which they certainly didn't let go unchecked.

"Hey, get off him!" said one of the workers.

"Hey, she's beating on someone!" said another.

Clay arrived just in time to ruin any chance for truth to prevail.

"This is your arsonist!" said Clay, pointing at me.

"Wait," I protested.

But the crowd was gathering and opinions were forming fast.

"This is the arsonist," one of the workers shouted back to the others. Someone had keys to the gate in the fence and opened it up right away.

Clay capitalized on the chaos. "She's got the fuses for the dynamite in her front pocket! Look! And the igniter in her right fist. Look!"

The crowd was looking at me. I was so out of breath I could barely speak.

"That's not . . . that's not true," I said.

"He's right," said a woman with tattooed forearms. "She's got fuse wire."

"No, I mean . . . it's not true that I'm the . . . that I'm the . . ." I couldn't finish my sentence. I had reached my absolute mental and physical limit.

Clay was in full force, grandstanding to the gathering crowd. "This woman has been trying to start fires all along the canyon. *On the day of your rally!* You tell me—is that a coincidence?"

More and more people were gathering.

Clay continued. "Your families, your friends, all conveniently clustered in one vulnerable location."

The crowd was growing hostile. There were awful names being shouted at me. This was their day to vent frustration, and now, thanks to Clay, this was their day to route it toward me.

I tried to step away from the growing circle.

"Not goin' anywhere, miss," said a man in a cowboy hat, rifle in hand. Folks in this part of the universe carried guns. Proudly.

"Please," I implored them. "I need to call an ambulance. My husband needs an ambulance."

"Stop lying!" said Clay.

"Yeah," said a worker, joining in the mob mentality. "Stop lying."

"She's a radical!" said Clay. "Hired by Drake to sabotage the strike!"

I started to struggle against the grip of the crowd but more and more people were shoving me back to the center. The two fires roared behind me.

After all I'd been through—was this really how I was going to go out?

The chorus of discontented voices grew and grew until someone said, "Kill her."

And someone else shouted, *"No, you kill me first!"*

CHAPTER 29

AND THAT CHANGED everything.

It was a thunderous voice, slightly ragged, but resounding with confidence and conviction that I've only heard emanate from one person. My husband.

"Me first!" roared Aaron. "Kill me first!"

The crowd all stopped. Hushed itself. They slowly opened their ranks to let him take center stage. He had Sierra in his arms. Knees buckling as he walked, he'd expended his last breath to walk up the hillside.

"Me . . . not her," he said one last time.

He knew what he was doing—the locals reacted instantly.

"Aaron Cooper," said the woman with the forearm tattoos, as if his name were holy.

"It *is* him," said someone else with equal awe. "It *is* Aaron."

They couldn't believe what they were seeing. I couldn't either. Whatever it was. Him. Their savior. He stood in the middle, commanding all their attention, all their respect.

"This is my wife," he said. "Her name is Miranda. Today she faced a monster. And that monster . . . that monster is standing right next to her."

"Quiet!" shouted Clay. Then he addressed the crowd. "You can't trust him!"

"Clay and his cronies rammed us off the road," continued Aaron, pointing at Clay. "Then he tried to kill her. Then, when he knew he couldn't cover any of it up, he had Jed try to kill all of us."

"This man is a liar!" said Clay, pointing his finger back at my husband.

"This man is Aaron Cooper!" said a woman from the back.

She had a small child with her. She nodded toward Aaron like he was her favorite brother. "He's defending my home and my family." Then she turned to Clay. "I'd trust him over you." Then she nodded to Jed to add, "Over both of you!"

"So would I," said another local.

"So would I," said another.

"Aaron Cooper's been helping us for almost a year," said the guy in the cowboy hat. "I'd trust him with the life of my newborn."

The workers and residents had taken his side, our side, which felt amazing, truly.

I finally spoke up. "I can tell you what this man did. I can tell you every detail."

Clay had reached his threshold. With the flames of hell whipping around behind him, he aimed his rifle directly at my chest and shouted his war cry, *"Liar!"*

I saw each split-second elapse individually. I heard each millimeter of his index finger begin to pull that sliver of metal. A flurry of gunshots went off. And I swear I felt each bullet go inside me.

CHAPTER 30

BUT THAT WAS an illusion. The others fired, Aaron's defenders and now mine. A total of fifteen rounds from four different guns. I don't think anyone missed. Every single shot pierced Clay Hobson in the chest before he ever squeezed his own trigger.

The bullet-riddled man teetered backward, took two clumsy steps, paused, coughed up blood, then fell into the trench behind him, into the roaring inferno of the rig, where instantly the dynamite sticks in his vest combusted.

Boom.

Luckily, our crowd was on the opposite edge of the blast radius. Clay Hobson wasn't spared. His body was obliterated, while the rest of us remained dazed but still on our feet. Aaron had instinctively clutched downward, curling himself over Sierra. She was shell-shocked, but she would see her fifth birthday.

The one person now trembling in our midst was Jedediah.

The crowd had fully aligned itself with Aaron, defending him, and thereby me. Jed's goons were nowhere to be seen, successfully evaded by my determined husband.

"Set your gun down, Jed," said the tattooed woman.

Jed didn't seem popular here. Maybe everyone saw through him.

The man in the cowboy hat cocked his revolver. "Jedediah Branch, I don't care how high up you are on the food chain. If you move one molecule of that index finger, I will shoot you in the throat."

Jed was pale. He lowered his weapon slowly.

I gingerly made my way over to Aaron. I wanted so badly to hug him but he looked frail enough to crush. I didn't even want to exhale in his direction. Instead, I took my place at his side.

Jed was covered in oil, head to toe, doused by the spray of snuffing out the first derrick. One of the men looked directly at Jed, pulled out a pocket lighter and flicked it without ever breaking eye contact, holding the flame aloft like a torch.

Jed trembled in horror. The implication was terrifying. These people might actually burn him alive. He dropped to his knees, to face, of all people, Aaron.

"No. Please," Jed began to grovel. "Please don't."

He must've been convinced Aaron would condemn him. I had to be honest: seeing my husband hold our child, thrashed, bruised, teetering on the edge of death, mere yards away from the man responsible for the agony of it all, I almost wondered if he might actually give the word.

Almost.

But I knew better. I knew what Jed didn't know.

"You asked me to speak at the rally on behalf of Drake, but you found out I was going to blow the whistle on the whole operation. So you ordered me killed. You ordered my family killed. All so you could keep getting kickbacks from Drake Oil while these laborers got sicker and sicker, poisoned by the drinking water in their own homes."

Aaron stared at Jed.

"You want me to call them off?" said Aaron to the judge.

Aaron isn't a murderer.

"I'll make you glad you did," said Jed. He kept his movements slow and cautious, well aware of the muzzles pointing at his vital organs. His desperate gaze turned to me. "Please, Miranda. Anything you want."

"There's nothing you can say," I told him.

His ghostly face then peered around the group, frantically calculating.

"I'll say it," said Jed. He took a deep breath. "I did what you saw other judges do. I obstructed justice. I was paid to rule in favor of Drake Oil." He clasped his hands as if in prayer. Imploring. "But I can make it right. Help me make it right."

It had no value, this sad speech. Under duress, stating something he'd later dispute, it had no legal weight. This was just another stunt. But the moral victory definitely tasted sweet.

What was bizarre was that everyone was staring at me just as much as they were staring at the judge, wondering what kind of verdict I would render.

"Help me, Miranda," pleaded Jed.

I said, "My family will be giving you back your $145,000."

I let that sit for a second, watching his confusion.

"The bonus your people paid us?" I continued. "You'll be getting all that back. Starting with..." I began to fish in the pockets of my jeans. Here came all the cash I had on me, some bills and two coins, a grand total of six dollars and eleven cents. I tossed the wad toward Jedediah, then added, "The rest is coming soon."

In the distance were sirens.

I looked over at Aaron. He emitted a frail half chuckle, his best version of a laugh. Which meant, given the state he was in, that he found me hysterical.

"There's an ambulance for you, Mr. Cooper," said the tattooed lady, kindly. She was pointing to the front gate at the far end of the ranch, ready to assist him down the road.

I still didn't want to hug my husband for fear of toppling him over, but before I could tell him no, he put Sierra on the ground and embraced me. Sierra glommed on to us to make it a three-way group effort. We held. We held tight.

We held our family as if we'd just learned what the word meant.

EPILOGUE

THAT DAY FELT like a year. And that's how long it would ultimately take to ram this monstrosity of a case through the Arizona court system, where Aaron had been summoned to testify, where I was now waiting out in the hallway for him.

Sierra was orbiting around the corridor like an urban tumbleweed. She'd abandoned her career in kangaroo development and moved on to portrait photography, snapping pictures of random faces wherever we went.

"There," she said, pointing into the courtroom. The door had opened briefly, giving her a glimpse of the distant witness stand and her daddy taking a seat. "Daddy! He's handsome."

She could hardly comprehend how important this was. He was about to provide landmark testimony that would essentially bury the oil titan for good. I could hardly comprehend it myself. All nine active members of the board would sink. The CEO, the previous CEO, the army of vice presidents, *Jedediah* and all the other judges who were bought off, the late Clay Hobson, everyone whose hands were dirty.

It got too much for me to watch, to be honest. The trial recognized case after case of ravaged families, and last week, while sitting in on testimony from a balding mother of three, two of whom were in caskets, I wound up getting escorted out of the room. For yelling at the defense.

I'm the reason gavels were invented.

As for Aaron's culpability, our infamous Tuesday in the canyon helped sway any public doubt as to whether we'd duly suffered. I mean, let's not forget, Aaron was the one person who tried to drown this demon the moment he learned it existed.

"Mommy, that lady is staring," said Sierra, having just snapped a photo down the hall. She leaned over to show me a woman on her screen, a woman who was now approaching in a high-heeled cadence that echoed across the marble. She was indeed staring. At me.

Soon her stilettos came to a crisp halt right in front of my chair. She was tall, tall like a statue-of-democracy tall, her business suit failing to hide a well-chiseled figure.

"Miranda Cooper," she said to me. A question with no question mark.

"Uh," I replied.

"My apologies for being abrupt. My name is Kelly Miles. I have a job offer."

"Oh."

"My team fights the kind of battles I think you'd appreciate. And we happen to need a geologist. Someone to cover the Caspian Sea. Someone like you. Someone hard to stop."

Hard to stop. Is that my new slogan?

"Ah." The only reply I could think of besides *uh* and *oh*.

She looked like she could dent a concrete wall just by glaring at it. I got the feeling she wasn't offering me a job so much as telling me she already hired me. The Caspian? Isn't that Russia? And missiles?

"I . . ." I didn't know what to say. "I like your . . . confidence . . . but . . ."

"But you're declining," she said. Another question with no question mark.

I looked over at Sierra as if she might teleprompt me. Sierra was riffling through her latest photos. Some seventy-five pictures in seventy-five seconds. No help.

"What I am is..." I said, "honored. And, yes, declining. But thank you."

She smiled. "My card." She handed me her business card. "You can throw it away as soon as I'm gone. Nice to meet you, Miranda Cooper. You did well."

She started walking away. And within ten more photos from Sierra, our strange visitor had disappeared around the corner.

I looked down. I contemplated the card. A new frontier. Wild terrain. The thrill of the hunt.

And I crumpled it up.

21ST BIRTHDAY

James Patterson
& Maxine Paetro

When a distraught mother pleads with San Francisco Chronicle reporter Cindy Thomas to investigate the disappearance of her daughter Tara and baby granddaughter Lorrie, Cindy immediately loops in SFPD Sergeant Lindsay Boxer. The prime suspect is Tara's schoolteacher husband, Lucas Burke, but he tells a conflicting story that paints Tara as a wayward wife, not a missing person.

While the city's chief medical examiner, Claire Washburn, harbours theories that run counter to the police investigation of the Burke case, Assistant District Attorney Yuki Castellano sizes up Lucas as a textbook domestic offender – until he puts forward a theory of his own that could connect the dots on a constellation of killings.

As the case grows into something far bigger than any of them could have imagined, the four friends will need each other to help unpick the truth from a web of lies.

AN ALEX CROSS THRILLER

DEADLY CROSS

James Patterson

When two prominent figures in Washington, DC are found murdered, lying half naked in a car, the shocking story dominates tabloid headlines.

Kay Willingham was a glamorous socialite and ex-wife of the US vice president. Randall Christopher was a high school principal with political ambitions, as well as a wife and family.

Alex Cross knew both victims well. Especially Kay, who had once been his patient – and maybe more. As Cross travels to Alabama to investigate Kay's past, he is drawn into a world of corruption and secrets, and left facing a desperate choice between breaking a trust and losing his way . . .

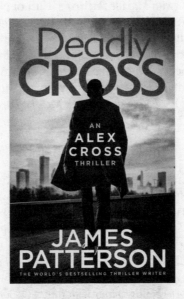

Also by James Patterson

ALEX CROSS NOVELS

Along Came a Spider • Kiss the Girls • Jack and Jill • Cat and Mouse • Pop Goes the Weasel • Roses Are Red • Violets Are Blue • Four Blind Mice • The Big Bad Wolf • London Bridges • Mary, Mary • Cross • Double Cross • Cross Country • Alex Cross's Trial (*with Richard DiLallo*) • I, Alex Cross • Cross Fire • Kill Alex Cross • Merry Christmas, Alex Cross • Alex Cross, Run • Cross My Heart • Hope to Die • Cross Justice • Cross the Line • The People vs. Alex Cross • Target: Alex Cross • Criss Cross • Deadly Cross

THE WOMEN'S MURDER CLUB SERIES

1st to Die • 2nd Chance (*with Andrew Gross*) • 3rd Degree (*with Andrew Gross*) • 4th of July (*with Maxine Paetro*) • The 5th Horseman (*with Maxine Paetro*) • The 6th Target (*with Maxine Paetro*) • 7th Heaven (*with Maxine Paetro*) • 8th Confession (*with Maxine Paetro*) • 9th Judgement (*with Maxine Paetro*) • 10th Anniversary (*with Maxine Paetro*) • 11th Hour (*with Maxine Paetro*) • 12th of Never (*with Maxine Paetro*) • Unlucky 13 (*with Maxine Paetro*) • 14th Deadly Sin (*with Maxine Paetro*) • 15th Affair (*with Maxine Paetro*) • 16th Seduction (*with Maxine Paetro*) • 17th Suspect (*with Maxine Paetro*) • 18th Abduction (*with Maxine Paetro*) • 19th Christmas (*with Maxine Paetro*) • 20th Victim (*with Maxine Paetro*) • 21st Birthday (*with Maxine Paetro*)

DETECTIVE MICHAEL BENNETT SERIES

Step on a Crack (*with Michael Ledwidge*) • Run for Your Life (*with Michael Ledwidge*) • Worst Case (*with Michael Ledwidge*) • Tick Tock (*with Michael Ledwidge*) • I, Michael Bennett (*with Michael Ledwidge*) • Gone (*with Michael Ledwidge*) • Burn (*with Michael Ledwidge*) • Alert (*with Michael Ledwidge*) • Bullseye (*with Michael Ledwidge*) • Haunted (*with James O. Born*) • Ambush (*with James O. Born*) • Blindside (*with James O. Born*) • The Russian (*with James O. Born*)

PRIVATE NOVELS

Private (*with Maxine Paetro*) • Private London (*with Mark
Pearson*) • Private Games (*with Mark Sullivan*) • Private:
No. 1 Suspect (*with Maxine Paetro*) • Private Berlin (*with
Mark Sullivan*) • Private Down Under (*with Michael White*) •
Private L.A. (*with Mark Sullivan*) • Private India (*with Ashwin
Sanghi*) • Private Vegas (*with Maxine Paetro*) • Private Sydney
(*with Kathryn Fox*) • Private Paris (*with Mark Sullivan*) • The
Games (*with Mark Sullivan*) • Private Delhi (*with Ashwin
Sanghi*) • Private Princess (*with Rees Jones*) •
Private Moscow (*with Adam Hamdy*)

NYPD RED SERIES

NYPD Red (*with Marshall Karp*) • NYPD Red 2 (*with
Marshall Karp*) • NYPD Red 3 (*with Marshall
Karp*) • NYPD Red 4 (*with Marshall Karp*) •
NYPD Red 5 (*with Marshall Karp*) •
NYPD Red 6 (*with Marshall Karp*)

DETECTIVE HARRIET BLUE SERIES

Never Never (*with Candice Fox*) • Fifty Fifty (*with
Candice Fox*) • Liar Liar (*with Candice Fox*) •
Hush Hush (*with Candice Fox*)

INSTINCT SERIES

Instinct (*with Howard Roughan, previously published as* Murder
Games) • Killer Instinct (*with Howard Roughan*)

THE BLACK BOOK SERIES

The Red Book (*with David Ellis*) • The Black Book (*with David Ellis*)

STAND-ALONE THRILLERS

The Thomas Berryman Number • Hide and Seek • Black
Market • The Midnight Club • Sail (*with Howard Roughan*) •
Swimsuit (*with Maxine Paetro*) • Don't Blink (*with Howard
Roughan*) • Postcard Killers (*with Liza Marklund*) • Toys (*with
Neil McMahon*) • Now You See Her (*with Michael Ledwidge*) • Kill
Me If You Can (*with Marshall Karp*) • Guilty Wives (*with

David Ellis) • Zoo (with Michael Ledwidge) • Second
Honeymoon (with Howard Roughan) • Mistress (with David
Ellis) • Invisible (with David Ellis) • Truth or Die (with
Howard Roughan) • Murder House (with David Ellis) •
The Store (with Richard DiLallo) • Texas Ranger (with Andrew
Bourelle) • The President is Missing (with Bill Clinton) • Revenge
(with Andrew Holmes) • Juror No. 3 (with Nancy Allen) • The
First Lady (with Brendan DuBois) • The Chef (with Max
DiLallo) • Out of Sight (with Brendan DuBois) • Unsolved
(with David Ellis) • The Inn (with Candice Fox) • Lost (with
James O. Born) • Texas Outlaw (with Andrew Bourelle) •
The Summer House (with Brendan DuBois) • 1st Case
(with Chris Tebbetts) • Cajun Justice (with Tucker
Axum) • The Midwife Murders (with Richard DiLallo) •
The Coast-to-Coast Murders (with J.D. Barker) •
Three Women Disappear (with Shan Serafin) •
The President's Daughter (with Bill Clinton) • The Shadow
(with Brian Sitts) • The Noise (with J.D. Barker)

NON-FICTION

Torn Apart (with Hal and Cory Friedman) • The Murder of King Tut
(with Martin Dugard) • All-American Murder (with Alex Abramovich
and Mike Harvkey) • The Kennedy Curse (with Cynthia Fagen) • The
Last Days of John Lennon (with Casey Sherman and Dave Wedge)•
Walk in My Combat Boots (with Matt Eversmann and Chris
Mooney)

MURDER IS FOREVER TRUE CRIME

Murder, Interrupted • Home Sweet Murder • Murder Beyond the
Grave the Grave • Murder Thy Neighbour • Murder of Innocence •
Till Murder Do US Part

COLLECTIONS

Triple Threat • Kill or Be Killed • The Moores are Missing •
The Family Lawyer • Murder in Paradise • The House Next Door •
13-Minute Murder • The River Murders • The Palm Beach Murders

For more information about James Patterson's novels,
visit www.penguin.co.uk